Solitary

—

K.Wiley Sider

ISBN: 1940950007
ISBN 13: 9781940950006
Library of Congress Control Number: 2014931818
Devilwood Press, Ellicott City, MD

This book is dedicated to my beautiful daughters and patient husband who held my hand, encouraged me to keep going, and told me everything was going to be fine while supplying me with bottomless glasses of wine.

"The things people say of a man do not alter a man. He is what he is. Public opinion is of no value whatsoever. Even if people employ actual violence, they are not to be violent in turn. That would be to fall to the same low level. After all, even in prison, a man can be quite free. His soul can be free. His personality can be untroubled. He can be at peace. And, above all things, they are not to interfere with other people or judge them in any way. Personality is a very mysterious thing. A man cannot always be estimated by what he does. He may keep the law, and yet be worthless. He may break the law, and yet be fine. He may be bad, without ever doing anything bad. He may commit a sin against society, and yet realize through that sin his true perfection."

- Oscar Wilde, *The Soul of Man Under Socialism*

Chapter 1

BUM RAP

The surface of a person's life rarely reveals the life they are truly living. Like the humble servant who hides great wealth, or the high society couple who are, in truth, penniless. To the world they are one thing, but their lives—their real lives—are often something else completely.

Abby knew she was a fraud. On the surface she was the beloved daughter of highly educated parents. She was gifted with beauty and poise that had been cultivated by a lifetime surrounded by the very best her parents could afford. In someone else's eyes she might be judged extraordinarily fortunate. But underneath she was living a life much less than others might credit her for. She knew deep in her heart that, despite what other people saw when they looked at her, she was anything but exceptional; she was ordinary.

Abby felt her inadequacies keenly as she got ready for another night out with the same friends in pretty much the same places. Though she'd had a couple of serious boyfriends since her high school sweetheart went off to play football at a college across the country, Abby was currently unattached, and feeling like something was wrong with her. All but a small handful of friends had gone away to bigger and more notable colleges while she'd stayed in the town she grew up in, and went to the private college her parents taught at that nobody had ever heard of. Only ten minutes from her home she had received free tuition and a generous grant for her current graduate program from one of her parents' friends. Even her summer job interning for one of the local professors had turned out to be nothing more than proofreading his abstracts. The only thing she still enjoyed was her daily run along the unfinished highway near her home. She'd just returned from her run when her closest friend, Marnie, texted her about going out.

Abby sat at her dressing table brushing the tangles from her hair when her cell chirped next to her. She set her hairbrush aside and picked up the phone to check the text. Abby had left it up to Marnie to make the final decision about where they were going to meet up later since party spots were limited in the small city of Springfield. There were plenty of dive bars, one so-called Irish pub, and exactly one dance club. Abby's friends were already out trying to find the best place to see and be seen while Abby got ready. She was running late because she'd had to work until 8:00 p.m.

Coco Lane popped up on the screen. Abby shrugged. It was as good a place as any other bar falling somewhere between grungy and semi respectable. It had the advantage of being near everything else, though. So it was at least a good start.

Abby brushed the last of the tangles from her long, straight brown hair, checked her makeup, and then went downstairs to say goodbye to her dad.

By the time Abby arrived at the pub, it was crowded. She scanned the crowd and found her friends crushed around one of the few tables in the far corner. She waved back as Marnie called over. As she crossed the pub, Abby greeted several old high school friends and some college friends who had stayed on campus for the summer. Holding court at his own table was a guy Abby had graduated with, Mark Massie, who was locally famous for being both the son of a wealthy local judge and a drug dealer. Abby stopped when he called out to her.

"Hey, Abs, what's up?" he stood up and kissed her on the cheek. Despite his unsavory profession, Mark was endlessly charming and had been raised well. Abby had known him since kindergarten. Their mothers had been close friends till Abby's mom passed away.

"Hey, Mark," she answered. "I haven't seen you in forever. What's going on?"

Mark shrugged then sat back down. "Nothing, just the usual," he answered. "You wanna sit with us?"

Abby glanced at Mark's stoner friends and sycophants. "No thanks," she replied. "Marnie's already wondering what's taking me so long."

"Talk soon?" he asked. Mark looked tired.

Abby nodded then waded through the throng to her table of friends. She should have realized they would only have beer at the table. She turned and wove her way back through the crowd to the long antique bar. It was packed with twenty-somethings and a few old-timers who tolerated the crowd instead of finding another hangout. Abby waved at Scott, the bartender, who gave her a smile and walked over.

"What? No beer for you?" Scott joked.

Abby shook her head. "Could I have a Dirty Dog?"

"Sure thing," Scott answered and moved off to make her drink.

Abby was so absorbed in watching the ebb and flow of people, she didn't notice when someone moved into the space next to her. Abby glanced over and noted a guy about her age. He was really good-looking in a clean-cut, military way.

He smiled at her, showing even white teeth that had most likely paid for his orthodontist's car. It was her habit to name people in her head, and "Mr. Grin," instantly came to mind.

"Hey," he said.

Abby smiled back but said nothing. She preferred to give nothing away when dealing with the opposite sex. Even though Abby was one of those effortlessly beautiful girls whose skin never broke out, who never gained weight, and who always managed to look perfect regardless of the situation, she was rarely approached by anyone worth dating. The guys who typically hit on her were either trying to impress their friends, or they were more interested in her looks and couldn't care less if she had a brain. This guy was definitely dateable.

"So this place is hoppin'," he continued. He was unfazed by her lack of an answer.

Abby shrugged and took her drink from Scott. "It can be," she answered. "Have fun."

Marnie moved over so that Abby could sit next to her.

"Who was that cute guy at the bar?"

Abby shrugged. "Just some guy." She didn't want to admit that she was interested...or desperate.

Marnie scanned the crowd for him. "Well, if he wants to come over here he can sit next to me if you're not going to go for it."

As they sat drinking and laughing, the pub began to clear out as patrons left for greener pastures in other clubs and bars in town. Mr. Grin seemed to be watching Abby and occasionally looked like he was about to come over, but didn't. Abby saw several tables of friends getting up to leave. Marnie took it as a cue to gather her group and move on as well. As the only one at the table with a paycheck, Abby offered to settle up their tab. At the bar, Scott was cleaning up after a bachelorette party that had made a mess on the bar with shot glasses containing something pink and foamy.

"Hey," Abby called Scott over. "I need to pay you."

Scott threw down his rag. "Sure thing. I'll be right there."

Abby was pulling out her wallet to check her cash situation when Mr. Grin reappeared at her elbow.

"Hey," he smiled. "You seem to know a lot of people here."

Abby shrugged without answering. She'd really only talked to Mark and her friends. Mr. Grin moved closer and leaned over to whisper in her ear.

"You know where I can score some bammy?"

Abby stared at him. "Some what?"

"Bammy…ganja? Some grass."

Abby moved away from him. Mr. Grin suddenly wasn't so interesting now that she knew he was a pothead. "Oh, that's not really my thing. You should ask Mark Massie. That's more his thing."

Mr. Grin moved back and smiled. "Awesome, could you introduce me to him?"

Abby scanned the pub and saw Mark pushing the door open and walking out. "He's at the door. If you go now you might be able to catch him."

Mr. Grin frowned. "OK, but I don't know him. I don't want to walk up to random people and ask them for pot."

Abby sighed as she handed Scott the cash for her party's bill. "All right then. Come on."

Mr. Grin followed her to the door. Abby pushed it open and pointed out Mark who was standing across the parking lot talking to what could have been Mr. Grin's twin. "He's right there. Mark!"

Abby was looking at Mark when she felt the steel of the handcuffs snap over her wrist. Mr. Grin wasn't so friendly anymore. "You are under arrest for the attempt to sell and traffic marijuana." Abby started to protest as Mr. Grin continued to recite her Miranda rights. She tried to get Mark's attention, but she saw that he too was being placed under arrest.

Her ordinary life had just ended.

Chapter 2

THE CHAIN

Abby rested her head against the window and watched the landscape creep by. Her striped jumpsuit reflected in the glass coloring the world in stripes of gray. Her eyes watered with unshed tears, but her cuffs were chained to the floor of the bus, preventing her from raising her hands any higher than her waist.

Flat fields of soybeans crawled slowly across the horizon as the bus made its way to the Maysville Correctional Facility for Women. Abby knew she was lucky to be going to a federal prison and not the old state reformatory known for overcrowding and daily violence. She was somewhat frightened at the prospect of prison, but she was more tired than anything else. The bus had left the county jail so early it had still been dark outside. Despite her fear, Abby was anxious to get it over with. She'd already spent eighteen months in and out of the county jail while awaiting her indictment, and then her trial. Her attorney had explained that because she knew that Mr. Grin (real name Brian Pierce) was looking to buy marijuana, introducing him to Mark made her an accomplice. She'd heard from her attorney that, because Mark's inventory during their investigation was more than a thousand kilos and he'd been arrested before, Mark was going to prison for twenty years. She'd been lucky that he'd only had a hundred kilos with him or she'd be going away for ten. When the prosecution offered her a reduced sentence, she took it and received a sentence of five years just for telling Mr. Grin where he could buy pot. Silver linings were thin, but if she didn't look for them, she'd end up on the floor, checked out of the world permanently.

Abby didn't have a seatmate, but one of the women she'd spent time in the county jail with was seated across from her. Janet had been arrested for prostitution and possession. She was going to Maysville for a reduced sentence of three years. She was probably the closest thing to a friend Abby had since all of her friends from home had avoided her after her arrest. Janet snored audibly and Abby noticed she'd wet herself. She was still coming off her addiction and battling a raging urinary tract infection, so Abby couldn't fault her for her accident. So far the ride had taken over four hours with stops to pick up other transfers, but no stops to pee.

She turned back to the window as the bus slowed, then turned into a long drive-way. In the distance, Abby could see the prison. It looked like a really large high school surrounded by layers of fencing. Weirdly, the land surrounding the prison was also ringed with fences topped by razor wire. Women in bright yellow cotton scrubs were dotted about the fields. Abby idly wondered what they were doing, and then realized she didn't care.

As the bus slowed to a stop, one of the female corrections officers (Abby had named her Fat Guard) got up and walked along the aisle, unlocking the bolts that chained the prisoners to the floor. Another corrections officer, or CO who Abby nicknamed Bald Guard because her hair was so light and so short got up and stood watch at the top of the aisle in front of the driver's cage. Abby wondered at all the precautions. Of all the prisoners on the bus, Abby was pretty sure she was the worst offender, yet she was the last person who would try to storm a guard with a shotgun. From the conversations going on behind her, Abby guessed all the other women were going in for much lesser crimes like kiting checks or theft. Some chick in the back had stolen a social security number, but she was still only going away for a year.

Abby had been assigned a seat toward the front because of her offender status, so she was the first one off the bus. She carried her paperwork and a small blue duffel bag filled with a few books, TSA approved toiletries, and some extra clothes as she followed Bald Guard across the small parking lot to stop in front of a thick, gray metal door. Her fellow inmates lined up behind her. The sign next to the door read "Intake." Abby groaned inwardly. She knew what to expect. The prison consultant her attorney had hired to explain the prison process had already told her. Bald Guard checked Abby's name off the passenger manifest then sent her in through the door.

As expected, intake was an ordeal. After she'd been afforded a visit to the ladies' room where she was ordered to pee in a cup, Abby was interviewed, exam-ined, and ordered to exchange her striped county jumpsuit for the blue scrubs the prison provided. Especially humiliating was the nurse visit, which included a cav-ity search that inspected the depths of every orifice of her body. Abby wondered why they didn't just install the X-ray scanners airports had. Innocent people had embarrassing images of their bodies put on public display while prisoners got the privilege of being poked and prodded behind the semi privacy of a faded blue curtain and half wall. After drug and pregnancy tests, Abby was interviewed for any special needs she might have. After her photo was taken she was sent to property inspection. She was grateful that she didn't have anything that needed to be confiscated and that her shoes had passed the metal detector wand. Abby's dad had given her high quality running shoes to wear to the prison. He must have done his homework because any shoes with metal in the toes or arches would have been confiscated.

After another interview about approved visitors, sexual preferences, enemies and religious affiliations, Abby was sent to wait outside in a large courtyard with her fellow bus mates. Janet was already there napping on top of a picnic table. The pee stained jumpsuit was mercifully gone. Social security number girl sat at the end of the bench and cried quietly. Abby didn't blame her. She felt like crying, too. From a distant yard, inmates crowded the fence and called out to them. Abby heard calls of "fresh fish" and "hey baby" and even a couple of offers to suck someone's dick. Their calls only made the girl cry harder.

Abby wanted to tell them to fuck off, but she knew better. Instead she shoved her bag under Janet's legs for safekeeping and began to jog around the courtyard. It was half the size of a high school football field so Abby was able to get a good pace going during the two hour wait. She'd hit her stride when she heard Fat Guard call her name. Abby jogged back to the table where Janet handed over her things. Then she followed Fat Guard in and received her photo ID, approved visitors list, housing assignment, and a small pile of clothes and linens. Abby looked at the single name on her visitors list. She doubted her father would be coming to visit. She was the only child of only children, and her parents had had her late in their lives. Her father was past seventy and suffering from early Alzheimer's and COPD. Though he was still able to function relatively independently, his short-term memory was worsening. Luckily there were church families who could care for him while she was gone. If one of them brought him to see her near the holidays, Abby would be grateful. She shoved the paperwork into her packet and followed Fat Guard down the hallway.

Chapter 3

DRIVE UP

Maysville was one of the newest prisons in the state. It was built in the shape of a wheel with one- and two-story wings of dormitory-like suites in the spokes. Some suites housed six women each and some less. Most units had suites that surrounded a central area with a glass guard office and fixed tables and benches in the center. Inmates with issues were typically sent to Administrative Segregation, which was called "ADSEG," to figure out where they would be safest while inmates who were an immediate threat to the general population were sent directly to the disciplinary segregation unit or "DSEG". Since Abby didn't have any previous associates in the correctional system, she was sent directly to her housing unit. Fat Guard led her to B Unit, and then handed her off to a tall, stocky redhead Abby immediately named Big Ginger. Big Ginger took Abby's paperwork and gave her a small speech about conduct as they walked into the unit. Abby nodded silently as she followed Big Ginger to her assigned suite. She was happy to see Janet enter the unit behind her. At least she'd know someone.

Abby set her bag and linens down on the only unmade bunk and looked around. The suite was a long rectangle. It was spotlessly clean with bunks lined up in an L-shaped pattern and a small bathroom containing only a sink and commode located in the inside corner of the L. There were six bunks in all and a desk and fixed stool near the door. Storage was limited to lockers at the end of each stack of bunks. Abby's bunk was a top bunk in the farthest corner of the suite. It was a surprising bit of luck since it afforded her a view of the entire suite. As she started making up her bed, women began to file into the unit. Abby looked at the cheap Timex her dad had provided for her. "It must be lunch," she thought as she pulled the thin white sheet across the meager mattress.

"What up, new girl."

Abby turned to see a tiny black woman at the door to the suite. She looked young and old at the same time. To Abby's relief, she was smiling.

She smiled back. "Hi, I'm Abby."

The tiny black woman moved out of the way as two other women filed past her. Both were Hispanic and chattering away in Spanish. They took the bunks at the opposite end of the suite.

"I'm Sheronda." The tiny black woman moved over to Abby. "Damn girl, you is tall. You need help?"

Abby shook her head. "I'm done. But thanks."

Sheronda picked up Abby's duffel and looked through it. "You ain't got nothin' special in here, right?"

Abby shook her head. "Just books and some clothes…socks…stuff like that."

Sheronda opened the locker attached to the foot of Abby's bunk and shoved her bag inside.

"It's lunchtime. Let's go eat and I'll give you a tour of our lugshurius commodations." Sheronda gestured elegantly out the door, and then chuckled at her own joke as she left the suite. Abby followed.

Sheronda walked fast, but she was so tiny that Abby had no problem keeping up with her. As she walked, she gave Abby a running narrative of life in B Unit.

"So you got lucky with us in our suite. You got good cellies, even though we all in for serious time. Like me. I'm ten in for twenty-five for attempted murder," Sheronda paused and whispered. "Stabbed my man in the dick for tryin' to fuck with me. Sometime a girl ain't in the mood." Abby nodded respectfully and Sheronda resumed her walk. Other inmates were following along and giving Abby sidelong glances. Abby ignored them.

"Then we got the two 'Spanic cousins, Rosita and Rita. They in for shoplifting and fencing. They speak like two words of English so you don't need to worry about them. Just watch your shit 'cause they steal in here too."

"Then we got Tanya, but she go by Mad T cause she look so pissed off all the time. She's in for a jolt for killin' her man when she find him messin' wit her baby girl. She coulda got off, but she kept cashin' his disability checks, so they gives her twenty-five to life. She's a bull, but she won't like you. She likes dark girls, but only one of her girls lives with us. That's Marianna. She's one of Mad T's wives or daughters. Both is LURDs." Sheronda glanced at her sideways. "You know what that is?"

Abby nodded. LURD was an acronym for "lesbian until release date." They were women who developed sexual relationships with each other in prison, but who were straight on the outside. The prison consultant had prepped Abby for the uglier side of prison by going to great lengths to explain what Abby should do if confronted.

"Marianna's half Puerto Rican, half a bunch of other shit. In for drugs." Sheronda led Abby to the entrance to the cafeteria where women were already lining up. Abby could see the big window along the back of the room was open, and kitchen inmates were getting ready to serve.

"What about you?" Sheronda asked.

"Trafficking." Abby answered. "Five years but eighteen months served at county." Sheronda shook her head. "Mandatory is such bullshit. Were you holding?"

Abby shook her head. "No, just pointed out the dealer."

Sheronda snorted. "Man, you is dumb. You didn't ask if he was a cop?"

Abby felt dumb. "No, it never occurred to me."

Sheronda chuckled as they followed the line into the cafeteria. It was smaller so Abby figured it served just their unit. They were early so they were able to grab a tray right away. Sheronda chattered as they moved along and got their food. Abby was surprised that the food smelled almost good. The food in Springfield's jail had the institutional smell and taste of canned vegetable soup regardless of what was actually served.

Inmates with gloves and hairnets stood behind steaming pans of food. There was a choice of hotdogs in buns, baked beans, corn, and grilled cheese sandwiches. For dessert there were chocolate chip cookies and pudding cups.

Abby took a grilled cheese and some baked beans but passed on the dessert. Sheronda gave her a pointed look, and then loaded up Abby's tray with the remaining options before filling her own. Fully loaded, Abby followed Sheronda over to a table already filled with women.

"Shove it, girl." Sheronda pushed in and left enough room at the end for Abby. The other women barely gave Abby a passing glance after Sheronda introduced her to the table. Two of the women across from Abby got up to leave in time for Janet to sit across from her. Abby introduced Janet to Sheronda, and then gave her friend a closer look. Janet had gone really pale and was trembling. Abby looked around the room and saw that Big Ginger had taken a position along the wall not far from their table. She was about to say something when Janet slid off the bench into a seizure. Women scattered as Janet's body pounded the cement floor. Abby jumped up and moved to turn Janet onto her side in case she vomited. Big Ginger came over and moved the inmates farther away. Amazingly, Sheronda sat and ate calmly while Abby tried to prevent Janet's head from bashing into the concrete. Big Ginger knelt next to her and gave Abby a pointed look.

"She's detoxing," Abby told her. "They didn't treat her at county."

Big Ginger shook her head in disgust, then pulled her radio from her shoulder. A minute later a couple of COs, and what looked like orderlies, showed up with a stretcher. Abby was surprised to see they were all male. The two COs stood by as the orderlies picked up Janet and secured her to the stretcher. Big Ginger took over holding Janet's head, which was still thrashing from side to side as the orderlies carried Janet out. One of the male COs, a huge bald black man walked across the room and took up position near the door while the other one, a younger white guy who looked more like a Calvin Klein model than a prison guard, held up the wall near Abby's table.

"Nice friend you got there," Sheronda mumbled through her food. "Good conversationalist."

Abby took Janet's tray over to the section of the wall where used trays were dropped off to be cleaned for the next meal. The trays already there were so gross, Abby hoped she didn't get a kitchen assignment.

When she got back to her table, Sheronda was eating her beans.

"So lemme tell you a little 'bout B Unit." Sheronda pointed out the different cliques around the room. "Most of these chicks call them they's families. Like there's a dad who's in charge and they got wives and kids. We calls them bull daggers or daddies. Mad T's over there with her girls." Sheronda gave a slight nod toward a table near the door where a truly large black woman held court over half a dozen dark-skinned girls. "Then you got Kelsey and her crew." Sheronda nodded at a table on the other side of the room. "You wanna watch out for her. She's a bitch and she likes white girls like you. You turn her down and it might get ugly."

Sheronda was a little more subtle when indicating Kelsey's table. Abby had no problem figuring out which one was Kelsey. Like most queen bees, Kelsey was very pretty. She was a little on the large side and extremely loud and expressive. Abby had no problem picturing her in a high school lunchroom torturing the lesser mortals who crossed her path. She was surrounded by a motley crew of sycophants, most of whom were blond-via-bottle. Abby noticed they all sported a lot of ink on their arms and some even on their faces.

Sheronda read her mind. "She marks them like that. Lucky for them she don't suck at it. You join up with her she gonna bleach you yellow and draw on you."

Abby shook her head. "I'm not interested." Sheronda snorted but said nothing.

"Then over there you got Alfreda. She go by Fred most times. She got all the spics Mad T don't got. She a real dyke, like on the outside too. You wanna watch her in the shower. She gonna try to fuck you whether you like it or not. Most times she's nice about it, but you don't wanna piss her off. She like a man when she fight."

Abby looked past Kelsey who was already giving her the side-eye to a woman who could have easily passed for a man. Alfreda was short and stocky with a dark complexion and black hair that had been buzz cut. She, too, was giving Abby too many looks. The women surrounding Alfreda all chattered in Spanish.

Abby looked away when Sheronda elbowed her. "Finally, you got Grandma." Abby followed Sheronda's thumb as the woman pointed to the table behind her where an elderly woman sat with women who would have been the nerds and outcasts in high school. "Her real name's Agnes, but she act like everyone's grandma so thass what we call her. She nice but people stay away from her 'cause she crazy. She killed a cop trying to save some tree or something. She get life. Then when some chick at her other joint try to fuck her, she kill her too. She get life again. She look like an old lady, but she dangerous. Mad T don't even mess with her."

"What about everyone else?" Abby asked.

Sheronda shrugged. "Some just be friends, some just pair up. Some move around families. Don't be movin' round too much, though. It make the daddies mad." The other women at the table nodded in agreement. "You don't like girl fuckin' you go with Grandma. She holy so she don't make nobody fuck her or each other for fun."

Abby turned back to finish her grilled cheese while Sheronda finished her beans.

One of the women at the table leaned over and whispered, "Don't look now, but somebody got a man lookin' at her."

Several of the women at the table sniggered and glanced over at the guard leaning against the wall near their table. Abby turned to see that the young Calvin Klein model was indeed looking at her. His expression was stony and Abby doubted he was looking at her with anything remotely resembling interest.

"That's Sergeant Quinn. We calls him Pretty Boy." Sheronda made kissy faces and noises at Sergeant Quinn who smiled and looked away. "Ima gonna make him my boyfriend. Ain't that right, Pretty Boy." Still smiling, Sergeant Quinn shook his head. Abby regarded him for a minute. He looked like a Quinn, but not a sergeant. In her head she dropped the sergeant altogether.

Lunch was ended by a loud buzzer that called the women to bring up their remaining trays. Abby moved with the rest of the crowd to the door where the guards herded them out to a large courtyard with a section of fixed picnic tables under a wooden roof, basketball courts, and what looked like a walking path. Sheronda resumed her orientation.

"COs we got is all the same. They's all in the brown shirts. We calls them officer to theys face. That big guy is Gray. He cool if you stay in line. You get outta line he pepper spray you fast. Then we got sergeants. They's in black. We got Pretty Boy you seen already. Then we got Sergeant Redfern, the chick that helped your friend. She nice for a guard. She likes to help people. She big but she real polite. Then we got Ramirez, White, and Montgomery. They's all officers 'cept for Montgomery. She a sergeant like Quinn. They ain't here till late shift. You goin' ta see other COs too, but they all rotate. Like Singh, we only see her sometimes. We also got two captains. They's in the black too but theys got more stripes. Captain Dennis be the day captain and he real strict but fair. Captain Hannah like to help people like Red does. She tryin' to save us all. She do late shift, but guarantee she's gonna try and talk to you before lockdown."

Sheronda sat down at a table near the outside of the group with the same ladies who were at the lunch table. Everyone but Sheronda took out yarn and crochet hooks.. Quinn took up a position near them.

"See, I tole you Pretty Boy be likin' me. He always gotta be nearby." Sheronda looked at Abby who was still standing. "You gonna sit or what?"

Abby looked over at the walking path. "How long do we have?"

Sheronda shrugged. "Hour or so. Why?"

"I've been sitting all morning. I'm going to go for a quick run first."

Sheronda looked at her like she'd just sprouted another head. "You crazy, girl. Ain't nobody runs in this place. That's why they's all fat."

Abby smiled. "Save me a seat OK? I'll be back." Sheronda shrugged and turned her attention to one of the ladies from their table.

Abby moved past the crowd of women settling into their various groups. She heard a couple of quiet catcalls but ignored them. The walking path was deserted as was the grassy area in the center of the yard. Only the basketball courts had a few women tossing desultory balls while they talked. Abby picked up her pace and headed toward the far end of the courtyard where the walking path followed the perimeter fence. Abby started to count her paces. After one full circuit, she estimated the full perimeter to be a little over a quarter mile. Her average run was five miles, so she'd have to circuit twenty times to make the run worth it. As she ran, Abby felt the world fall away. She could no longer hear anything but the pounding of her feet on the path and the sound of her breathing. After being cooped up for so long, it felt good to stretch. Abby lengthened her stride and picked up speed, feeling the breeze lift her ponytail off her neck. When she hit her twentieth circuit of the track, she slowed to a trot, and then a walk. Sheronda was staring at her when she made it back to the table. In fact, most of the women were staring at her.

"What?" Abby asked.

"Damn, you is the fastest white girl I ever seen." Sheronda shook her head in disbelief. "You is like Flo-Jo."

Abby sat down next to her. "I ran track in high school and college," she said by way of explanation. "I was training for a marathon when I was arrested."

"How long is that?" one of the ladies sitting at the table asked. Her hands were filled with a half-finished hat.

"About twenty-six miles," Abby answered. "Though I've done a few 5K and 10K races, I've only run two full marathons."

"Jesus Christ, girl." Sheronda fanned herself dramatically. "I got tired just lookin' at you. And you ain't even breathin' hard or nothin'."

Abby shrugged and pulled out her ponytail. Pieces of hair had come loose and were sticking to her neck. She finger combed her hair back into place and put her hair into a twist at the top of her head. An elderly black woman sitting in front of her paused in her crocheting and leaned over. "That boy's been staring at you somethin' fierce this whole time," she whispered.

Abby wanted to look behind her but felt the blush rising up her neck to her face. Sheronda turned instead. "Hey, baby," she called out. "You wanna cuddle wit me? You know you want to. No? OK, maybe later."

Sheronda turned back to the table with a smirk. "That boy watchin' our girl somethin' bad." The other ladies nodded in agreement. She turned to Abby and looked her over. "You must be somethin' special. He and me been here a long time and he ain't never looked at any of the girls. And some been tryin' *hard*."

Sheronda's Greek chorus nodded in agreement with lots of "mmhmm" and "you know that's right."

Abby was rescued from the teasing by the loud buzz that called the women back into the unit.

Sheronda followed her in. "You got yer job yet?"

Abby shook her head. All inmates had some form of employment at the prison. She'd learned during intake that Maysville was a profitable turf farm, so some inmates worked outside. Other jobs included the kitchen, laundry, or an admin job like the library. The prison also had a sewing shop that made the prisoner's scrubs and even the guard's uniforms. Abby had learned from her attorney that the turf farm and sewing shop paid the most, affording prisoners who worked in those areas a higher quality of life. Each inmate had an account, called their book, which held any money they earned at the prison as well as any money their families sent them. They used the money to buy things like toiletries or food from the small commissary. Abby's father had loaded her book, so she was in good shape.

As Abby made her way back into B Unit, an older woman in civilian clothes stepped forward. "Abby Blackwood? I'm Emma Bronwin. I'm your case manager here." Emma indicated the table nearest the guard office. Abby sat down.

"I've been going over your file to determine where to place you. Typically drug convictions are placed in the recovery and treatment section, but I'm going to be honest, you're a bit of a problem." Emma opened the file in front of her and looked over the report. "It appears that, despite the crime that put you here, you're not actually a drug user. In fact, your file indicates quite the opposite. I see active participation with your church as a youth leader, work with Habitat for Humanity, as well as your studies toward…is it nursing?" Emma looked up.

"I was going for a master's degree in clinical nurse management." Abby answered. "I was going to specialize in pastoral psychiatric counseling for eldercare and hospice."

Emma shook her head. "And your conduct during your incarceration at the county level has been noted as exemplary as well. I'm a little concerned that it says you've competed as a fighter, but even that doesn't indicate any behavioral issues. So you might see my problem." Emma closed the file and looked at Abby. "Inmates who come to us from certain types of socioeconomic situations are accustomed to the kind of work we typically assign. However, when we get someone with your level of education and intellectual capacity, we find that the adjustment to manual labor can be difficult."

"I don't really know what to tell you," Abby said honestly. "I don't mind working hard. I've participated in several mission trips to Louisiana where I helped to rebuild areas damaged by Katrina and to Africa to build schools."

Emma considered her for a moment. "With your educational background, I'd like to put you in as an instructional leader, but it's too early, and it would put you in an awkward position with the other inmates. The best I can do right now is to assign you to the cleaning crew. Even though it only works half shifts, we can put you on the office crew with Sheronda. You'll be paid $1.50 per day, and it'll go straight on your book at the end of each week. You'll report to Sergeant Redfern in the morning. She'll get you set up."

Abby shrugged. "OK."

Emma put out her hand. "It was a pleasure, Abby."

Abby took her hand and smiled. "Pleasure's mine."

Emma shook her head as she stood up. "Let me know if you have any problems, OK?"

Abby nodded and stood up as well.

As her case manager left, Abby felt a presence just behind her. She turned to see the queen bee, Kelsey, regarding her with a smirk. Her band of bottle-blondes were crowded behind her.

"So we got a new girl with us." She moved around Abby, looking her up and down as her group of wannabes giggled like schoolgirls. Kelsey stopped in front of her. Though she was at least thirty pounds heavier than Abby, she was a good six inches shorter. "I saw Sheronda giving you the lay of the land. She tell you about me?"

Abby said nothing. She simply nodded and narrowed her eyes. Kelsey reached over and brushed the front of Abby's breast with her fingertips. It was a bold move, considering how close they were to the guard booth. Abby caught her wrist before she could continue.

"I don't do girls," Abby said quietly. "We're not going to have a problem are we?"

She watched as Kelsey's expression turned to rage. She moved to pull her wrist away, but Abby had an iron grip on her. Kelsey's girls had fallen silent.

"Are we?" Abby repeated. Kelsey considered her position in that moment and chose to save face.

"Of course not," she replied with an artificial laugh. "I just wanted to welcome you. If you need anything, just ask."

Abby let her go, but held her gaze steady as Kelsey moved off with her cronies. When Abby turned away, she noticed Quinn behind the glass of the guard booth watching her closely. His face was expressionless. At once, Abby was furious that he'd watched the whole exchange and had done nothing to intervene. Physical contact between inmates that was sexual in nature was expressly forbidden, and in Abby's case, unwanted. She stalked off to her suite to get out from under his scrutiny.

Chapter 4
SHAKEDOWN

Abby wondered if her encounter with Kelsey was the beginning of an unpleasant and unwanted rivalry. She'd been a reluctant participant during her freshman year of high school when girls freshly minted from middle school were all jockeying to be the most popular. In college, it was girls who were determined to get their Mrs. rather than their BAs. Abby was so lost in thought as she headed toward the door to her suite, the buzzer that sounded throughout the unit startled her. Women began to flow out of the suites to line up outside. Sheronda pulled Abby aside.

"Time to get counted," she told her, and the two women stood alongside the rest of their suitemates.

A very large and very loud black guard came striding across the common area. "Move it, ladies. I don't want to see anyone takin' their time." Abby was impressed with his sheer volume. He reminded her of a drill sergeant.

"Thass Dennis," Sheronda whispered.

"I said move it, ladies." Captain Dennis took up position in the center of the common area. "One minute and anyone not front and center is going to Lock."

"He mean it too," Sheronda whispered. Captain Dennis looked over and gave her a pointed look.

"I'm gonna overlook you talkin', Sheronda, since I know you're just tellin' that new girl what's what. But you're gonna zip it now, right?"

Sheronda zipped it.

Captain Dennis turned back to address the unit. "This is a toss, ladies." Groans went up all around as Gray and Quinn went into each suite and searched for

19

contraband. Big Ginger and another guard stood outside each suite and kept watch over the ladies while the remaining COs stood along the unit. Just outside the door was a plastic storage bin that served as a receptacle for anything they might find. Sure enough, in the first room they found hooch—liquor made with bread, sugar, and fruit—and homemade cigarettes.

Several other suites yielded homemade tattooing needles and ink, lighters, and even a couple of weapons.

In Abby's suite, Quinn pulled her bag from the locker and thumbed through her books. He glanced at the titles then looked over at her briefly before moving on to the other lockers. Rosita and Rita's lockers held an astonishing amount of junk food and clothing, but nothing illegal. None of the other lockers yielded anything either.

As the COs finished, Captain Dennis addressed the unit. "Now you know when we find shit, we gotta search you," he bellowed. "Full cavity for you ladies."

There was a collective groan from the women as the female COs led each inmate, one at a time, into a cubicle that only had a pink curtain for a door. Inside the inmate was required to strip down to nothing, even pulling hair clips and ponytail holders out. One guard searched shoes and clothing while the other checked the inmate. Big Ginger did the physical search and Abby could see through the gap in the curtain as she ordered the inmate to lean forward and run her fingers vigorously through her hair. She ordered the inmate to open her mouth wide and lift up her tongue, pull her ears forward, and then lift her arms. Big Ginger spun her around then ordered the inmate to lift each breast checking her thoroughly. Then, most humiliatingly, she directed the inmate to spread her legs apart, spread her butt cheeks, squat three times, and cough hard. Finally, Big Ginger ordered her to turn around, lift her feet, and wiggle her toes. When the all clear was called, the inmate was allowed to dress and return to the common area where she was ordered to sit along the wall just outside the suites.

Regardless of whether or not an inmate had contraband, they were all subjected to the cavity search. Abby was shocked that some of the fatter inmates hid contraband like cigarettes, lighters, and in one case, a paper shiv, under their breasts and in the fat folds of their bellies. She felt sick knowing that her turn was soon. Most of the inmates were heavy set and their searches took longer. Sheronda's was short since she was so tiny. Then it was Abby's turn. She stepped into the cubicle and Big Ginger turned to face her.

"Sorry about this," Big Ginger muttered, much to Abby's surprise. "I know you just did this at intake, but we can't skip you."

"It's OK," Abby reassured her and began to undress. Abby's body was lean from running, and she was somewhat self-conscious that her breasts were small compared to the other women in the unit. Through the gap in the curtain, she could see the male COs had their backs to the cubicle with the exception of Quinn. Though he was mostly in profile, Abby knew he could see her out of the corner of his eye. She turned away as much as she could and Big Ginger moved so that only Abby's backside was on display.

At the end, Big Ginger moved again so that she blocked Abby's view of the commons while Abby put her clothes back on. Abby smiled at her then walked out to sit next to Sheronda.

When all the searches were done, four women had been discovered hiding contraband in various orifices and fat folds. They were sent to DSEG for charges. Abby knew they'd stay there as punishment.

At the end of the ordeal, Captain Dennis sent the ladies back to their suites to clean up.

In the suite, Abby put her things back in her locker and remade her bed. Mad T came up to her as Marianna set about cleaning up their space.

"You Abby, right?" Mad T was only slightly shorter than Abby, but easily a hundred and fifty to two hundred pounds heavier. Abby nodded.

"We keep it clean in here, OK? No funny stuff. You bring in contraband, I'm gonna get you kicked out and sent to D Unit." Mad T gave her a long look until Abby nodded.

"D Unit be where all the problems go," Sheronda said. She had finished cleaning and was resting on her bunk. "They be all like anger issues and people who be a little bit crazy. Like bad crazy."

"I'm not going to bring anything in," Abby promised. She pulled out one of her books, a collection of stories by Neil Gaiman, and settled onto her bunk to read.

Dinner was less eventful than lunch with Janet still in the infirmary. On offer was a choice of meatloaf, mashed potatoes, salad, and boiled chicken breast with apple crumble or a pudding cup for dessert. Abby took the boiled chicken and salad as Sheronda loaded up with everything using both hers and Abby's trays.

The COs had changed shifts at toss, so Abby assumed it was Ramirez, White, and Montgomery who manned the walls and door. All were women. So was Captain Hannah, who took a seat in front of Abby. In surprise, Sheronda's spork paused halfway to her mouth.

She was a very attractive black woman with short-cropped graying hair. Abby pegged her for a loving grandmother.

"I wanted to introduce myself and ask you some questions, if that's OK?" Captain Hannah had a deep, mellow voice.

Abby put her own spork down. "Sure."

"I understand from your file that you are a churchgoer," she gave Abby a smile.

Abby nodded. "Yes, ma'am."

"But you are also a competition fighter. Could you explain that?"

"I don't know why it says that. I trained in the Keysi and Krav Maga. They are tactical self-defense methods. We didn't compete or have tournaments. We had exhibitions to demonstrate the techniques, and I taught young women how to defend themselves." Abby moved her tray out of the way. "Some of our students went on to mixed martial arts competitions, but I stayed in training. I'm not sure who put competitive fighting in my file. I never competed."

"But you are skilled at this...what was it again? Keysi? Krav Maga?"

Abby nodded.

Captain Hannah gave her a smile that only slightly softened the look of steel in her eyes. "I just want you to understand that we don't condone any fighting of any kind here."

"Yes, ma'am. Though Keysi and Krav Maga aren't about initiating conflict, they're about ending the attack," Abby reassured her.

Captain Hannah nodded as she stood up. "Good to know." She patted Abby on the hand. "Welcome, then. I know you're going to do well here."

Sheronda stared as the older woman walked away. "Damn girl, how much trouble you gonna be?"

Abby picked up her tray. "I was hoping to avoid trouble. I was hoping to be invisible."

Chapter 5

JIGGING

The women were allowed to go wherever they wanted after dinner, so Abby went out to run in the yard. This time she doubled her plan and worked on ten miles. She managed to finish in time for a short shower. Back in her suite, Abby exchanged her running shoes for rubber sandals, grabbed her towel and toiletries kit from her locker, and made her way to the showers. She was inwardly terrified. She'd heard stories about the things that happened in the showers like beatings, gang rapes, and even murder.

As she passed a suite farther down, a voice called out. "Hello…Abby?"

Abby turned to see Grandma coming to the door of her suite. "My name is Agnes, but most of the ladies call me Grandma. Do you mind if I walk with you to the showers?" Grandma asked.

"Not at all." Abby waited while Grandma collected her things.

"I wanted to speak with you, but we've had such an eventful day, I haven't had the time."

Grandma was a small woman, somewhere in her sixties or seventies, with iron gray hair styled in a curly bob.

"I see you've been placed with Sheronda," Grandma noted. Abby nodded. "She'll be a good friend to you." Abby smiled but said nothing. Grandma continued, "I've been told you are a good Christian."

Abby shrugged. "I'm not sure good Christians end up in prison."

Grandma laughed. "I'm sure you know your Bible, my dear. Even our Lord and Savior ended up in prison. You're in good company."

Abby had to laugh at that.

As they neared the entrance to the showers, Grandma put her hand out to stop Abby.

"Have you engaged in activities with other women?" she asked tactfully.

Abby shook her head. "I'm not interested in that. It makes me uncomfortable to even think about it," she admitted.

Grandma smiled. "Then I must warn you, the showers are a place of rampant debauchery. If you stay close to me, no one will bother you." Grandma moved to enter the bathroom, but Abby stopped her.

"Can I ask why?"

Grandma patted her hand and smiled reassuringly. "I'm a psychopath, dear. I should have been paroled years ago, but I stabbed a woman who tried to rape one of my girls." Grandma gave Abby's hand a squeeze and went into the showers.

Inside, Abby saw that Grandma was right about the showers. Full on nudity was on display, and even though about half the women were actually showering, the other half were engaging in heavy flirting or performing actual sex acts on each other.

Grandma stopped and regarded the inmate known as Fred with the woman she shared her shower stall with. The woman stood under the spray, her head back as Fred kissed her neck. Her nipples stood out as Fred pinched and rolled the nipple on one breast. Then she moaned as Fred moved her hand between the woman's legs. Grandma stayed a moment longer as Fred's fingers moved deftly over the woman's engorged sex.

Abby's face was flushed with embarrassment as she turned away to find an empty shower stall. Grandma pulled her to the end where another one stood empty.

"This one's mine," she said as she turned on the water. "No one but me or my girls come to this one. *They* all know to stay away." Grandma put her things on a small shelf built into the wall and hung her towel on a hook underneath it.

"You go first, dear," she smiled. "I'll wait here. Then when you're done I'll take my turn."

Abby undressed and placed her clothes on the shelf. Some of the women turned to watch her, but they turned away at Grandma's glare.

Abby took the shortest shower she'd ever taken in her life. When she had rinsed, Grandma handed over her towel. "Dry off in there and I'll give you your clothes. The less you tempt them the better."

Abby did as she was told, and then switched places with Grandma. With no shower curtains, only the location of the stall and Abby's body gave Grandma any sense of privacy. Her shower was mercifully brief as well, and Abby turned to hand her a towel. She saw that Grandma had had both breasts removed in a radical mastectomy. Her thin chest was shrunken from the loss of muscle tone and huge scars crisscrossed her chest.

As Grandma dried off and proceeded to dress, Abby watched the other women in the room. Some were gossiping and giggling as if it was some sort of sorority house, while others treated the session as an opportunity to display their bodies. Kelsey and her girls had come in. They were in various stages of undress and engaging in an impromptu twerking contest. Kelsey laughed and moved from one girl to the next, grabbing their asses and grinding against them until they squealed. Abby knew the show was for her. Kelsey kept glancing over each time she put her fingers between their legs.

As much as she opposed girl-on-girl sex for herself, Abby had to admit it was an intriguing show.

By the time Grandma was ready to leave, Kelsey had one of the girls on her knees in front of her. Kelsey's hand was tangled in the girl's hair as her tongue lapped at the hairless slit between Kelsey's legs. She was already shaking as Abby and Grandma left.

"Do you shower every day, dear?" Grandma asked. Abby nodded. Grandma smiled at her as they stopped at the door to her suite. "Then come pick me up whenever you're ready and I'll go with you."

Abby was relieved. "Thanks." Grandma smiled and reached out to give Abby's hand a squeeze then turned and went into her suite.

In Abby's suite, all of the women were ready for bed. Sheronda looked up from her bottom bunk as Abby put her stuff away.

"Grandma be jiggin for you?" she asked.

Abby shrugged. "I don't know what that is."

Sheronda thumbed through her magazine. "She be a lookout for you, like when you showering or going to the toilet."

Abby nodded.

"That's what I thought." Sheronda closed her magazine. She held her place with her thumb. "It ain't allowed, but them COs let Grandma do it 'cause it be for protection, not fuckin'. You is lucky."

Abby agreed, and then pulled out a book and climbed on her bed. She'd only read a couple of chapters before it was lights out. She didn't think she was going to be able to sleep on the thin mattress, but in no time she was out.

It was still dark when she awoke. She was confused about where she was at first, but soon realized she was in her bunk in her suite. A groan near the floor told her what had awakened her. Abby turned over and looked down to see Marianna completely naked on Mad T's lower bunk. She had the body of a centerfold with large breasts and a flat, toned stomach. Mad T kneeled on the floor at the end of her bunk, her tongue working at the cleft between Marianna's legs. Rosita, also naked, was at the top of the bunk near Marianna's head. She squeezed the other woman's breast with one hand while her other one covered Marianna's mouth to stifle the moans that could get them into trouble. Rita was barely visible at the far end of the suite, but she was clearly naked from the waist down and masturbating as she watched Mad T.

She might not like contraband, but Abby could tell Mad T loved sex: her hand was deep inside her scrub pants.

Abby's face grew hot as she watched the three women. She glanced down at the bunk beneath her and saw that Sheronda too was watching and working her sex furiously under her sweat pants.

Abby moved her hand under her waistband and pressed her fingers against herself. She moved her middle finger slowly along her cleft. It was already hot and she could feel the moisture filling her panties. She only needed a few strokes before she was shuddering from a quick but intense orgasm. At the same time, Marianna began to moan with her own. Abby glanced down as Mad T pulled away, her fingers still working vigorously between her legs. She looked up at Abby as she too started to orgasm.

"You wanna be next?" she panted. Abby shook her head and rolled over, spent.

Abby woke up the next morning tired and achy. It was going to take her a while to get used to the hard bed and late night interruptions.

She slid off the top bunk, and then put on her prison blues and a soft gray hoodie she'd brought from home. She sorely needed to go for a run. Her body was used to hitting the road first thing in the morning for track practice, and she was feeling anxious about not being able to go outside.

Everyone in her suite was still asleep as she took her toothbrush and toothpaste into the small bathroom. She was rinsing when she heard the heavy *thunk* of the door lock disengaging. A minute later, a buzz sounded throughout the unit and her suitemates all pushed out of their bunks with groans. Mad T appeared in the doorway and gave Abby a long look.

"You ain't gonna say nothin', right?" she asked. Abby didn't know what she was talking about at first then realized Mad T meant their late night rendezvous.

"No," Abby answered. "What's to say?"

Mad T looked at her suspiciously at first. "You playin' me?"

Abby moved past her to put her things back in her locker. "No. It's none of my business."

Mad T seemed satisfied with that. "You all right then, girl. You need some lovin' sometime, you let me know. I'll hook you up."

Abby smiled at the gesture. "Thanks. But I don't dig girls."

Mad T looked over at Marianna and the two shared a smirk. "You like to watch then? OK. You watch."

Abby said nothing about that. She had liked watching.

Chapter 6

RANGE RUNNER

After breakfast, there was a count, and then another small shakedown. With the previous offenders still in DSEG, there was no contraband found, so there were no body searches. Abby reported to the common area outside the guard office where Big Ginger was waiting.

"You ready for your first day of work?" she asked. Abby nodded and the two waited for the rest of the crew.

Sheronda walked up yawning. "You gonna clean with me, girl?"

Big Ginger answered for her. "She's with you. You're going to be doing the admin offices from now on."

Sheronda's eyebrows went up. "Cool…easy job then."

The rest of the women arrived and Big Ginger took roll. Besides herself and Sheronda, the crew included some of Grandma's girls, Sheronda's knitters, and a couple of the older women who typically cruised the periphery of the groups. Abby suspected Sheronda was in charge of her own clique but had neglected to mention it.

After roll, Big Ginger and Gray led the group out of the unit to a locked closet that held a dozen cleaning carts. Each woman got her own cart. Then they were led down several locked halls to the administrative section of the prison. The admin wing looked a lot like what one would see in a large high school. There were several offices. The largest was the chief administrator's office, or warden. It was flanked by the offices for the assistant corrections administrator and the chief of security. Farther along the hall were the offices for the prison's case managers and psychologist.

Big Ginger stopped with Sheronda and Abby in the reception area while Gray took the remaining women down another hallway.

Big Ginger looked at Abby. "Have you cleaned before?"

Abby shrugged. "At home and sometimes at work."

"Well, here all you need to do is dust, empty trash cans, and vacuum. You two will clean during admin staff meetings, so you should be able to get everything done." Big Ginger pointed out the offices on the left. "Abby, you take those. Sheronda, you're on the right."

Abby found cleaning to be a quiet activity. It was mindless work, but in a way that was good. She found herself settling into a groove as she dusted the wall of bookshelves. At some point, Sheronda poked her head in.

"You doin' all right?" she asked. Abby nodded. "Just make sure you dust them plants too. Warden like her leaves shiny."

Abby looked up at the row of philodendrons that covered the top of the bookshelves. She was tall, but there was no way she could reach the top leaves. Luckily, there was a small stepladder attached to her cart. Abby started at the end, and after a time had all the leaves clean and shining.

It took most of the morning to finish their section. They were still vacuuming when the warden and her staff started to come in. Big Ginger and the rest of the crew were waiting for Abby and Sheronda when they finished. Gray led the women back to the closet and checked in each cart, making sure nothing was missing. Every job used some type of tool that was checked out then checked back in to make sure the inmates weren't using their tools as weapons. Housekeeping had little to weaponize except cleaning chemicals. Gray checked bottle levels on each cart. Luckily all of them passed.

It was midday and time for lunch. Abby followed Sheronda into the cafeteria and loaded up on everything. Lunch that day was beef vegetable soup, turkey sandwiches, potato chips, or celery and carrots, with brownies and the ever-present pudding cup.

They sat at the same table as the day before, which further confirmed for Abby that Sheronda was in charge of her own crew.

"Oh look, my boyfriend's comin' to sit wit me," Sheronda cooed. Abby turned to see Quinn in position near their table. He looked over at Sheronda and smiled, but looked away without saying anything.

Sheronda turned back to the table and helped herself to Abby's soup. Abby took the turkey and cheese off the bread and rolled it up.

"Girl, how you gonna live with so little food?" one of the ladies asked.

Abby shrugged. "I'm not used to eating like this. At home I ate mostly organic food; healthier stuff."

"You mean like a vegetarian?" Sheronda asked. Abby shook her head.

"No, I eat some meat, like boiled chicken breast or ground turkey, and lots of fresh fish." Abby finished her turkey and cheese then started on her celery. "I ate food that was really high in protein, but in small quantities. What's really important are high quality foods like whole grains, fresh fruit, and vegetables with flaxseed or chia. It would be great if I could get some kefir and kale. But it's not likely going to happen here."

"Not unless you can get the commissary to get it for you," Sheronda offered. "But I doubt it. They just got junk food an' shit."

"You can file a request for special diet consideration," one of the ladies suggested. "I got it for my diabetes and high blood pressure. Ask your counselor next time."

Sheronda took Abby's brownie and pudding cup. "We ain't got a fridge in our suite though. Ain't nobody got that much money."

Abby was surprised. "We can have a fridge?"

Sheronda nodded. "Yeah, like a small one. We can have a hot plate too, but nobody got money for that neither."

Abby thought for a moment then asked, "Where do you get them?"

"Commissary," one of the other ladies answered for Sheronda since her mouth was full.

Abby turned to her. "Can you take me there after lunch?"

"Sure, B Unit can visit the commissary after two today," Sheronda answered with her mouth still full.

After lunch it was not just Sheronda and Abby, but also all of Sheronda's friends who accompanied them to the commissary line. Posted on the wall was a list of everything that one could get with paper and small golf pencils to write down requests. Abby looked over the list and marked off things she thought she might need in addition to the mini-fridge and hot plate. She'd noticed that neither Sheronda nor any of her friends were getting anything. While they waited, Abby handed the list to Sheronda to check off what she needed. When it was Abby's turn, she handed the list to the guard at the window who looked at it in surprise.

"You've got a lot of stuff here," he said. "You new?" Abby nodded. "You have help carrying it?"

Abby nodded again.

"I need your ID," he said. Abby pulled the lanyard that held her ID over her head and handed it to him.

He scanned it into his computer and Abby understood that the items she was getting would be paid for out of her book. She wasn't sure how much money her father had put on her account, but she was sure it was considerable.

Inmates pulled the items from the shelves and placed them in bins that ran along a rolling track on the other side of the windows. When the bins were filled, a second commissary guard checked them, and then pushed the items through the only opening in the glass wall. Abby waited as he pushed the fridge through first. The other ladies in line looked at Abby enviously as Sheronda's ladies took possession of it. Sheronda took the hot plate and the bag of dishes and pans. Abby took the bag of toiletries she was sure to need shortly.

"We gonna get a TV too?" Sheronda asked.

Abby laughed. "Maybe next time."

Back at the unit, Abby and Sheronda set up the fridge and hot plate on the empty desk in the corner. Abby locked everything else up in her locker. For security, Abby had bought a heavy padlock to secure the cabinet. When everything was secured, she attached the key to her lanyard.

Sheronda put the things that Abby had bought her into her own locker, and then smiled as Abby handed her a lock as well.

"Why you bein' so nice to me?" Sheronda suddenly seemed suspicious.

Abby didn't want to offend her, but she had to ask. "You don't have much money on your book, do you?"

Sheronda shook her head. "Ain't got family to send me nothin', and workin' don't pay shit." Sheronda fell onto her bunk. "I can get soap and a razor and that's it. They charge full price for shit in commissary, but they don't give you fair pay for workin'. And since theys so many cons here, we only work like half a day, so we only get paid half. It's like they want you to suffer."

Abby laughed. "I know, right? It's like being in prison."

Sheronda gave her a dirty look then laughed with her. "Yeah, right…but thanks, you know? You was cool to do that."

"No problem," Abby answered then left to go for a run.

Chapter 7

FLIPPING THE SCRIPT

After the first few days, Abby easily fell into the rhythm of prison. Timing was regiment-ed, as were their activities and life on B Unit was predictable, if not a little boring. The unit population was evenly divided between lifers and prisoners with longer sentences, and those who were only serving a bit, or a short sentence. It was rare when a B Unit inmate needed to go to DSEG, which the inmates called "Lock," for fighting or contra-band. After a while, Abby could tell who was going to be a problem. With the exception of the chronic troublemakers like Fred and Kelsey, the problem inmates were usually short-sentence, repeat offenders who had already served multiple sentences which con-tributed to the recidivism statistic. They were the ones most likely to pick fights in the yard or bring in contraband. They were also the ones most likely to be "cell warriors," inmates who made a lot of threats when suites were in lockdown, but had very little to say when out among the general population. Abby knew from the other women that these cell warriors were really irritating and often privately beaten up by their suite-mates just to shut them up. One of Sheronda's crew had to threaten her noisy suitemate by putting her crochet hook up to the woman's eye one night, just to get some sleep.

After a few weeks, Janet finally returned. Abby could tell she was clean but shaky. She was assigned to a suite just down from Abby's. Being young and blond, Janet was immediately recruited into Kelsey's group. Abby was angry that Kelsey took advantage of Janet's tenuous grip on sobriety to manipulate her, but she under-stood that Janet's addictions were born out of a need to escape her horrible past. Kelsey supplied Janet with enough hooch to keep her sedated, and Janet did whatever

Kelsey told her to do in order to keep it that way. It wasn't long before Kelsey's brand showed up on Janet's arms, further cementing her place in the group.

Periodically they would get a real troublemaker in the unit. Although the most serious offenders who were a threat to general population were sent directly to Lock, there were a limited number of cells in Lock to accommodate them. When DSEG was full, transfers were sent wherever there was room. Abby was a couple of months into her sentence when one such problem child showed up.

Her name was Dana and she looked ordinary enough, like a high school student who had not yet grown into her prettiness. Sheronda called her a "whigger." It was a term used to describe a white girl who acted like a black girl. Some of the younger women couldn't help it, but Abby could tell with Dana that it was an affectation. It seemed like Dana could turn the behavior on and off like a light switch. She was in for aggravated assault with five years added to her sentence for attacking another inmate. According to Dana, she'd been transferred from another prison for her own protection. Abby suspected the opposite was true.

Right away Dana set out to redefine the cliques in the unit, which did not sit well with the daddies. Even Kelsey demurred when Dana tried to move in on her family. Worse yet, Dana chose to bait the COs every chance she could. Abby watched as Big Ginger and Captain Hannah both tried to befriend the angry young woman, which only made her angrier. She refused counseling sessions and balked at work assignments, calling them stupid. Extremely confrontational, she would verbally abuse anyone who looked at her sideways, which was pretty much everyone. The only job she would take was kitchen duty.

During general population, Dana would rant, going from preppy white girl to whigger at the drop of a hat. Sheronda would translate her slang until even she had to give up. Dana seemed to be coming up with her own language. Abby wondered if the girl might be bipolar or even schizophrenic. She knew from Big Ginger that the unit COs had already requested her transfer out of B Unit. But with limited space it was going to take some time. With so many problem children, even the Intensive Management Unit, or Hole, where the most dangerous inmates were housed, was full.

So Big Ginger and Captain Hannah kept trying to befriend the girl. They couldn't see that every attempt made Dana angrier and more resentful. Abby wanted to tell them to stop, but chose to mind her own business.

Then, weirdly, Dana grew calm. Abby was in the common area helping Sylvia, one of the ladies in Sheronda's crew, complete a revised visitation request when Dana came in to speak to Big Ginger.

"I wanna talk to my case manager," she announced.

"I can see if she's available," Big Ginger answered. "I have to give her a reason though."

Dana's face went stony. "I just need to talk to her about some stuff."

Big Ginger regarded the young woman for a moment then shrugged. "OK, let me give her a call."

As Big Ginger turned away, Abby saw Dana reach under her shirt and pull something out. Instinctively, Abby jumped up. But by the time she reached the young woman, Dana was shoving her fist into Big Ginger's side. Abby grabbed Dana's arm and snapped it back, breaking Dana's arm at the elbow. She tried to force Dana to drop the paper shiv she was holding. It was dripping with Big Ginger's blood.

Sylvia began to shout for the other COs as Big Ginger fell to her knees. Her face was pale, and the bloodstain on the side of her shirt was growing.

Despite her broken arm, Dana continued to struggle to get to Big Ginger. Abby put her in a headlock and pulled her to the floor then wrapped her long legs around Dana to prevent her from getting up. In frustration, Dana started screaming. Over her screams, Abby could hear an alarm sounding through the unit.

Quinn rushed to Big Ginger's side while Captain Dennis ran to assist Abby. Dana still held the bloody shiv, and despite her broken arm, was trying to stab Captain Dennis. Abby gripped Dana's wrist in an effort to protect both Captain Dennis and herself.

"Turn away, girl," he said to Abby as he pulled his OC spray off his belt. Abby twisted so that her face was as far away from Dana's face as possible. Captain Dennis stepped on Dana's wrist and Abby's hand then sprayed the girl straight in the face. Splatter hit Abby, and she cried out from the burning; but she kept her hold on the girl as Captain Dennis pulled cuffs from his belt. Seconds later the SRT were surrounding them. Their Tasers trained on both women.

"Roll over, hon," Captain Dennis ordered. Abby flipped the girl so that he could pull Dana's other arm out to cuff her hands behind her back. Dana still tried to buck her way out of Abby's hold, but Abby held tight. She couldn't see

Captain Dennis, but she knew from the sounds he was making that he struggled to pull the young woman's legs together. To help, Abby moved her legs lower and tightened them around Dana's knees. She heard the sound of a zip tie closing, and then Captain Dennis told her to let go. Dana had been effectively hobbled.

Abby relaxed her grip then pushed the young woman off. The side of her face and neck burned from the pepper spray, and Big Ginger's blood stained the cuff on her shirt.

Dana lay on the floor, fighting against her restraints despite the broken arm Abby had given her and a face full of pepper spray. Abby pushed off the floor then stepped away from Dana. Mindful of the Tasers still trained on her, she put her hands up. She clasped her fingers together on her head while Dana continued to struggle on the floor.

"Put your hands down, girl," Captain Dennis ordered. Abby dropped them and stepped aside as two of the SRT officers pulled Dana off the floor. Orderlies were already strapping Big Ginger to a gurney to take her to the hospital. Another orderly led the way as SRT officers strapped Dana to an emergency restraint chair, and then rolled her to the central infirmary. Quinn escorted Abby to a small treatment room off the main common area where one of the prison nurses waited to check her for injuries.

"How much spray did you get?" she asked, as she looked Abby over for wounds. "Any in your eyes?

"Enough," Abby answered. "None in my eyes. I need some milk and some dishwashing detergent."

"I brought some," the nurse replied pulling a cart up to the table. She diluted the detergent in a basin of warm water. "How do you know that?" she asked.

"I did a rotation in the emergency room," Abby admitted. She hated giving anything away about her past since it usually invited more questions. "I saw the aftermath of a lot of bar fights." She gritted her teeth against the burning. Quinn was watching her closely. The last thing Abby wanted was his pity.

In another minute, the nurse had everything she needed. She bathed Abby's face and neck with milk to soothe the searing pain of the spray. The nurse used a dishwashing detergent and water mixture to cut through the capsicum oil, and then reapplied the milk. The burning soon stopped. Abby's skin was red along her right ear and part of her cheek and neck where she'd been hit; but the pain had dulled considerably. The nurse had cut away Abby's prison top, which had caught part of the spray. Abby's tank top underneath was clean.

The nurse cleaned the blood from Abby's hand to make sure there wasn't an injury.

"It's not my blood," Abby told her. "It's Big Gin…I mean Sergeant Redfern's. I think Dana got her kidney."

"They're airlifting her to nearest trauma center," Quinn replied.

Abby looked over at him. "They're not taking Dana to the same place are they?"

Quinn shook his head. "She'll go to the local facility. You destroyed her arm."

Abby didn't care. "There's something wrong with that girl. She's either deranged or she's on something."

"They think she's been inhaling from one of the kitchen refrigerators. They found damaged coils." Quinn said.

Abby and the nurse looked at each other and nodded. "Regular inhalant abuse can cause psychotic episodes," Abby said to Quinn.

"Did she cough a lot?" the nurse asked. "Or clear her throat?" This time it was Abby and Quinn who both nodded.

"That's probably it, then." The nurse bathed Abby's hair and scalp in the detergent then the milk. When she finished she declared her done.

Abby stood up and thanked the nurse, and then turned to Quinn. "Now what?"

Quinn looked uncomfortable. "I have to take you to ADSEG. Your case manager is there waiting to take a report from you, then they'll decide what to do."

Abby was furious. "You have surveillance video. Why am I in trouble?"

Quinn led her out. "You probably won't be. Captain Dennis has already put in his part for you. I'll do mine when we get there. They'll know what happened and let you go."

Abby knew he was lying. She had badly broken Dana's arm. They weren't going to overlook that. She also wasn't surprised when he snapped handcuffs on her for the transfer. Regardless of the fact that she had been trying to prevent further injury to Big Ginger, Abby had physically assaulted another inmate. She brooded over the situation she had put herself in as Quinn led her down cold cement hallways peppered with barred doors and windows crisscrossed with wire.

Abby's case manager, Emma, was waiting for them in ADSEG. Quinn removed the cuffs and went to file his own report.

Abby sat down in front of Emma, rubbing her wrists.

"Well, you've had an exciting day." Emma pulled out Abby's folder. "Tell me what happened."

Abby recounted the day's events as Emma took notes. Emma was still writing when she finished.

"I won't lie to you," Emma began, "it could go either way. On the one had you used excessive force on the girl and broke her arm. But if you hadn't intervened, Sergeant Redfern might have been killed." Abby sat silently as Emma regarded her. Then she handed Abby the paperwork to sign. "You'll be spending at least tonight in DSEG," Emma informed her. Abby shrugged, but said nothing. Emma seemed nonplussed by Abby's stoicism. "I'll probably know by tomorrow what they're going to do with you."

Emma got her papers together and stood up. "What you did was very stupid, but if you hadn't done it…well, let's just say you did a good thing. Sergeant Redfern is highly regarded here. A lot of people are going to be happy with you." Emma reached over and patted Abby on the shoulder then left. As Abby watched her go, she had the feeling that Emma wasn't one of those people.

One of the DSEG COs showed up at Abby's elbow. "You need to come with me," she said, but not unkindly. "I have a transfer coming."

Abby got up and followed her to the disciplinary unit. The CO stopped at a cell closest to the central guard office and waved Abby in. She heard the door close behind her and the lock engage.

Where ADSEG was just a smaller version of the units, DSEG was a whole unit of single cells furnished with nothing but a bunk bed, an attached shelf desk, an exposed toilet, a sink, and a stall shower. Meals were distributed in Styrofoam containers through a slot in the door. Inmates were handcuffed for transfers. Whereas general population in B Unit included over a hundred prisoners, DSEG held only thirty in each isolated section. Only two to three inmates at a time were allowed out onto a small courtyard surrounded by walls and a twenty-foot high fence topped with razor wire. The courtyard was divided into sections by fencing so that inmates were kept apart during their hour. DSEG was almost full and extremely noisy with women demanding their free time or attention from the COs or case managers. Women in DSEG were typically problem prisoners with a wide variety of behavioral issues. Some were violent while others took their anger out in more creative ways. The favorite was gassing. An inmate would dilute her feces in a cup of urine and let it sit. When it was good and fermented, she would throw it at whoever happened to be nearest her food slot. One resident of DSEG was a chronic gasser, and the unit reeked of her bodily fluids. Abby hoped she would get her hour soon. The smell was overwhelming, and she was so pumped with adrenaline, she really needed to run it off.

Sure enough, an hour later Quinn showed up and the door to Abby's cell opened.

"I'm taking you for your hour," he said. Abby didn't respond. She wondered why it was Quinn and not one of the DSEG COs. She followed him out to the largest section of the small, walled courtyard that was half the size of B Unit's. She took deep breaths of fresh air, trying to get the unit's stench out of her nose.

When Abby turned to start her run, Quinn put out his hand to stop her. "I wanted you to know, Dana nicked Redfern's kidney…just like you said. She's in surgery, but they think she's going to be fine." Abby stared at him for a second then nodded. Without a word, she turned away and began to run.

When her hour was up, Quinn led her back to her cell. As Abby entered it, he called her back to the door.

"Since you're only here temporarily they're not moving your things." He reached behind him and pulled out a book. "I don't know if you've read this one, but it's all I have with me." Abby took the book and looked down. It was a well-worn copy of *Good Omens* by Neil Gaiman. It was one of her favorites. She'd loaned it out and hadn't been able to get it back before leaving for prison.

"Thanks." Abby was surprised and more than a little bit touched.

Quinn gave her a short nod then turned and locked the cell.

Chapter 8

JACK UP

Abby ended up in DSEG for a week. Despite the fact that their daughter tried to murder a guard and was now looking at a life sentence, Dana's family insisted that charges be brought up against Abby for breaking her arm. They also threatened to sue her personally. To appease the family, Abby was called before a disciplinary committee to hear charges and sentencing. The committee informed her that she was guilty of committing bodily harm against another inmate. Abby was given an additional one-year sentence that was subsequently suspended. She thought the whole thing was stupid, but accepted it with grace. Luckily, the hearing officer ended her stay in DSEG and ordered her back to B Unit. Quinn waited at the door to the hearing room to take her back.

They were silent as they made their way through the prison. It wasn't until they reached the doors to B Unit that Abby remembered his book.

"Wait, I need to go back to Lock. I left your book there," she started. Quinn reached back, pulled the book from out of the back of his waistband, and handed it to her.

She stared at the book as they walked back into B Unit. She stopped at her suite and turned to him. "Why are you doing all this?"

Quinn looked at her for a second. "Doing what?" he answered then walked away.

Abby's suitemates and friends were happy to have her back. Although it took several showers to get the smell of DSEG off her skin, it didn't take any time to fall back into the rhythm of prison.

Big Ginger wasn't due back for a few weeks so Quinn took over as escort for the cleaning crew. Sheronda was especially glad to have Abby back. She'd had to put up with another cleaning assistant while Abby was gone, and the girl just hadn't lived up to Sheronda's high standards. She maintained a running monologue of all the events Abby had missed as their group picked up their carts and made their way to the admin wing.

Montgomery took the rest of the crew off, while Quinn stayed with Sheronda and Abby. Sheronda gave him a pointed look, then wiggled her eyebrows at Abby before going off down the hall to start her offices.

Abby pulled her cart into the warden's office at the top of the hall and set about dusting her plants and bookshelves. She was so absorbed that she didn't hear Quinn walk in. It wasn't until she felt his hand reach under her pant leg that she realized he was so near. His touch startled her so badly that she almost fell off the stepladder. She grabbed the end of the shelf to regain her balance and looked down. From her vantage point, she could see only the top of his head as he gazed, not at her, but at his hand resting near her ankle. She could feel the heat of his palm warming her skin, and then his thumb moving across her calf. Abby remained motionless as his thumb traveled back and forth across her skin, but her heart pounded in her chest. A long minute passed then he removed his hand and walked out. Abby sat on the top step to catch her breath. She knew her face was flushed; she could feel it burning. When she felt settled again, she turned back to the shelves to finish her work.

When they were finished with all the offices, Abby and Sheronda dragged their carts back to check-in with the rest of the group. She kept looking at Quinn, but for once, he wouldn't return her gaze. Instead, he stared straight ahead. His expression was stony, almost angry.

All the carts passed check-in and the cleaning crew was returned to B Unit. Abby wanted to talk about Quinn to Sheronda, but she didn't really know what to say so she kept silent as they went to lunch. Quinn took up his usual position near her table, but continued to look away. Abby picked at her lunch before giving all of it to Sheronda. She was relieved when lunch was over and she could go out to the yard to run.

After a week in DSEG, it felt good to get in a long run. Abby spent her hours after lunch and dinner sprinting along the path. She felt everything fall away as she ran: the buildings, the fences, and the people all became a blur as she ran faster and faster.

At the end of her run, she slowed to a walk then stopped. Exhausted, she bent over and panted. Abby had never run so fast for so long before. She knew she looked like a crazy person, but she didn't care. DSEG had been claustrophobic, and she needed to run off all the anxiety she was feeling.

As the women flooded into the unit, Abby grabbed her things and went to Grandma's suite. Grandma was ready and waiting for her when she walked up, and the two women set off toward the showers.

While she was stuck in DSEG, a new shaving cream had appeared in the commissary. It had been a requested item, not because of its superior shaving capabilities, but because the cap was rounded like the top of a dildo. Tape or latex gloves held the cap on and women were already putting it to use. Fred had fashioned a type of harness from strips of fabric and was enthusiastically fucking one of her girls with it. Others watched with their hands between their legs as they waited to let Fred attend to them as well. Abby looked away as Grandma looked on in disgust. Life in B Unit was like living in one long porno sometimes. After a while it got boring until someone came up with something new...or someone new.

Abby took a quick shower, and then switched places with Grandma. She was talking to the older woman when she felt hands on her hips. Then something hard pressed at her backside between her legs. Abby spun around, almost knocking Fred down as the woman slipped on the tile floor.

"Hey, baby," Fred cooed. "You wanna give it a try?"

She was about to answer when Grandma flew out of the stall, naked and dripping, shampoo still in her hair.

"You get away from her, you faggot," Grandma roared. Fred's shocked expression was comical for a moment. Grandma always sounded so educated and reasonable. Abby moved to put herself in front of the older woman as Fred prepared to retaliate. But she needn't have bothered. Grandma struck fast, hitting Fred square in the throat and putting her down on the floor before anyone could say another word.

"You think I give a shit about you?" Grandma snarled over the choking woman. Fred's makeshift dildo stood straight up as if the encounter were exciting rather than terrifying. "I will cut you so fast you'll be out of here tits up, you fucking freak."

All the women, naked and dripping, watched in silent shock.

"What's going on in here?"

Everyone turned to see White standing in the doorway with her hand on her pepper spray.

"Nothing," Fred coughed. "I just slipped."

White stared at the naked woman with a look of disgust on her face. "Get up and take that off."

Fred gave Grandma a fearful look then did as she was told. White stayed as the other women soberly finished up their showers. Grandma stepped back in the shower to rinse off, then she dried and dressed. She and Abby left Fred under the watchful eye of the sergeant.

"It really wasn't that big of a deal," Abby said as they returned to the common area.

Grandma gave her a look. "Unless they are stopped, women like Alfreda will continue to harass you. They will keep upping the ante until they feel comfortable enough to rape you. And she will. Each time she makes a play she gets closer and closer to pulling people into her depravity. She won't try for you again. She knows I will kill her if she does."

Captain Hannah and Quinn waited for Grandma near the guard office. As if she was expecting them, Grandma gave Quinn a gracious smile and followed him out of the unit. Abby wasn't surprised to hear the buzzer call for a count.

"Line up, ladies," Captain Hannah called out. "It's a toss."

Abby set her things on her bunk, knowing it would be useless to put anything away. Then she went back out to stand by the door.

She and her suitemates watched as COs confiscated all the dome-lidded cans of shaving cream. Most were taped for use as dildos. Mad T was pissed and not quiet about it.

"Fuckin' Fred," she fumed. "So fuckin' stupid. Now we all gotta give it up." She'd just picked hers up from the commissary and had been looking forward to giving it a try.

Quinn had returned from escorting Grandma to stand guard during the search.

"No more shaving cream, ladies," Captain Hannah announced. "You're going to have to go back to your old stuff." Several women shot Fred dirty looks. Mad T looked murderous.

When the toss was over, Captain Hannah addressed the group again. "Body searches."

At that point, Abby had been subjected to so many body searches that it was fairly routine. She felt weird this time though, as if she was undressing for Quinn. Though his back was to her, she realized her reflection could be seen in the glass of the guard office. Without Big Ginger there, there was no one to hide behind, and she could sense that he was watching.

When she was done, Abby walked past Quinn with her face turned away, ignoring the looks from the other women. She knew they talked about her, even Marianna who had the looks and body of a successful porn star.

When they were dismissed, Abby lay down in her bed to read.

Chapter 9

JUICE CARD

For the next few mornings, Quinn kept his distance while Abby cleaned. After a week of nothing from him, she found him standing right behind her when she stepped off her ladder. She turned and stared into his face with their bodies only inches apart. Instead of looking at her, Quinn looked at the spot near her ear that had been burned by the pepper spray. It had mostly healed, but there were still red marks where she had gotten the worst of it.

Abby remained still as his hand moved her hair away from her cheek then gently touched the burn just below her ear. She jumped, not because it stung, but because he was touching her. Her breath quickened as he leaned over and pressed his lips on the spot. She turned slightly and closed her eyes, inhaling. He smelled like soap and man and a faint woody scent, as if he'd worn aftershave the day before. She shivered as he pulled her collar away from her neck and kissed the burn below. She trembled as his lips traveled over the marks the spray had left on her.

In the distance, the sound of Sheronda's vacuum stopped, and Quinn pulled away abruptly. Abby was flushed and panting when he turned and left the room.

She wanted to talk to him as the group gathered to return and check in their carts, but she knew he would just ignore her, so she remained silent.

She stayed that way for the rest of the day.

Throughout the weekend, Abby would close her eyes and relive the feeling of his lips on her neck. They had rotating weekend guard staff, so Quinn did not work most Saturdays and Sundays. She was able to daydream without interruption.

On Sunday, Abby lay in her bunk dozing when Mad T walked up and tapped her on the leg. She looked down at the woman in surprise. With little in common, Abby and Mad T typically avoided each other.

"I heard you been helpin' people with paperwork," she said.

Abby swung her legs off her bunk and dropped to the floor. "Yeah, some. Why? Do you need help?"

Mad T nodded. "I gotta put in a diet restriction request, and I don't know how to do it."

Abby shrugged. "OK. That's easy enough. You want to go out in common?"

Mad T nodded and grabbed her form then followed Abby to one of the tables near the guard office. Abby pulled Mad T's form over and looked at it. It looked like a first grader had tried to fill it out. The form was full of misspellings and grossly incorrect grammar.

Abby knew better than to question Mad T about it. "Can I erase some of this?" she asked instead. Mad T looked around then nodded. Abby erased the entire page and began to fill it out for her, asking for answers for some of the questions only Mad T could answer.

When the form was complete, Abby slid it across the table. Mad T took it with as much gratitude as she could muster for a proud woman. Before she could get up to go, Abby reached over to stop her.

"Can I ask you something?" she began tentatively.

Mad T smirked. "That was a question. But OK."

Abby leaned over and lowered her voice. "Do you want me to help you with your reading and writing?"

Mad T's face turned mulish for a moment then relaxed.

"You can do that?"

Abby nodded. "We can use my Bible so it looks like Bible study."

Mad T nodded. "That be cool."

Abby smiled. "We'll start tomorrow."

Mad T smiled and got up from the table. "Cool. You's cool."

Chapter 10

DEDICATED

The next morning, Abby was surprised that Gray stood guard while she and Sheronda cleaned while Quinn took the other group off. Abby assumed their encounter had been another isolated incident.

She ignored him as much as he ignored her on the way back. Abby noticed he kept to the other side of the cafeteria during lunch. If Sheronda noticed, she didn't say anything.

After a short run, Abby sat with Mad T at one of the courtyard tables and started working on her reading. She was glad she'd brought the Bible she'd used with her church group. It was a youth Bible that had been translated into more modern vernacular, making it easier to understand. She began with Genesis and worked with Mad T on word and sentence structure. The other woman was a quick learner, but after an hour, Abby wondered if she might suffer from dyslexia. She seemed unable to recognize the difference in letters like b and d and attached letters from one word to another. Luckily, Mad T seemed to be enjoying herself. For Abby, it was an opportunity to stop thinking about Quinn.

Abby and Mad T continued working at the common tables after count then again after dinner. Abby didn't even notice when Quinn left for the day.

The next morning he stood at the top of the hallway as Abby and Sheronda set about cleaning.

Abby had finished the warden's bookshelves when she turned to see Quinn at the door. As Sheronda's vacuum went on in the distance, Quinn closed the door behind him and crossed the floor in seconds. Abby was shocked when he pulled her into his arms and pressed his lips against hers. All her pent up frustration released as he pulled her close. His lips moved over hers. Abby's breath caught as his tongue ventured past her lips and his hands moved under her clothes. One pressed the small of her back, his fingers venturing under her waistband, while the other moved up under her tank top to cup her breast. Abby rarely wore a bra since her breasts were so small. His thumb quickly found her nipple and moved across it, sending shivers throughout her body. Abby moved her hands up and twined her fingers in his hair.

Quinn moved his lips down her neck, then groaned as the sound of Sheronda's vacuum shut off. Panting, the two stepped away from each other quickly. With Quinn's arousal evident, Abby gathered her things and stepped out of the office, leaving him to compose himself.

They ignored each other again as they returned to the unit. This time for fear that their latest encounter would be obvious. Abby thought they'd been successful until Sheronda pulled her aside in their suite.

"Girl, that boy be crushin' on you hard," she whispered. "You be likin' him too?"

Abby nodded, afraid to say it aloud.

Sheronda smirked. "I knew it. That boy never like nobody before. And believe me, they be plenty of girls who try."

Sheronda's smile faded. "You fuck him yet?" she whispered.

Abby started. It never occurred to her that things would go that far. She shook her head.

"He get in trouble if he get caught. They'll arrest him and put him in the man's prison." Sheronda chewed her lip for a second. "I jig for you so's you don't get caught, but you gotta watch yo self. Lemme think."

Quinn stood near the guard office watching as Sheronda walked out. He gave Abby a long look. When she nodded, he shook his head and turned away.

The next morning Quinn took the other group while Gray stayed with Abby and Sheronda. As it happened sometimes, the staff meeting had ended early, so most of the offices were occupied. Abby and Sheronda had to work around the staff. Sheronda pulled Abby into the hallway as she was about to enter the warden's office.

"Lemme take this one," she offered. "Me an her go way back."

Abby let her go and moved down the hallway.

When they were finished, the warden walked out as the crew was assembling for the return to B Unit.

"Sergeant Quinn," she called. "Please have Captain Dennis come see me."

"Yes, ma'am," Quinn answered then herded the women back to check-in.

Once in B Unit, Abby pulled Sheronda aside. "What's going on?"

Sheronda shrugged. "Warden and me had a convo about how inconvenient it is to be cleanin' when they's in there. I tol' her I can't get nothin' done when peoples be underfoot."

Abby stared at her friend. "And?"

Sheronda gave her a sly smile. "So, she be thinkin' we clean after they's leavin."

Abby stared at Sheronda. "But they leave at five. What would be the point of changing?"

Sheronda rolled her eyes at Abby's apparent stupidity. "Then you an' Pretty Boy won't be interrupted."

Abby stood there and stared at Sheronda. "But he leaves at three every day. He'll be gone by then."

Sheronda smirked. "Well, that's up to your boy, ain't it?"

Sure enough, Abby's cleaning schedule switched to late afternoon, and a week later Quinn switched to overnight shifts. Abby found out from Sheronda that, because of child care issues, Montgomery had asked to move to days. Quinn was more than happy to oblige.

They hadn't spoken since their last encounter, so when Quinn stayed with Abby and Sheronda, Abby didn't know what to expect.

Sheronda pulled her cart down to the opposite end of the hallway and pointedly closed the door to the room she was working in. Abby was pretty sure it was just a conference room with little to do in it except polish a table and vacuum.

Abby pulled her cart into the warden's office and started with the plants. Quinn appeared in the doorway as she finished. She stepped off the ladder and stood watching him. At first he looked everywhere but at her. He seemed to be struggling with a decision. When he finally looked up, his face was inscrutable, not happy, sad, or angry.

Abby stared back. He was only slightly taller than she was, maybe six feet. His complexion was darker than she had realized, as if he spent most of his time outdoors, which she knew not to be true. His hair was an even brown, neither light nor dark. He'd be invisible if it weren't for his eyes. They were an unusual blue. Like the color of the sky reflected in water. He was exceptionally handsome. Quinn had the kind of face found in men's magazines on models wearing thousand dollar suits in Milan. And where most male COs in the prison were either huge body builder types with thick necks and bulging biceps, or fat and soft with full-term pregnancies hanging over their belts, Quinn was almost thin, with a runner's build similar to Abby's.

Abby wanted him to talk to her, to explain things to her. She wanted him to say anything. The silence in the room was becoming uncomfortable for her.

She was about to speak, when Quinn crossed the room. He stopped just in front of her. Instead of taking her in his arms, he put his hand against her cheek then kissed her, almost chastely, on the tip of her cheekbone. Then, without a word, he turned and left the room.

Abby stared after him. She had a million questions but couldn't articulate a single one. Abby had the horrible feeling she'd just been dumped then she chided herself for being so stupid. He was a guard and she was an inmate. Never before had Abby felt unworthy of a man's attention, until now.

With a heavy heart, Abby finished her work then left to meet the rest of the crew. Once they'd gathered, Quinn led the way back to check-in. Sheronda gave Abby a pointed stare, but Abby just shook her head and looked away. Back in the unit, Abby and Sheronda went to get a late dinner. Abby wanted just a quick bite so she'd have more time to work with Mad T. Sheronda had other things in mind though.

"What the fuck's going on?" she demanded once they set their trays down.

Abby shrugged. She really didn't want to talk about it.

"Come on, girl," Sheronda coaxed. "What happened?"

Abby shook her head and stared at her tray. She'd lost her appetite for her meal. "I think he realized that I'm just an inmate."

Sheronda snorted. "Bullshit."

Abby looked up. "No really. I *am* just an inmate. I'm definitely not worth getting in trouble over."

Sheronda looked skeptical. "We'll see about that."

Abby pushed her tray over to Sheronda and left the cafeteria.

Outside, Abby ignored everyone, including Quinn, and set off for her run. She didn't even bother to count her paces or her circuits. Instead, she imagined she was running free, without walls or fences surrounding her. Only the sound of her footfalls, her breath, and the pounding of her heart sounded in her ears. Tears threatened to spill, but Abby refused to cry. She'd never cried over a man before in her life, and she wasn't about to start now.

She instinctively knew she was past the ten-mile mark when she heard a faint buzzer in the distance. Slowing, she trotted then stopped. When she felt like she had her breath back she walked back in. With the days growing shorter, there were fewer women outside. Quinn still stood guard near Sheronda's table, but Abby ignored him as she went in.

Days and then weeks passed without anything more from Quinn, so Abby filled her time with calls to her dad and helping Mad T and several other women with their reading and writing. She had also joined Grandma's Bible study and church group, which met with a volunteer pastor several times a week. Abby was raised in the Episcopal Church, but since the Episcopal priest only came once a month, Abby attended Grandma's nondenominational group between his visits. Grandma might call herself a psychopath, but in Abby's experience, she was a loving one. Her meetings typically involved several readings, a sermon, and the opportunity to discuss things of concern to the inmates. As much as she enjoyed the meetings, Abby found comfort in the familiar when the Episcopal priest came. His visits were closer to actual worship services, including well-loved hymns led by two young women on guitar. Sometimes Abby would close her eyes and let the presence of love and forgiveness wash over her. She would emerge from those meetings with a sense of peace.

Abby was returning from church services when she saw that Big Ginger had returned to the unit. Most prisoners looked upon the CO staff as a necessary evil. With the exception of the enigmatic Quinn, Abby found them to be a dedicated and caring group who performed their jobs with consummate professionalism. Big Ginger was no exception. She gave Abby a big smile as she walked into the unit, and to Abby's great surprise, Big Ginger walked over and gave her a huge bear hug. Contact between COs and inmates was strictly forbidden, but Captain Dennis stood nearby watching, so Abby felt OK about returning Big Ginger's hug. She had been a big woman, but during her time in recovery, Big Ginger had lost a lot of weight and muscle tone.

"I think you've gotten smaller," Abby joked when the other woman pulled away. "Are you sure you didn't come back too early?"

Big Ginger rubbed her hand across her face. Her eyes were wet. "Probably, but I just couldn't stay away any longer. I was going crazy sitting at home watching my mom worry about me."

Abby smiled. "I'm really glad you're going to be OK."

Big Ginger's smile faded, her expression turned serious. "Listen Abby, what you did…well, it went way above and beyond what anyone would do." Abby started to protest, but Big Ginger put her hand up. "Wait, let me finish. I know that if you hadn't been there that girl might have killed me. I've had to search my heart to forgive her.

Captain Dennis said she was huffing refrigerant, so maybe she wasn't in her right mind. But what you did..." Big Ginger's eyes filled with tears, and Abby found herself on the verge of shedding some tears herself. "I don't know what you did to get here. I'm pretty certain it was a big mistake," she said finally.

Abby interrupted her this time. Big Ginger's pity and regard were misplaced. "I broke the law. It was a stupid mistake, but I deserve to be here, Big...I mean Sergeant Redfern."

Big Ginger chuckled. "I know you call me Big Ginger. I don't mind. It's actually kind of funny because my mom's name is Ginger. And I hate my real name."

Abby was mortified. Most people wouldn't find her name game amusing.

"What's your real name?" she asked to be polite.

Big Ginger looked around to make sure no one was nearby. "Roberta, but my family calls me Robby."

Abby stared at the poor woman. "Robby Redfern?"

Big Ginger nodded. "Exactly. Imagine what high school was like. I got called 'young man' and 'Rob' so much I thought I'd go crazy. So I'll take Big Ginger any day." She chuckled. "I guess I didn't help things by becoming a prison guard either. It's not the most feminine job. Anyway, what you did really means a lot to me and I'll never forget it." Big Ginger reached out and gave Abby another hug.

"Oh my God, get married already," Sheronda exclaimed as she crossed the common area.

Abby and Big Ginger laughed as they parted. Both were wiping tears from their eyes.

Chapter 11

DOPE FIEND MOVE

For Abby, one of the hardest parts about being incarcerated was knowing that her father was getting worse and there wasn't anything she could do about. Abby had received a prepaid phone card in the morning's mail so she decided to give her dad a call to see how he was doing.

The unit's phone bank ran along a wall near the cafeteria. It was never empty and when Abby walked up several women were already there talking to family or running scams to earn some extra money. She chose one at the very end and sat down on the small metal disk that protruded from the wall and served as a seat.

She dialed through the prison phone system and entered the phone card number then her dad's number. She waited through all the clicking and recordings then sat patiently as the phone rang at her father's house.

It seemed to take a long time and Abby was about to hang up when her father finally answered.

"This is Callum Blackwood."

Abby smiled. "Hey dad. It's Abby."

She could hear a long pause and worried they might have been disconnected. It had happened before. She was relieved to hear her father still on the line. "Abby? She's not here right now. May I take a message?"

Abby frowned. "Dad? This is Abby. Are you ok?"

"Oh! I'm fine honey. Are you well?"

"I'm well, Dad. How are you feeling?"

Abby could hear her father chuckle. "Oh, I'm feeling OK but I could be better. You know I was just telling your mother I should probably go see Dr. Rosenstein about this weird feeling in my chest. I've been having a hard time catching my breath lately."

Abby closed her eyes and pressed her thumb against the spot between them. "You were talking to mom?" she asked with her eyes still closed. Abby's mom had been dead for years.

"I'm not supposed to tell you but she's planning your graduation party. What time are you coming home? Will you be here for dinner?"

"No Dad," Abby answered. "I'm not going to make it for dinner. Has anyone from the church come by today?"

"Today? No. Were they supposed to? They've been coming by a lot lately. I guess to see your mother. Oh, someone's at the door now. I'll see you at dinner."

Abby stared at the phone. Her father had hung up. "Love you dad," she said quietly into the dead phone line then hung up.

She knew it was pointless to call back so she wiped her eyes and went back to her suite.

She was about to pull herself up when she found a book on her bunk. Abby pulled it over and looked at the cover: *The Ocean at the End of the Lane* by Neil Gaiman. It was a hardcover too, so it must have been a new release. Without access to the Internet or even a bookstore, Abby had no way of knowing. No one was in the suite to ask where it had come from, though she suspected Quinn. It was a welcomed diversion from the stress of trying to make sense of her dad's situation. She worried that he was deteriorating and hoped that his friends at the church were on top of it. She was immensely grateful to have something to distract her. Abby put her things away and crawled up into her bunk to read.

After dinner she had planned to thank Quinn, but he was conspicuously absent from both the cafeteria and courtyard. In his place was a rotating guard Abby had seen only once before. As handsome as Quinn but beefier, the guard acted like the lone frat boy in a sorority house filled with horny coeds.

Women who normally acted like raging lesbians, turned into coquettish sex kittens around the guard, and he seemed more than happy to play along. After her run, Abby sat next to Sheronda.

"Who's the new guy?"

Sheronda glanced over at him then looked away. Her face was a mask of disgust. "Thass Pike. He from D Unit. He only come over when they's short and whiles your boyfrien' be out, they's short."

"Why is Quinn out?" Abby wondered aloud.

Sheronda gave her a look. "Girl, ain't my day to babysit," she huffed. "Why you lookin' at that boy anyway? You wanna date him too?"

Abby shook her head. "Ugh, no. I've already dated guys like him. I'm done."

Sheronda's group all nodded in agreement with their usual chorus of "mmhmms" and "you know that's rights."

Abby went into the suite early to read more of her book before count.

Quinn stayed gone for several days, leaving Pike in his place. Sheronda had sussed out from Big Ginger that Quinn had gone to help his brother in Maryland and wasn't expected back until the following week. Behavior on the unit descended to an all-new low as the ladies competed for Pike's attention. Women who'd never even bothered with shampoo were sporting full makeup, and there was a rush at the commissary for hair dye. Perfume wasn't available, so the women made do with a spray-on hair conditioner that smelled less like flowers and more like cucumber and melon. During Pike's shifts, the unit smelled like a healthy fruit salad.

When Quinn came back, Abby was hoping to be free of Pike, but he stayed on so that Big Ginger could go to her postsurgical follow-up to make sure her kidney was functioning properly.

Seeing them together, Abby noted distinct differences between Pike and Quinn. Both were good-looking, but where Quinn kept his distance from the inmates and interacted only when necessary, Pike strutted the unit like a peacock, inviting attention, even encouraging it. The ladies were more than happy to oblige. She also noticed that the other COs kept their distance, taking up positions as far away from Pike as possible. Abby could tell Captain Dennis was not a fan, especially when Pike took it upon himself to call for a toss. Abby suspected it had less to do with suspicion of contraband and more to do with Pike's desire to watch the ladies get searched.

Abby fervently hoped that no one was holding, but as luck would have it, Kelsey was brewing hooch in shampoo bottles, and several other ladies were stashing cigarettes and lighters.

With Big Ginger gone, it fell to two COs from outside the unit to fill in. One was Bald Guard who Abby hadn't seen since intake. The other was a tiny dark-skinned woman who would be impossible to hide behind.

While most COs stood still during search, Pike wandered around acting like he was questioning the ladies. Abby saw him steal glances at the search cubicle now and then.

When it was her turn, Abby walked over to Bald Guard who surprisingly smiled. "You're the girl who saved our Bobbie." Instead of using her potentially insulting nickname, Abby took the time to learn her name. Her badge read "Hamilton."

Abby nodded and went in to undress. Hamilton conducted the body search while the tiny guard whose name Abby learned was Singh, searched her clothes. Hamilton stood in such a way that, for the most part, Abby thought no one could see in. When she looked up though, she was mortified to see Pike staring straight at her, her body in full view. She tried to turn but Hamilton was asking her to squat. With her face burning with humiliation, Abby completed the search as fast as possible. From beyond the curtain, Abby heard a pointed throat clearing. Captain Dennis must have noticed Pike. When she looked up again, Pike's face had disappeared. She left the cubicle as fast as she could, her face down as the women around her tittered.

Pike was back the next day, this time filling in for Ramirez at the evening shift change. Abby wished fervently that everything would go back to normal and he would leave. She was glad to see Big Ginger filling in for White to make up for the time she missed. The two of them escorted Abby, Sheronda, and the rest of the cleaning crew to their shift.

At the admin wing, Pike stayed while Abby and Sheronda started their rooms. Abby was starting on her last office when Pike appeared in the doorway.

"So you're Abby." Pike stepped in and gave her a look she was sure he'd practiced in the mirror. "I've noticed you back in the unit. I wanted to introduce myself but there's always so many people around, so I haven't had a chance. I'm Mike."

Abby said nothing, but inwardly wondered how much his parents had hated him to name him Mike Pike.

"I thought we should get to know each other," he said as he stepped in farther.

"Why would you think that?" Abby moved around the desk.

Pike looked surprised. "I just want to be friends. Everyone needs friends." He moved closer. "I could be a really good friend to you."

Abby backed up as far as she could go in the small room.

"I've got enough friends. I need to finish." Abby was trained to defend herself, but she knew if she hurt a guard she'd catch far more trouble than she had for hurting Dana.

Pike looked around and stepped in front of her. "Looks done to me." He moved closer and backed her up against the wall, pressing his hips against hers. Abby could feel his raging erection. His hands started to pull up her shirt.

"No," Abby shook her head and pushed his hands off her. "No, no, no. Get off."

Pike moved his face closer to hers. "Come on, pretty girl, we can be really good friends."

"No, no…" Abby kept trying to push him away, but Pike was leaning his weight into her and she couldn't get leverage. "I don't want to hurt you," she warned.

Pike chuckled. Then he shoved his hand against her mouth, cutting her lip against her teeth. She could taste blood on her tongue. His mouth moved against her ear. "Shh, this won't take long." He was pulling open his belt when he suddenly flew backward. Big Ginger had pulled him by the shirt collar and thrown him down on the floor. She stood over him, the fabric of his collar still in her hand. Her other hand pulled her radio off her belt. A minute later, Captain Hannah and Quinn appeared in the doorway. Pike lay on the floor proclaiming his innocence, but his undone belt and the blood on Abby's face revealed his lies. Sheronda stood in the doorway, eyes wide, and her mouth a perfect "o."

Moments later the small office was filled with COs. Two of the SRT held Pike between them as the warden was called in. Abby was questioned first. She described his attempt to molest her, which elicited protests from Pike who gave a much different story. He accused her of stealing from the office. Pike said she fought him when he tried to restrain her. The fact that Big Ginger was a witness to his rape attempt seemed lost on him. The warden ordered Pike cuffed then ordered Quinn to take Abby to the infirmary as the lower part of her face was already swelling.

Halfway to the infirmary, Quinn stopped and pulled Abby aside. He took her chin in his hand and looked closely at the wound on her lip. She could tell she'd not only busted her lip, but the inside of her mouth as well.

"Why didn't you break his arm?" he asked quietly.

Abby stared at him. She struggled to answer. "I got another year for defending Sergeant Redfern. What do you think they'd do to me if I hurt a guard?"

Quinn had no answer for that. He tucked her hair behind her ear then ran his fingers along her jawline, stopping before her injured mouth.

"I'm sorry," he whispered.

Abby moved her chin out of his hand. "For what? You didn't do this. You didn't do anything."

Quinn dropped his hand and looked at her. On his normally stoic face was an expression of infinite sadness.

Abby couldn't take it anymore, she turned away and took herself to the infirmary.

After being bandaged and gifted with a gel icepack that she could refreeze, Abby was escorted back to the unit by Big Ginger who gave her the rundown of what happened after she left. Pike had been taken away and charged with felony institutional sexual assault and felony attempt at a criminal rape threat. Big Ginger had seen enough to secure the charges regardless of Pike's claims otherwise. Back at the unit, Abby found that Sheronda had been busy telling everyone that Pike had beaten Abby up when she spurned his advances. Though some of the women were surprised Abby had turned down their dream guy, most were furious with Pike; especially after seeing Abby's face. Inmates were always quick to take each other's side against a guard. By the time she'd reached the unit, Abby's lower lip and jaw were swollen and purple. Mad T was especially pissed and vowed to castrate Pike if he ever came back. Big Ginger reassured her that Pike was most likely going to his own prison.

Even with the painkillers, Abby's face was throbbing. She thanked Big Ginger and went to lie down.

The next day, Abby was called to the admin wing to give a deposition of the events of the previous day. She was videotaped, and even though the infirmary had taken pictures, she was photographed again from every angle. They even took pictures of the inside of her mouth. Big Ginger had already given a statement and would be called to testify if the case went to trial. Pike had been given the option to plea to a lesser charge, but he was still claiming innocence.

Abby knew she should be angry, but she was in so much pain she didn't care. All she wanted was her bed. Instead, she was taken to the infirmary where they determined she had contracted an infection, either from the bacteria in her mouth or bacteria on Pike's hand. The thought of something disgusting going from Pike's hand into her mouth made Abby want to throw up. Under the visiting doctor's orders, the prison's PA put her on antibiotics and kept her under observation in the infirmary. The nurse who'd treated Abby's pepper spray burns came by often to change her ice packs and chat with her.

It was several days before the swelling went down, and an additional week of antibiotics before the doctor would release her back to B Unit. When Abby was discharged, all that was left was a yellowing bruise below her lower lip, and a raw spot in her mouth where the cut was still healing.

Chapter 12

ANOTHER CRAB BITCH

During Abby's time in the infirmary, little had changed on B Unit except that some faces had gone and there were some new faces among them. Kelsey had been sent to DSEG for fighting over a new blonde. One of Mad T's girls had been paroled, and Montgomery had been placed on medical leave due to complications with her pregnancy. Abby was embarrassed that she hadn't even noticed the woman was pregnant. Big Ginger and Quinn were taking on some of her shifts until new COs were brought in. Abby suspected Captain Dennis of stalling on any new assignments. He was a man who embraced routine and disliked change of any kind.

Little had changed in her suite. Mad T still ruled the roost, but she had missed her tutor. She was proud to show Abby the progress she'd made in filling out some of her own paperwork. Abby looked it over and pronounced it perfect, earning a big grin from the other woman. Sheronda's yarn crew came by to welcome Abby back and to ask about Pike. Though he'd seemed popular, women from D Unit were coming forward saying he'd victimized them as well. The charges against him grew and grew, and the plea bargain was pulled. Pike finally admitted his guilt, and Abby was glad to hear he was going away for a long time.

One girl, Brandi, wasn't so happy with Abby. She was one of those short-sentence repeat offenders who'd been in Pike's unit before her discharge several months earlier. She was back on a parole violation and assigned to B Unit where she immediately set out to discredit Abby.

Abby and Sheronda were at breakfast when Brandi showed up at their table. She had a sidekick with her, a young girl Abby had never seen before.

"Hey." Brandi had stopped a couple of feet from their table, but called out as if she was across the yard.

"The fuck you want?" Sheronda asked the girl.

Brandi gave her a withering look. "I ain't talking to you. I'm talking to her."

Abby turned to look at Brandi. "Yes?"

Brandi sneered. "Yes?" she mimicked. "Ain't you a princess."

Sheronda turned to the table. "Oh Lord, we got us another whigger." Brandi got scornful looks all around. The girl behind her looked uncomfortable.

"You shut the fuck up," Brandi took a step closer. "I'm talking to this bitch. I wanna know why you been lyin' on my man."

Abby was confused. "What are you talking about? What man?"

"Pike. I'm talkin' 'bout Pike." Brandi put her hands on her hips and gave Abby a pointed look. "You know you lyin'. He never raped nobody."

Abby stared at the girl. "I don't give a shit about Pike. And I don't answer to you."

"Excuse me?" Brandi affected a look of shock. "You wanna say that to my face?"

"I'm looking right at you, so clearly I just said it to your face," Abby answered.

The girl behind Brandi took another step back. Sheronda was watching her.

"Hey, girl," Sheronda called to her. "Why you backin' up this crab bitch?"

The girl shook her head, refusing to answer. She seemed to be reconsidering her alliance.

"Move on, girl," Sheronda told her. "You don' wanna be fakin jacks with this bitch."

The girl glanced at Brandi then took Sheronda's advice and ditched her friend.

Deflated, Brandi watched her go. With her imaginary muscle gone, she tried to save face. "Pike was my friend," she whined, her ghetto persona gone. "Now he's in trouble because of you."

Abby was incredulous. "Pike's in trouble because of what he did. Not just to me, but to a lot of women. You do know that over forty women here have given depositions against him." Abby picked up her tray and walked over to Brandi who immediately started backing way. Abby stared at her until the girl looked away. "That's what I thought."

Abby walked away leaving Brandi glaring behind her.

The next few weeks became the Brandi show. She seemed to be everywhere, working the unit like a skilled politician. Brandi was remarkably adept at adopting the language patterns of whoever she was talking to. She created a familiarity with the women in a surprisingly short amount of time. The lifers and women serving a jolt, or a longer sentence, weren't impressed. They'd seen versions of Brandi over and over again, but the younger ones serving bit sentences were in her thrall. With Kelsey in DSEG, Brandi took over her girls in no time. She easily slid into the queen bee role.

Brandi was also a hustler, running multiple scams out of the prison, including an elaborate pen pal operation. It involved men desperate for attention who would send her money and gifts with the goal of meeting her upon her release. She used photos of women she'd never met, and her ability to adopt different personalities to appeal to different tastes worked to her advantage. Worse, she scammed their telephone numbers by convincing the men to hit star seventy-two on their phones, effectively handing over a wide-open phone line. Brandi would then let the other inmates make calls for a hefty fee.

Abby watched the show with slight amusement. She'd known girls like Brandi before. Competitive and manipulative, their only mission seemed to one-up the person they felt was their greatest competition. In Brandi's case, that was Abby.

For the most part, Abby didn't care. She knew who her friends were, and none of them had bought into Brandi's show. She could tell that frustrated Brandi, but Abby figured the girl would burn herself out eventually, or that someone would do it for her. Girls like Brandi made more enemies than friends.

Abby also noticed Brandi was one of those girls who needed a lot of attention, especially from men. Eventually she set her sights on Quinn. Though she told herself that the man who fell for Brandi deserved Brandi, Abby couldn't help but be bothered by the girl's efforts.

To his credit, Quinn seemed uninterested in Brandi's attention, and went out of his way to avoid her. Whenever Brandi asked him for an escort, Quinn turfed her to one of the female COs. She soon turned to blatant displays of sexual aggression in front of him. She would complain about imaginary aches and pains in her breasts and groin, and then she would rub the "aches" in front of Quinn. Other times she would blast music from her suite and demonstrate a remarkable skill at stripper dancing, twerking in front of him or using the common tables as a stage. Abby was at a table helping one of Mad T's girls, Tyana, study for her GED when Brandi started another one of her shows. She had turned on some hip-hop and came out of her suite with her blues pulled up and secured with ponytail holders to show off a reasonably voluptuous body. Quinn immediately sequestered himself in the guard office as Brandi climbed up onto a table and started gyrating.

Abby and the other women watched in amusement as Captain Dennis came striding into the common area.

"What are you doing, girl? This ain't no club!" he bellowed. "Get off that table and turn that shit off."

Brandi slid off the table and danced over to Captain Dennis who was not amused. "Girl, I said turn that off or you're going to Lock."

The other women tittered as Brandi stomped to her suite. A second later, the music was turned off and Brandi spent the rest of the day pouting.

Things took a turn for the worse when Kelsey returned from her stay in DSEG. She was less than happy that her girls had taken up with someone else. It became a battle of the queen bees with Brandi the definitive loser. Brandi may have been an artful scammer, but Kelsey was a master at prison survival. It all came to a head during dinner when Brandi tried to coerce Kelsey's girls back to her table. Kelsey had had enough. The entire room watched as she got up from her table, stalked over to where Brandi sat, and with one punch, laid her out cold. Abby was impressed. Of course, Kelsey went back to DSEG, but after her stay in the infirmary, Brandi was transferred out of the unit.

Chapter 13

PUNK CITY

After the Brandi incident, things slowly returned to normal. Abby divided her time between work, church, and tutoring. Once Tyana had passed her GED exam, Abby had so many women asking her for help that Captain Dennis went to Emma, her case manager, to get Abby set up in a classroom. For two hours every day, Abby taught the basics of the GED test and covered each section then offered practice tests at the end of the week. She found many women had profound learning disabilities, and tried to work with them on an individual basis. Her success rate was good, though some women couldn't overcome their behavioral issues to study effectively. Before they could complete their education, they needed to learn anger management and coping skills, something Abby didn't feel qualified to instruct. The prison offered group counseling and drug therapy and though medical intervention was better at Maysville than everywhere else, it still relied on the women to comply with their treatment. Abby recognized that some of the women probably needed antidepressants or Adderall to function normally, but she did the best she could to encourage them to pursue medical help. After the GED instruction, she added another hour of class time to teach life skills with the hope that the women would be better able to succeed at their interpersonal relationships with the staff and each other.

Abby continued to find gifts on her bunk. Usually books, chocolate, and CDs, which prompted her to buy a CD player; then after Mad T complained that the music wasn't old school R&B, some headphones. The music was eclectic, ranging from The Branches to Simon and Garfunkel to Bon Iver.

She was immersed in her latest gift, *The Perks of Being a Wallflower* by Stephen Chbosky, when Big Ginger appeared in the doorway.

"Abby, Father Duncan wants to see you." Big Ginger's face was drawn. Abby knew instinctively that something was seriously wrong. She set her book aside, slid off her bunk, and then followed Big Ginger out.

Father Duncan waited in the space typically used for worship services. He stood up and crossed the room when Abby walked in.

"I'm so sorry, Abby," he said, taking her hands in his. His expression was mournful. "St. Simon's rector just called me... your father's passed away."

Abby stared at the man. Intellectually she knew her father wasn't well, but in her heart she had always assumed he'd be fine, at least until she got out.

"What happened?" she asked.

Father Duncan shook his head. "I don't know the exact details, but it appears he had pneumonia and didn't know. One of the visiting ministry volunteers found him on the floor unresponsive. By the time they got him to the hospital it was too late."

Abby nodded. Her face looked grief-stricken. "He had an alpha-1 antitrypsin deficiency. Pneumonia would have been devastating," Abby said. She let go of Father Duncan's hands and fell into the nearest chair.

Father Duncan shook his head. "I'm so sorry. I've contacted the warden. She'll need to speak with you shortly."

Abby looked up. "About what?"

"The warden decides whether or not you go to the funeral," Big Ginger said from the door.

It never occurred to Abby that she'd be allowed to leave the prison. Since she'd been there, no one had left for anything other than discharge or transfer. As nice as it would be to go home, Abby knew it wouldn't matter. The last person tethering her to the world was gone.

"Abby?" Big Ginger called from the doorway. Abby looked up.

"The warden is ready to see you," she said quietly. Abby got up and followed her out.

As they arrived in the admin section, Abby was surprised to see Quinn waiting there. He wasn't scheduled to arrive until the afternoon at shift change. He followed them into the warden's office and took up a position behind her as she sat in the chair the warden had indicated.

Warden Abellard was an older woman who'd worked in the corrections system for over thirty years. She was tough, but she took good care of her prison and her staff. Other than the incident with Pike, Abby had only met her occasionally as she was cleaning, and not at all since the change in her shift time. She was one of those ageless women with clear, unlined skin the color of milk chocolate that glowed warm and molten. Her hair, cut in a stylish bob, was a combination of white and steel gray. Abby always found that color combination to be extremely attractive. Her natural expression was benevolent, but Abby knew her to be extremely tough.

Warden Abellard gave her a kind smile. "Miss Blackwood, please let me offer you my condolences."

"Thank you," Abby answered quietly.

"We have an unusual situation with you, Miss Blackwood," the warden continued. "Because we are a medium security prison, we do not typically grant inmates bereavement leave. However, I have reviewed your file, and between your efforts on behalf of Sergeant Redfern and your contribution to your fellow inmates, your conduct here has been admirable, stellar even. And the officers on your unit, as well as your case manager, have all offered their recommendations toward allowing you to attend your father's funeral." The warden looked down at the papers on her desk. "Am I correct in understanding that your father was your only family member?" she asked.

"Yes, ma'am," Abby replied. It was difficult to speak around the lump in her throat.

"Then I feel strongly that you should be allowed to attend his funeral and finalize any affairs related to his passing. Quinn and Redfern have volunteered to accompany you, as has Father Duncan. Given the distance and the time of the funeral, I'm granting you an overnight furlough, Miss Blackwood. You or your father's estate will be responsible for all costs. Do you understand?"

Abby was touched by the gesture. Her eyes teared. "Yes. Thank you so much, Warden. I am so grateful, you don't even know."

Warden Abellard stood with Abby and walked her to the door. "You're welcome, Miss Blackwood. Again, my deepest condolences. Have a safe trip."

As they returned to B Unit, the enormity of Abby's situation hit her. With her dad gone, she had no one. She had no family and no friends other than the women on the unit.

Big Ginger stopped her at the phones and handed her a piece of paper. On it was the name of the woman who coordinated St. Simon's visiting ministry and a phone number.

"They want you to call right away," Big Ginger said quietly. "I'm going to go get our transportation set up. Funeral's day after tomorrow, so we'll leave tomorrow afternoon."

Abby took the message then went in to make her calls.

Mad T, Sheronda, and the other ladies were especially kind when Abby returned to the unit at lunchtime. Abby wasn't hungry, so Sheronda graciously offered to finish her lunch. Instead of eating, Abby went out to the yard. Storm clouds surrounded the prison, so the tables and lawn were deserted. Raindrops started to fall and thunder rumbled in the distance as she slowly walked to the far side of the yard. The turf fields past the perimeter fence glowed an exaggerated green as the sky turned dark. Abby sat at the corner and stared out with her fingers caught in the wire and the rain mixing with the tears that poured down her face.

Her heart ached as a universe of emptiness opened up inside her. Her mind was numb to anything but the hope that if she stayed long enough, she would begin to melt and the rain would wash her clean away. The storm flew across the fields and was raging directly over her. She did not see the lightning as it arced across the sky, nor did she hear the footsteps coming up behind her over the thunder that shook the world around her. It wasn't until Quinn kneeled and put his hand on her shoulder that she realized she hadn't washed away, but sat drenched as lightning and thunder fought above her.

Quinn didn't say anything and Abby didn't need him to. She pressed her cheek against the back of his hand and let her hot tears fall. Quinn let her rest for a moment, and then he put his other arm around her and pulled her up. Abby didn't protest, but let herself be led back inside.

Captain Dennis and Big Ginger stood in the doorway. Sheronda, Mad T, and the other women stood behind them. Sylvia held a towel and wrapped Abby in it as she stepped in.

"We need to take her to ADSEG," Captain Dennis said quietly. "She needs to go under watch."

Mad T shook her head. "Meaning no disrespect, sir, but ain't no one gonna take care of her there. She'd just be sittin' alone. She's better here with us." Sheronda and Sylvia nodded. Then all the women nodded.

Captain Dennis and Quinn looked at each other. Then Quinn nodded as well.

"Very well then, ladies," Captain Dennis acquiesced. "She's relieved of duties for today. Redfern, you stay on her door."

"Yes, sir," Big Ginger answered. Then she guided Abby off to her suite.

True to their word, Abby was never alone. The women sat with her in shifts. Sylvia and Sheronda were first as Mad T went off to her job in the laundry. Sylvia had brought Abby a blanket she'd crocheted, but Abby barely noticed when Sylvia pulled it over her. Tyana came and sat at the end of Abby's bunk with her hands resting on Abby's icy feet, warming them.

Every so often, Redfern would look in on the women then she would resume her post at the door. At shift change, Singh took over.

Marianna brought in dinner with the help of Brandi's former sidekick, the unfortunately named De-lisha, but the tray sat untouched. Sheronda tried to get Abby to eat, but was unsuccessful. Soon she had to leave for cleaning crew, so Grandma took her place.

While the others sat silently, Grandma took out her Bible and began reading aloud. As she began with the book of Psalms, Abby remained immobile. Grandma's voice was quiet as was the rest of the unit. The words fell on Abby, calling to that part of her that knew, despite her mistakes, despite her losses, that she was still a child of God.

Abby hadn't moved until Grandma started a passage from the book of Philippians.

"It is my eager expectation and hope that I will not be put to shame in any way, but that by my speaking with all boldness, Christ will be exalted now as always in my body, whether by life or by death. For to me, living is Christ and dying is gain. If I am to live in the flesh, that means fruitful labor for me; and I do not know which I prefer. I am hard pressed between the two: my desire is to depart and be with Christ, for that is far better; but to remain in the flesh is more necessary for you. Since I am convinced of this, I know that I will remain and continue with all of you for your progress and joy in faith, so that I may share abundantly in your boasting in Christ Jesus when I come to you again. Only, live your life in a manner worthy of the gospel of Christ, so that, whether I come and see you or am absent and hear about you, I will know that you are standing firm in one spirit, striving side-by-side with one mind for the faith of the gospel, and are in no way intimidated by your opponents. For them this is evidence of their destruction, but of your salvation. And this is God's doing. For he has graciously granted you the privilege not only of believing in Christ, but of suffering for him as well, since you are having the same struggle that you saw I had and now hear that I still have."

Abby turned to look at Grandma as she paused. The older woman regarded Abby thoughtfully.

"This speaks to you because you are giving up hope. And in giving up hope, you are failing the women here who look to you for guidance." It was a gentle scolding and Abby felt ashamed. Grandma continued, "Blessed art those who mourn, dear, for they shall be comforted. But, you cannot leave this world on your own account. You can cry, shriek, rage…whatever it takes to cope. But you must live your life."

Grandma set aside her Bible and stood next to Abby's bunk. "Come on. Let's get you cleaned up. You have a busy day tomorrow." Abby slid off the bunk and let Grandma lead her to the showers.

Chapter 14

FURLOUGH

For the rest of the evening and the next day, Abby was never alone. Sheronda helped her pack her duffel with the few things she might need for the trip. Because she was leaving the prison while still serving her sentence, Abby was required to wear a bright pink jumpsuit that identified her as an inmate. However, because it had turned cool, Captain Dennis allowed her to put on her gray hoodie.

Grandma led her out of the suite where Father Duncan, Quinn, and Big Ginger waited. Abby turned and hugged Grandma, and then Sheronda and Mad T. The rest of the women of the unit gathered around her. They all offered words of comfort. Finally, it was time to go.

Abby had to leave the prison cuffed to chains around her waist and ankles. Outside, a dark blue SUV waited. Big Ginger helped Abby into the back and set her duffel next to her before getting in. Father Duncan got in the front as Quinn took the wheel.

Once they were past the last set of gates, Big Ginger unlocked the cuffs and removed the chains.

"Technically you have to wear them the whole time but...well, that's just ridiculous," she said as she placed them in the seat pocket in front of her. Grateful, Abby smiled then turned and stared out the window.

The heavy storm the night before had scrubbed the world and left behind a shining blue sky. It was nice enough that Quinn put down the windows so that everyone could enjoy the crisp breeze.

71

Abby had taken Grandma's words to heart. Though tears threatened to fall, she took comfort in the knowledge that there were still people who needed her.

The trip was relatively short compared to the time it had taken her to get to the prison months before. Abby credited it to Quinn's ability to go the speed limit rather than the creeping pace the prison bus took. They were in Springfield in just under three hours. Quinn called ahead to let the jail know they were arriving.

Abby was surprised to see Jane, her attorney, waiting with one of Abby's previous jailers, Deputy Stone, at the inmate entrance to the jail. Big Ginger put her wrist cuffs back on before she exited the vehicle.

"Is that really necessary?" Jane asked. "She's hardly a threat."

"It's OK," Abby assured her. Jane glared at Big Ginger then reluctantly let it go.

Deputy Stone checked Abby in then led the group to an interview room inside.

"So this is the schedule for your stay here," he began. "You'll spend the night here in lockup. Then tomorrow morning your escorts will pick you up and we'll take you to the funeral and the internment at St. Simon's. You'll return to the prison immediately following the burial. OK?"

Abby nodded.

He turned to Quinn, Big Ginger, and Father Duncan. "The church is offering to put you up in their visiting clergy apartments, if that's OK." All three nodded. Abby was glad. The trip was not at the expense of the state. In order to attend her father's funeral, she had to foot the bill for the county sheriffs too.

"First, though, Jane has asked to speak with you," Deputy Stone said, and then he herded everyone but Jane out of the room.

Abby and Jane sat across the table. "Before we start, I want to tell you how sorry I am about your father." Abby thanked her.

Jane pulled her briefcase up to the table and opened it. It was filled with papers relevant to Abby's case and her father's estate.

"I've prepared the paperwork for probate. As your father's only heir, you'll receive the remainder of his assets once any and all liens and taxes are satisfied." Jane pushed a pile of papers over to Abby who started to read them.

"In a nutshell, there isn't much left," she continued. "Much of your parents' retirement was paid toward your mother's medical bills. Your dad had a life insurance policy, but it isn't for much and the benefit is subject to estate taxes. He also took out an equity line of credit for your legal defense that needs to be resolved. The only way to do that would be to sell your father's house."

Abby shook her head. "I won't have anything to come home to if you sell the house."

Jane pushed over a paper that listed the debts her father's estate would have to pay. "I'm so sorry, Abby, but it's unavoidable. You don't have to decide right now. The state needs the application for a grant of probate within three months. When it's time for the house to be sold, the church has offered to do one of two things: pack up the entire contents of your father's house to be stored until your release, or sort everything for you and sell or donate the items. They are leaving that entirely up to you. I can say that if we close his estate appropriately, I'll be able to set up a trust for you with the remaining money so you'll have something to live on when you come out. Before his death, your father put a large amount of money into an account in your name for me to make appropriate purchases for you and to make deposits to your prison account, so that can't be touched and you'll receive any balance upon your release. And between the value of the home, and its contents, you should have enough to cover you for at least the first couple of years after you're released."

Abby sat and stared at all the papers in front of her. She felt numb and there was no way she would be able to make sense of any of it in her current state of mind.

"Can I let you know tomorrow?" she asked.

"Of course," Jane answered. "You can take as long as three months."

Jane gathered the papers and put them into an accordion file for Abby to keep.

"I'll see you tomorrow," she said then left.

Deputy Stone appeared in the doorway.

"You won't be staying in general population, but the only single cell we have available is the safe cell." The safe cell was where prisoners who were a threat to themselves were put for their own safety. Abby wondered if her placement had less to do with lack of vacancies and more to do with her grieving.

Deputy Stone led her down the hall and through the double doors into holding. The safe cell was a new addition that was built after one of the jail's inmates tried to kill herself by bashing her head against the edge of the bunk. She'd survived. Afterward, the jail installed a room where every surface was either padded or rounded, and the sink was set into the wall. Abby saw that even the toilet was padded. She stepped in and put her duffel and Jane's paperwork down as Deputy Stone closed the gate behind her.

"There's closed-circuit monitoring in here, so if you need anything just say it out loud. If you want the TV on, just ask and security will turn it on for you.

"I'll be one of the deputies taking you to the funeral tomorrow," he added. "You're required to have at least two county deputies as well as your prison escorts. There's a few of us here who were in your dad's scout troop, so we've volunteered to perform escort."

Abby gave him a small smile. "Thanks."

Deputy Stone smiled back. "No problem. See you in the morning."

Abby pulled her Bible from her duffel and settled in.

The next morning, Big Ginger, Quinn, and the county deputies arrived to pick up Abby. They were all in dress uniforms, making Abby feel shabby by comparison.

Big Ginger took her duffel as Deputy Stone put on her chains and cuffs. "Sorry about this," he murmured.

"It's OK," Abby replied.

Big Ginger helped Abby back into the prison's SUV as the county deputies got into their squad cars. Abby looked on in dismay as Deputy Stone pulled in front and the other county cars fell in behind them.

"Is that really necessary?" Abby asked. Big Ginger shook her head.

"You're like a visiting dignitary," Quinn offered from the front. "Just think of yourself as the president."

"The least they could have done was let her wear regular clothes," Big Ginger griped. "They do everywhere else." Abby silently agreed.

Springfield was such a small city that the trip was mercifully short. St. Simon's was located just north of the city center, only five minutes from the county jail. It was an old church surrounded by its own park and cemetery. As one of the first churches in Springfield, it had managed to keep a significant amount of its original land as the city grew around it. Abby's parents had been lifelong members, and served many roles at the church. As such, they had been afforded plots in the church's cemetery. Abby's mother was already buried there.

Stunned mourners met their caravan as they pulled into the drive that circled near the front of the church. Quinn stopped at the front door and got out with Big Ginger. As a unit, the deputies exited their patrol cars and assembled around Abby.

"I feel like a serial killer," she whispered to Big Ginger.

Quinn leaned over. "Remember, you're the president," he whispered then led Abby into the church. All but the first three pews were filled. The coffin that held Abby's father was already at the altar.

As the only living member of the family, Abby would normally have had the first row to herself, but the church had blocked off the first three rows of pews so all of the accompanying deputies could sit behind her.

Friends of Abby's mother and father filled the rest of the church. The only person there for Abby was her attorney, Jane, who had taken a seat near the back. As she looked around, Abby saw that, other than herself, Jane, and the deputies, no one else in the church was younger than sixty. None of her friends had come, though many of their parents were there. The people who were present were incredibly kind. Many came up to Abby to offer their condolences. Abby had known most of them her whole life. She tried to return their hugs, but her chains prevented her from lifting her arms. Her parents' friends had the good grace to ignore them and hugged her warmly. It wasn't allowed, but to his credit, Deputy Stone chose to ignore it.

Father Duncan was already there and dressed in a cassock. With him was Father Abbot, St. Simon's rector and her father's friend. His wife Margaret was with them. Abby had taught their grandchildren in Sunday school.

"Abby, we're so sorry," Father Abbot offered as his wife hugged her tightly.

"Thank you," Abby replied.

Margaret Abbot turned to the deputies. "May I sit with Abby?"

Big Ginger and Quinn looked at each other and shrugged. "Sure," Quinn answered. Margaret thanked him graciously, and then she led Abby to her pew. Big Ginger sat next to Margaret while Quinn took a seat next to Abby. The rest of the deputies filled in the pews around them.

Father Abbot began.

Since Episcopal funeral services are actual liturgical services, it was an hour or so before the service ended and her father's pallbearers were called to the front of the church to escort his coffin to the cemetery. It was a long walk, so the elderly men tasked as pallbearers employed a wheeled wooden cart to save their shoulders. The cart had been in use for over a century and had carried Abby's mother to her grave as well. Margaret Abbot led Abby and her escorts out after the coffin. The rest of the parishioners followed behind them.

Her mother's grave sat in the shade on a small rise that overlooked a paved prayer labyrinth her mother had commissioned for the church the year before she died. Her father's grave was next to her mother, though his name had not been added to their headstone.

Abby and Mrs. Abbot sat as the rest of the mourners gathered around. Quinn and Big Ginger stood behind Abby. Quinn rested his hand on the back of her chair.

Unlike the service in the church, the burial was much more personal. Several of Abby's father's friends had given eulogies in the church, but it was at the burial that Father Abbot chose to speak from the heart.

"I'd like to begin with a reading from first John." Father Abbot looked at Abby then began. "We are from God. Whoever knows God listens to us; whoever is not from God does not listen to us. By this we know the spirit of truth and the spirit of error. Beloved, let us love one another, for love is from God, and whoever loves has been born of God and knows God."

Abby's eyes filled with tears as Quinn's hand gently squeezed her shoulder. Her shackles chimed as Margaret Abbot took her hand.

"Callum Blackwood always knew God. Even through the burdens he bore from his terrible disease, he knew God. When faces became unrecognizable and names were lost, Callum still knew God. His love for God was immense and all enduring. It was eclipsed only by his love for Abby. Because as Callum knew God, and always remembered God, he always knew Abby. He always remembered her. He never forgot her face or her voice. Although she was far away in person, Callum kept Abby near in spirit…and never ever forgot her."

Abby wept openly as Father Abbot paused.

"Callum had a favorite reading, which I'd like to share with you now," he continued. "I am the good shepherd; I know my sheep and my sheep know me, just as the Father knows me and I know the Father and I lay down my life for the sheep. I have other sheep that are not of this sheep pen. I must bring them also. They too will listen to my voice, and there shall be one flock and one shepherd. The reason my Father loves me is that I lay down my life only to take it up again. No one takes it from me, but I lay it down of my own accord."

"We do not say goodbye to our friend. We say 'fare thee well until we meet again.'" Father Abbot stepped away from the lectern and handed Abby a single white rose.

Abby stood and laid it upon her father's coffin. As she stepped back, other mourners approached with roses as well, but only Abby's was white.

Abby turned to thank Father Abbot and to hug his wife when Jane approached.

"There are some things at Abby's father's house she might need. I don't know if it's permitted, but would it be possible for you to stop by there on your way back? Mrs. Abbott needs to know what to do with the contents of the house."

Big Ginger glanced at Deputy Stone who shrugged. "Our job here is done. She's in your custody now."

Big Ginger turned back to Jane. "We can stop."

Jane smiled. "Great. We'll follow you."

Deputy Stone retrieved his cuffs and chains from Abby. "Good luck, Abby," he said with a smile.

Abby thanked him, and then thanked the rest of the deputies as they left.

Quinn led Abby back to the car with Father Duncan and Big Ginger right behind them. Once inside, he gave Abby a pointed look.

"Oh, right," she said "Just turn left out of the drive. Then turn left again at the corner."

Following Abby's directions, Quinn drove the short distance to her previous home. It was only minutes from the church. The house was a small Craftsman-style home situated in an old neighborhood filled with mature trees.

Margaret Abbot and Jane arrived just behind them. Margaret stepped forward to unlock the door. Abby stepped inside and inhaled. Though the house was spotlessly clean, the air was stale with a faint hint of the pipe tobacco her father loved. Spare in furnishings, the only items that were clearly in abundance were the books Abby grew up with. Both her parents had been college professors. Her mother taught comparative religions and her father history. Abby saw a box on the dining table that held photos, some of her mother's jewelry, and what looked like a file of very old, but probably important, papers.

"I've told Abby about the estate issue," Jane said to the assembled group. Margaret Abbot nodded. "She knows the house needs to be sold."

Margaret reached over and took Abby's hands. "I'm so sorry, Abby. If there was any other way..."

"I know. It's OK," Abby reassured her. "I don't think there's a lot here for me to keep."

"Joseph Miller is a book dealer who works with the church. He's been in to assess what's here and has offered to list the more valuable books through his company. Other than the books, I've packed up everything I thought would be important," Margaret explained. "Your parents didn't keep much else. I've left your room intact if you want to go up there."

Abby looked over at Big Ginger who nodded. Then she went up the small wooden staircase to her bedroom under the eaves.

Her room was exactly as she had left it when she left for her sentencing. She'd tried to clean up so her father wouldn't have anything to do, but her laundry hamper still had clothes in it.

"You should pick some clothes to take with you," Big Ginger suggested. Abby walked over and opened the closet. She was shocked at the amount of clothes crammed into it. Her new reality certainlywas less materialistic. She pulled out jeans, worn twill pants, T-shirts, and a couple of woven shirts. A little more searching netted her favorite sweater, a soft gray cashmere blend that she'd had forever. Finally, Abby chose a pair of faded Sanuks and threw them on top of the tiny pile. She didn't want anything else from the room. She went into her parents' room and opened their closet. She took out an ancient Hermes scarf her mother had worn on special occasions and an old fisherman's sweater that had been her father's favorite.

Abby led the way back downstairs where Jane and Margaret were waiting. She walked past them to her father's den. It too was filled with books, but the only things Abby wanted from there were the pipe that lay on his desk and the blackwood chanter that sat on the bookshelf. She returned to the dining room and put everything in the box.

"Except for that box, you can sell it all," Abby said quietly.

Margaret walked over and hugged her. "I'll keep the box with me until you need it. And anything else I find."

Abby doubted there was anything else, but she thanked Margaret and Jane for all their help.

Big Ginger and Quinn led Abby out to the truck where Father Duncan waited. She waved at the women as they drove away.

They had been on the road for a while when Quinn asked, "What was that thing you put in the box?"

Abby looked over at him. "It's a blackwood pipe chanter for bagpipes," she answered. "It's the part that plays the melody. My dad was a piper before his COPD diagnosis. Most people think it's noise, but every true Scot cries at the sound of bagpipes."

Quinn nodded. They spent the rest of the trip in silence.

It was late afternoon when they returned to the prison. Abby and her things were searched, and then she was allowed to return to B Unit where everyone treated her as if she was made of glass.

It took time, but things gradually returned to almost normal. Abby couldn't shake the numbness that surrounded her, though. She went through her days in a state of complete languor. Sheronda and Mad T watched her closely. They were worried she would hurt herself. Abby was too tired to reassure them that suicide was the furthest thing from her mind.

She returned from her evening tutoring session to find another CD on her bunk. This one was open and there was a note taped to the top that read, "Mad T will love this." Abby smiled at the note, but frowned at the CD. She took it with her and went in search of Quinn.

She found him escorting one of Kelsey's girls back from the infirmary. He frowned as she walked up to him.

"I can't accept this," she said. Quinn frowned at her then at the CD. "I can't listen to it," she continued. "It'll be too hard."

"You said that if you're a true Scot then the bagpipes will make you cry," he said in answer.

Abby stared at him. "So?"

"You're walking around here trying to act normal but everyone can tell that you're numb." He handed the CD back to her. "You need to cry it out."

Abby stared at his back as he walked away.

In her suite, Abby put on her headphones, put the CD in her player, and turned it on. The first song was Amazing Grace, always a tearjerker. Abby lay back and stared at the ceiling. The tears were already filling her eyes.

She pictured the last time she'd heard her dad play. His piper group had marched in the Tartan Day parade in New York City. They had played "Scotland the Brave" with hundreds of other pipers and drummers. Abby had had the honor of being the standard-bearer at the head of the pipers. She'd worn traditional highland dress and carried the blue and white flag of Scotland. It was her proudest moment as she marched the streets of New York with thousands of people gathered along the parade route to watch.

As if on cue, "Scotland the Brave" came on, and Abby felt her tears fall. She closed her eyes and saw her father as he was at the parade: proud of his heritage and proud of his daughter.

Abby felt a hand on her leg. She opened her eyes to see Sheronda standing at the foot of the bed. Abby realized that it was time for cleaning crew and she had made them late. She quickly dried her face with her sleeve and followed Sheronda out of the suite.

Quinn and White led them to admin. This time Quinn stayed, and Abby and Sheronda started on their offices.

Abby was in the office Pike had cornered her in when Quinn appeared at the door.

"Are you OK?" he asked. His voice was quiet.

Abby nodded. Her tears were falling so much she'd been wiping them off the desk. Quinn crossed the room and gathered her in his arms. Abby cried as he held her tight. Her tears stained his shirt. When she had calmed, Quinn tucked her hair behind her ears and wiped the tears from her face.

"Oh my God, finally," Sheronda exclaimed from behind him. Quinn stepped away quickly as Abby laughed into her hand. A second later they heard her vacuum go on. Abby picked up her polish and rag and set to finishing up her work.

Back in B Unit, Quinn held Abby back as the others went to their suites. "I'm serious when I say you need to work through this. Dennis has been watching you and he's worried. He wants to put you on watch in ADSEG."

Abby had visited ADSEG and wished to avoid it at all cost. It was just too claustrophobic for her.

"I will," she promised.

Chapter 15

ACE BOON COONS

Abby did get better. Though there weren't any more moments of comfort from him, Quinn must have spoken to Mad T and Sheronda because they would not let Abby sit quietly for a single moment. Mad T's approach to Abby's mental health was especially effective as she was a natural comic. In fact, she was the funniest person Abby had ever known personally. She would tell stories about her family that were so funny, Abby had to wonder what happened in her life that landed her in prison.

Sheronda worked on Abby's inherent commitment to helping people. She brought in women who were too shy to ask for Abby's help and introduced them while handing Abby their paperwork or GED tests for review. By the time the two were done, Abby was almost back to normal. Only the CD of bagpipes could bring on the tears, and Mad T took care of that. One day it had only played for two minutes when Mad T snatched it out of the CD player, snapped it back in its case, and marched it across the common area to place it firmly in Quinn's hand.

"Please take that away," she ordered. "Ain't nobody need to listen to them killin' cats."

Even Quinn laughed at that.

One unfortunate side effect to the hilarity was the return of what Grandma called the "debauchery." Though they had been on their best behavior during Abby's mourning, both Kelsey and Fred were back to their sexual escapades. Grandma had hoped that the change for the better would be permanent, but the last trip to the showers proved that wasn't the case.

It was nothing to Abby who was immune to it by then, but it still made Grandma angry. Especially when it was Fred encouraging two of her girls to scissor each other in the shower stall. Abby was impressed by the sheer physicality of the effort, but otherwise she didn't care. She led the way to the far stall and didn't even bother to undress inside the stall as they had before. Abby was fairly certain that after hundreds of showers and strip searches, no one was interested in her nudity. She still covered for Grandma though, who wanted to preserve her modesty regardless of the disinterest from the other women.

Fred was trying to get her short chubby leg up as Abby and Grandma were leaving. Abby wanted to make a joke, but she knew Grandma would be less than receptive to her pointing out the ridiculousness of Fred's efforts. Instead she kept her mouth shut and walked her elderly friend back to her suite in silence.

Back in her own suite, Abby pulled out the latest book to appear on her bunk and tried to read, but her mind drifted to the weekend. Thursday was Halloween and her twenty-fifth birthday. She usually loved that her birthday fell on such a fun holiday, but that year she had little to celebrate and she assumed that inmates didn't typically celebrate what was really a children's holiday.

Abby set her book aside and watched the activity outside of the suite. She could see Quinn in the guard office typing on the computer. Captain Hannah stood just outside gently reading someone the riot act. Several women sat in the common area watching the TV mounted high on the wall. It sounded like the Food Network. It was usually that or Home & Garden Television. Every other Saturday they could watch a feature film, usually G or PG rated fare. Abby preferred independent films and thrillers, so she usually passed on the romantic comedies and kids' movies.

Abby put on her headphones and lay back to watch her very small world flow past her door with Amos Lee playing in her ears. Soon it was bedtime, and her suitemates started coming in for the night.

As everyone settled down, Abby pulled her earphones off at the end of the CD, rolled over, and went to sleep.

It was late when a cry woke her up. She lay for a moment wondering if she'd been dreaming. A second later another sound came from below her. Abby rolled over and looked down at Mad T's bunk. This time it was Marianna on the floor between Mad T's legs with her entire hand hidden. Abby had heard of fisting—the women on the unit certainly joked about it enough—but she'd never seen it before. Mad T had her head back and her eyes closed as Marianna slowly rotated her hand as if she was turning a doorknob. Abby glanced past her and saw Rita and Rosita on the other lower bunk masturbating each other. She could tell from the quiet snores beneath her that Sheronda was sleeping through it all.

Mad T moaned again, loud enough that Abby looked up to see if any of the COs heard her. She could barely see the guard office through the Plexiglas window in their door. She could see Captain Hannah sitting at the computer and part of someone who looked like Sergeant Ramirez. That meant Quinn and White were probably walking the unit. Neither was likely to do more than tap on the door, so Abby kept silent.

Abby looked over at Mad T and saw her looking back.

"Sorry, baby," she panted. "We tried to give you peace an' quiet when daddy died…but I gotta gets me some release."

"It's OK," Abby whispered.

Mad T nodded then closed her eyes and lay back.

Abby turned to the wall and went back to sleep.

Chapter 16

GOD SQUAD

As the week went by, Abby remained silent about the upcoming event. She noticed, though, that the women in the unit seemed excited about the holiday, which was a little strange since Halloween was more about kids dressing up and trick or treating. But it was the guard staff's firm belief that the more joy the inmates could find in things, the happier they would be. And happier inmates were compliant inmates.

The only person who did not appreciate Halloween was Grandma. She took the approaching holiday as an opportunity to lecture the other women on the threat of evil coming among them if they even acknowledged the day. For the most part, the other inmates let her rant, but Abby could tell it was beginning to wear on their nerves. Things came to a head in the common area where Kelsey had been mock trick or treating around the unit, accepting things like candy, coins, and in Abby's case, a paperclip. Those who didn't hand her something were crowned with a circlet of toilet paper. Grandma sat and fumed until she couldn't take it anymore.

As Kelsey circled around her, Grandma stood up and pointed at the girl. "Whoever makes a practice of sinning is of the devil, for the devil has been sinning from the beginning. The reason the Son of God appeared was to destroy the works of the devil. You are engaging in the devil's celebration and you will burn in his hellfire for an eternity."

Kelsey stopped and regarded the older woman. She was primed for an argument. "You mean to tell me you never ever took your kids trick or treating?" she challenged.

Grandma shook her head. "Of course not. I raised my children as good Christians. I taught them to turn their faces from the enemy. They celebrated the bounty of the earth instead and rejoiced in God's blessings in our lives. My children have never participated in Satan's holiday."

As much as she respected Grandma, Abby couldn't take it anymore.

"Actually, Satan doesn't have anything to do with Halloween," she said to the group. "October thirty-first to November first is a pagan holiday called Samhain celebrated by the pre-Christian druids of Scotland and Ireland to mark the end of the harvest season. Early druids believed the holiday was one of two days that their loved ones could come to visit them from the underworld. And even though a place was set for them at the feasts, it was really about honoring their dead and not about ghosts coming to visit. Since druids didn't understand or acknowledge the existence of the 'devil' as the early Christian church did, evil had nothing to do with the holiday."

Everyone, including Grandma was silent as Abby spoke, so she continued. "Samhain was Christianized in the year six hundred and nine, but was moved to November first in the ninth century by Pope Gregory who loved nothing better than to co-opt pagan holidays and rename them as Christian events. Early priests told the people they were trying to convert that Samhain was actually All Saints' Day, and to consider it to be anything else was an act of the devil. To prove their point, the church condemned early druids who refused to convert as possessed by the devil and executed them."

Abby looked at Grandma. "To celebrate Halloween as a harvest day is to celebrate its *pagan* history. To celebrate it as the early Christians did would be to condemn and murder people."

Grandma stared at Abby, her face a mask of confusion. "How do you know this?" she asked quietly.

Abby shrugged. "I was raised by two college professors. Religious history was a big topic in our house."

"But you're a good Christian," Grandma sputtered. "How can you believe this?"

"Because it's history," Abby answered. "The problem with many fundamentalists is that they try to revise history to suit their faith's agenda, or they ignore the parts that are unflattering. History is the truth of what happened in the past. Revisionist history is often an exaggeration or even an outright lie. Christ died to save man from his own sins, not to save man from the devil."

Abby braced herself for a dose of Grandma's wrath. Instead, the woman pushed herself up from the table and walked away.

"Was all that true?" Kelsey asked.

"It's history, which to me is true. I wouldn't have said it if I didn't think it was true," Abby said with a shrug.

Grandma had little to say over the next couple of days. Abby could tell the older woman was bothered by what she had said, but Abby wasn't going to apologize. She'd spoken the truth, even though it wasn't the truth Grandma wanted to hear.

It was during the next Bible study that Grandma questioned Abby further.

"Abby, you *do* accept the presence of Satan in this world, don't you?"

Abby shook her head. "Not in the way most people understand him, no."

"What do you mean?" she asked.

Abby thought for a moment. "The Old Testament has very little of the devil. In fact, the book of Job is one of the few references to Satan. The Hebrew word they translated as Satan could also mean 'adversary,' which could be anybody. It isn't until the New Testament that we saw see Satan represented as we understand him today. And because the Bible has been translated many times over, our information about the devil is colored by the opinion of the translators and the intent of their church."

Abby paused to see if Grandma was getting upset. To her credit, she seemed more interested than anything else. So Abby continued.

"If God created all things, and everything God made is good, why would God create something or someone whose sole purpose is to perpetuate evil in the world? Unless he didn't."

"He didn't?" asked one of Grandma's girls.

"Well, it's only my opinion, but no, I don't think God created the devil as he's represented in the New Testament. I think that the devil is either a fallen angel who challenged God's love for man, or the devil doesn't exist at all and *we* are ultimately responsible for the evil that exists in the world. I'm inclined to go with the latter."

"So you don't believe that Satan even exists?" Grandma asked.

"I believe that all good things come from God, so no. I truly think that the evil we see in the world comes from man, and the devil construct was created to give the church an enemy; someone they could use to control adherents through fear. And for the common man, the devil exists to cast blame upon and to deny personal responsibility for their actions."

"What about people who are possessed by the devil?" another girl, Jessica, asked.

Abby shook her head. "Most suffer neurobiological disorders. They are schizophrenic or bipolar. One famous exorcism, Anneliese Michel, was an epileptic who was starved to death by her exorcists. Others may have had behavioral disorders that were interpreted as possession, such as ADD or ADHD, autism, or even dissociative personality disorder. They are usually children or young people who are highly suggestible and their symptoms are more likely psychosomatic than the result of a demonic possession," she explained. "Unless the symptoms of their possession are accompanied by true occult phenomena like levitation or psychokinesis, they need a psychiatrist, not a priest. We also have to question why the devil would possess some unknown, relatively inconsequential person in the first place."

"What about Hitler?" Jessica asked. "Some people say he actually was the devil."

Abby shrugged. "Hitler was raised as a Catholic. He claimed to be a Christian and promoted religious instruction in schools. At the same time he ordered the deaths of hundreds of priests and nuns as well as the termination of Jews. Some historians theorized that he felt Christ's sacrifice was not just for salvation but also evidence of his betrayal by the Jews. And because the Catholic Church included the Jewish Torah as their Old Testament, they were just as guilty. I think he saw himself as the head of a whole new church. He was a delusional megalomaniac, sure, but not possessed. Himmler, on the other hand, was truly evil, so that might be a completely different argument."

"So you don't believe that the devil uses us to commit acts of evil?" Grandma asked.

Abby shook her head, "No. When God gave us free will, it came with the ability to do evil unto each other as well as good. If we commit an act of evil, it is because we chose to."

The small group sat and stared at Abby until Grandma announced that Bible study was over.

Abby picked up her Bible and walked toward the door where Grandma stopped her.

"I don't understand how you can study the Bible but not believe it," she stated.

"I'm a contextualist not a literalist," Abby explained. "I believe that somewhere in the deliberate mistranslations and outright propaganda, the word of God is hidden but still there. I cannot accept the Bible as the only history of the world. Dinosaurs existed even if they aren't mentioned in the Bible. I don't believe God created the world in seven days or put Adam and Eve in the Garden of Eden. No one was witness to the earliest beginnings of the universe, so anything written is just a story, a fable."

"And you think we are all ultimately responsible for the things we do," Grandma's voice was flat.

Abby thought for a moment then answered. "Yes, to a certain extent. There are people who do terrible things, but because of their psychological issues, they don't realize what they've done. And there are people who react so suddenly that their baser instincts have taken over for a moment, essentially overriding their intellect."

Grandma looked thoughtful. "But you're here."

"Yes, because I told an undercover police officer where he could buy drugs," she answered. "I broke the law, and as it is written, I deserve to be punished for that. But to blame the cop or my friend Mark, or even the devil, would be to avoid personal responsibility for my actions. I'm here to serve my punishment for my crime."

Grandma regarded her for a moment then asked, "Do you know why I'm here?"

"Sheronda said you killed a cop while protesting."

Grandma shook her head. "Being a protester didn't have anything to do with it. I was working with injured veterans in the city's free clinics at the time. I had a sister who was much younger than I…an 'oops' baby, if you will. She was still in high school long after I graduated from college and married. She was home alone when she heard someone breaking a window at the back of the house. She was about to call the police when a cop came to the front door claiming he saw someone running from the house. When she let him in, he raped her. He tried to strangle her, but left after she lost consciousness. Our dad found her when he came home from work. When she came to in the hospital, she told the nurses what happened and who had hurt her, but at trial they found her testimony to be unreliable. They said she'd been deprived of oxygen too long. So they let him go. She was only sixteen. She couldn't go back to school, and she couldn't hold a job. He took everything away from her. And he would have done it again. So I went up to his front door, I knocked, and I shot him." Grandma paused and looked away. It was obvious the memory still pained her. "I was so angry at him. I felt like the blood in my body was roaring in my ears. And when I watched him die in his doorway, I was so filled with joy I thought something was in me, making me do it."

"You thought you were possessed?" Abby asked quietly.

Grandma stood quietly for a second before answering. "I didn't have a name for it, but essentially that's how I felt. Like someone else was in me. Normal people don't do things like that. Our priest told me I had succumbed to the temptations of the enemy…and I believed him. I guess it was easier than believing that *I* could do something like that."

Abby watched as the older woman struggled with herself.

"You've given me much to question about myself and what I believe," Grandma said quietly.

"I'm sorry," Abby offered. "I never wanted to hurt you."

Grandma reached out and patted Abby on the arm. "Self-examination is never easy. Always necessary, but never easy."

Chapter 17

TEN-TEN FURLOUGH

With Grandma more subdued than usual, the ladies in the unit embraced the Halloween festivities with more gusto. Big Ginger even hinted at a special movie viewing. Abby hoped for an actual horror movie, but she knew it was unlikely. The prison followed a very short list of approved films. Any R-rated movies were typically comedies or action films that were so heavily edited they were barely worth watching. Big Ginger told her that all horror films were on the "not approved" list for excessive violence. Some were on the list because they supported criminal behavior.

Abby hoped it was at least something worth watching.

She was surprised at the enthusiasm with which the women approached their costumes. She didn't think there would be any dressing up. Some costumes, like ghosts, were not permitted at all. There was a run on toilet paper as many women were planning on wrapping themselves like mummies, Sheronda included. Some women were using sheets to make dresses or togas, while others were simply using their prison scrubs to dress as doctors or nurses. It was fun to watch from the sidelines, and nobody seemed to care that Abby wasn't interested in joining in.

The COs watched over their antics with rare indulgence. Excitement over Halloween offered a welcome distraction from the regular mayhem of petty disputes and sexual shenanigans. The only variable would have been Grandma, but after her conversation with Abby she'd kept a low profile, preferring to stay in her suite with her back to the common area; the only indication of her disapproval.

By Thursday anticipation was running high as the women looked forward to the evening's events. Abby still hadn't said anything about her birthday, and she hoped no one knew. She and Sheronda left for their cleaning shift with Big Ginger escorting them to the admin offices.

Abby enjoyed the mindlessness of cleaning. Their shifts had grown much shorter since they were there every weekday and the warden ran such a tight ship that everyone's offices were neat as a pin. Abby took her time dusting the warden's plants, stopping to watch the storm clouds roll across the turf fields. It looked like another whopper was on its way. Abby loved storms and regretted not having actual windows in the suite to watch them rage. Even the skylights in the ceiling were little more than smaller transom windows designed to offer some natural light into the unit.

By the time they returned from check-in, the common room was filled with inmates. The room was already dark from the storm, and rain pounded on the roof in a frenetic percussion.

Abby followed Sheronda into the suite and helped her with her costume. It took only two rolls of toilet paper to wrap her small body. By the time they were done, Captain Hannah was calling everyone into the common area. Abby sat down next to Mad T while the other women took seats on the remaining chairs and the floor.

"I'm excited to announce that we have a special evening planned for you!" she began. "I see all of you have been very creative with the limited resources at your disposal, and I am extremely pleased that we do not have anyone violating the small restrictions to the evening." Captain Hannah nodded at the guard station and Big Ginger rolled out a cart covered in a sheet.

"So to reward you for such good behavior, the sergeants have put together candy bags for all of you." Captain Hannah pulled the sheet from the cart to reveal dozens of candy bags filled with small chocolate bars, Hershey's kisses, and gummy worms. There was a round of thunderous applause as Big Ginger took the cart around and handed each woman a bag. Abby accepted her bag with thanks as Mad T tore into hers immediately.

"We also have a very special treat for one of you," Captain Hannah nodded again at the guard station. This time it was Quinn who pushed out a covered cart. "Not only are we celebrating Halloween, or All Saints' Eve for some of you, but we are also wishing Abby a very happy birthday!" Cheers accompanied the applause as Quinn removed the sheet to reveal frosted cupcakes for everyone. One special cupcake had a candle on top. Quinn lit it and brought it over to Abby as the ladies started to sing.

Abby smiled through her embarrassment. When they were done singing, Mad T and the other ladies urged her to make a wish. Abby closed her eyes and thought for a moment. What she truly wanted, to have her father back, she knew would be a waste of a wish. And to hope to go home felt as futile and empty as the home she'd be returning to. So instead she wished a successful future for each of the women in the unit with her. Then she opened her eyes and blew out her candle.

"Now we have one final treat for you," Captain Hannah indicated the televisions mounted high on the wall. "I understand that Abby is a big fan of horror films; however, due to their violent content, we hope this will be a suitable substitute."

Abby looked up as the screens went on. Then a roar arose among the women followed by enthusiastic applause. Abby smiled. It was the *Rocky Horror Picture Show*. Abby's favorite movie of all time. She was thrilled to see so many of the women playing along. The stormy movie scenes were punctuated by the storm raging above them.

Sheronda was riveted to the screen, having never seen the movie before. Abby laughed as she mooned over Tim Curry as Dr. Frank-N-Furter.

"Damn but that boy is pretty," Sheronda fanned herself. "He's getting me all hot an' bothered."

"Really? I thought you'd go for Rocky," Abby joked.

"Mm. I like me some muscles, but that Rocky's just way too white. But the doctor, now he's got some manly about him even with all that makeup."

Abby had to agree. Rocky might be the golden boy, but Tim Curry was a beautiful man.

When the movie ended, it took some time for the ladies to wind down. Abby helped clean up, and then Captain Hannah called for the evening count. As the ladies moved to the doors of their suites, most of them took off their costumes, while others traded their chocolates. Abby tossed her candy bag on her bunk then returned to the door in time to witness a commotion further down the row. Quinn ran by and stopped at Grandma's door where Big Ginger was on her radio. Captain Hannah emerged from the suite and declared an immediate lockdown.

As she moved into the suite, Abby started to worry. She'd never experienced a total unscheduled lockdown during the time she'd been there.

"Oh damn," Sheronda shook her head. "Somethin' gone way wrong." Abby stood just inside as the doors slid shut. She couldn't see along the suites. Although some inmates used mirrors to look along the row of cells, it was strictly forbidden. If they were caught, the violation would result in a trip to DSEG.

Abby returned to her bunk and pulled herself up. The ladies in the suite were surprisingly quiet. Even Rita and Rosita who usually chattered in Spanish till lights out were silent. Even the unit was quiet. The only sounds came from Grandma's suite. Abby closed her eyes and prayed that everything would be OK.

An hour later, it was lights out. They were still in lockdown.

Chapter 18

DOING THE DUTCH

Abby was already awake as the door locks disengaged just before wake-up call. Captain Dennis came out of the guard office ready to holler.

"Rise and shine, ladies," he bellowed as he moved across the common room. "Time to get up and get yourselves counted."

Mad T and Marianna rolled out of bed. Sheronda was already behind Abby as she stepped out of the suite. Both looked down toward Grandma's door. Gray was already there starting the count. Abby noticed Grandma wasn't outside the suite, and her stomach sank. She knew she'd have to wait until after count to ask about her.

Other than Grandma, everyone was present and accounted for. The group was released to get ready for breakfast. Abby walked over to the guard office where Big Ginger sat. Her face was drawn with extreme fatigue. She looked up as Abby approached, and then she got up to meet her at the door.

"Is Grandma OK?" Abby whispered.

Big Ginger shook her head. "She drank a bottle of rubbing alcohol last night. By the time we got her to the hospital it had already been absorbed. She's in a coma. It's not looking like she's going to make it."

Abby was shocked. "Why would she do that?"

"She left a note, Abby." Big Ginger looked away to where Captain Dennis was herding the ladies into breakfast. "It was a long note, but the gist of it was that, after talking to you, she realized she was ultimately responsible for the murder she'd committed and that she didn't deserve to live any sort of life when she'd taken someone's life from them."

"Oh my God, this is my fault," Abby took a step back. "I never meant to imply that. I should have just kept my mouth shut."

Big Ginger shook her head and placed a hand on Abby's shoulder. "Abby, Agnes was deeply troubled long before you got here. I've been here almost ten years and I've seen her go from almost normal to the extreme evangelical you met when you got here. You can't take the blame for this."

Captain Dennis approached. "Redfern, you need to go home and get some rest," he ordered then turned to Abby. "Go to breakfast, girl. If you need to speak with your case manager or the priest, we'll give them a call after." Abby did as she was told.

Though she wasn't hungry, Abby took a full tray of food and went to sit next to Sheronda. She noticed that Grandma's girls had left a space for her at their usual table. The girls themselves looked forlorn without their leader. They didn't seem hungry either and picked at their food.

As usual, Sheronda had the full scoop on what had happened. Abby wouldn't put it past her to have already memorized Grandma's letter.

"So that Jessica girl's been sayin' that Grandma stole that alcohol when she went in for her heart check-up yesterday mornin'. She been real quiet since talkin' to you about devil stuff. Jus' readin' her Bible and starin'. Then last night when we all be in the common, she tole her girls she just goin' to lay down 'cuz she was tired. They thinkin' she drank it when everybody leave for the party."

"But I don't understand why she would do it," Abby started.

"Because you told her there was no such thing as the devil," Jessica answered from behind her. Abby turned to see the tears already streaming down the girl's face. "This whole time she thought she was being unfairly prosecuted because she wasn't in her right mind when she killed that cop. But after talking to you, she started to think that she hadn't been punished enough. An eye for an eye."

"I'm so sorry," Abby apologized to the girls at the table. "I never meant to hurt her."

"She didn't blame you," Jessica answered. "She told us we couldn't blame you either."

Abby could tell by their expressions that they did blame her. In her heart, she blamed herself. She turned away and stared at the tray in front of her. Sheronda watched her. For once she was at a loss for words.

After breakfast, Abby went out for a run. It was so cold the yard was empty. The grass rimmed with frost from the rain that had frozen overnight. Dark gray clouds still hung over the prison. Abby walked over to the perimeter path then started to jog. She had long since given up on counting her paces. It no longer mattered how far she ran. Instead, she let her mind turn away from thoughts of guilt and rehashing her last conversation with Grandma. She ran until her heavy heart pounded in her chest. She ran until she was so exhausted she couldn't take another step. Fat flakes had started to fall, catching in her hair as she walked over to one of the tables to sit and stare out past the fences.

She knew Grandma was going to die, and she knew it was her fault. Abby's sense of self shattered in the face of the responsibility that was fully hers to bear. She had been so full of herself despite her current circumstances. What others saw as confidence, Abby knew in her heart was nothing more than hubris, an ugly desire to hold herself apart. She had always been treated differently and she had let her pride define her as something better, or if not better, then special, even though inside she felt plain and inadequate. She knew her need to be as others saw her was at worst, vain and selfish. But in truth, Abby's selfishness was hurtful, even damaging. She had callously flaunted her theories without regard to anyone else's fragile hold on reality. And now someone was going to die. Abby knew she was as guilty of Grandma's death as she would have been had she handed the old woman the bottle of rubbing alcohol and told her to drink.

Captain Dennis appeared at the door behind her and called her in from the cold.

The mood in the unit was somber. Even Kelsey and Fred, who'd had countless run-ins with Grandma, were subdued. Though some women were callous to the plight of others, suicide was felt keenly. And Grandma had been there so long that she'd become a permanent fixture in the unit.

It was just before noon count when Captain Dennis made the announcement that Grandma had died. The unit's various case managers came in to make themselves available to anyone who felt they needed counseling. Grandma's girls all availed themselves of the offer and Father Duncan arrived to meet with anyone feeling a crisis of faith.

Abby refused all offers of assistance and went to her suite instead. It was mercifully empty as she climbed up into her bunk and closed her eyes.

Hours later, Abby awoke to a hand on her leg. She rolled over to see MadT gently shaking her.

"Gotta get up, little girl," she whispered. "They called for a shakedown."

Abby rolled off her bunk then moved to the door of the suite where the other ladies were already waiting.

"They's taken Grandma's girls to ADSEG," Sheronda whispered to Abby, which earned her a glare from Captain Dennis. "Seems one said they's wantin' ta kill they-selves too."

"And they been talkin' bout you," Mad T added, earning her own glare.

Abby stayed silent as the COs went about tossing the suites. As usual, Fred had hooch and Kelsey had tattoo contraband. Other women were found to be holding illegal prescription pills and excessive amounts of commissary goods, which usually indicated illegal trade. Abby knew she had been under observation when the commissary reported the size of her purchases to her unit captains. In the beginning, both Captains Dennis and Hannah had watched her closely until they realized that Abby was giving away her purchases to inmates who did not have money on their books. They left her alone when they saw she did it without expecting anything in return. Sheronda managed the distribution to ensure no one was benefiting unfairly.

"Miss Blackwood," Captain Dennis waved her over. "Your presence is requested in ADSEG. You are relieved of duty for the remainder of the day. Gray will be escorting you over."

Abby nodded dully and followed Gray out of the unit. She was barely aware that she had been excused from the body search as well.

In ADSEG, Abby's case manager was waiting for her in one of the interview rooms.

"Have a seat Abby," Emma indicated one of the chairs across the table and Abby sat. "I'm sure you've heard about Agnes." Abby nodded. "We are talking with everyone closest to her. I wanted to ask you how you are feeling about what happened."

Abby shrugged. "I feel horrible. I feel like I should have said something to make her feel better about her situation."

Emma nodded. "That's natural. However, you may not be aware of this, but Agnes had some profound psychological issues. Her problems were not bad enough for her to be determined mentally unfit to serve her sentence in a correctional facility; but her issues got her transferred here as soon as Maysville was available for inmates."

"I'm pretty sure she was bipolar," Abby suggested. "Was she being medicated?"

Emma nodded. "That was part of the reason for her transfer. Maysville was constructed to accommodate inmates with relatively nonthreatening mental disorders so that the state could monitor treatment more closely." She closed the file in front of her and looked closely at Abby.

"When I read through her last letter, it occurred to me that we may have overlooked you."

Abby was confused. "What do you mean?"

"Well, Agnes described a situation that bears further investigation. She admired you for your intelligence and your strength. She respected you more than Tanya, Kelsey, or Alfreda, citing your assistance to your fellow inmates. However, your work with the women in the unit and your generosity creates a situation where the other inmates are beholden to you, so I have to assume that you are either positioning yourself as a bull, or even worse, trying to take over the whole unit."

Abby was incredulous. "Grandma said that in her letter?"

"Not in so many words, but the inference is there. I have to say, personally, that it is quite subtle in you, but I can see her point. This all looks highly manipulative. And now someone is dead."

Abby was speechless. She had never even thought about why she was helping the women of the unit. It was something she had always done in her church and in the community. Had Grandma seen something in her that she couldn't see herself?

"My report has gone out to all of the COs in your unit. It's only fair that you be advised that you are under closer scrutiny at this point. Any infractions will result in a permanent transfer to DSEG. You are removed as an instructional leader, though you may remain in your current work assignment with the cleaning crew. Removal of additional privileges will be at the discretion of your unit captains. You have twenty-four hours to appeal this report. Please sign here." Abby scribbled her name at the bottom of the report. Then Emma nodded behind Abby and a moment later Gray appeared at her side.

Abby was silent on the way back to the unit. As Gray led her to the guard office for check-in, Abby could tell that the staff was looking at her differently. Big Ginger in particular looked confused, and Abby thought she detected a hint of an expression of hurt.

She walked up to Captain Dennis and asked permission to go out to the yard even though it wasn't necessary. Inmates who weren't assigned to work duty elsewhere in the prison were relatively free to go where they chose within the unit. Captain Dennis granted her request.

As Abby made her way outside, a freezing gust of wind blew across the cement patio. She was glad she'd worn her hoodie as she made her way to the path. At the perimeter fence, she quickened her pace and began to run.

It was getting dark when Captain Dennis appeared at the door and called out for Abby to come in.

"Shift change, girl," he said. His tone was gruff and formal. "You need to report for count."

Abby was silent as she moved past him into the unit. At the suite, the ladies were already waiting. Abby stood still and silent, ignoring the whispers around her. After count, she went into the suite and pulled trail mix out of her locker. She had missed lunch during her disastrous meeting with Emma.

Mad T and Sheronda came in, followed by some of Mad T's family. They congregated around the lower bunks and looked at Abby expectantly. Abby looked back.

"Well?" Mad T asked. "What they say?"

Abby shook her head. "Emma filed a report against me based on Grandma's suicide letter. She interpreted it to mean that Grandma was accusing me of manipulating everyone here to do what I want. I've been removed as an instructional leader and I am under observation. If she feels like I'm trying to take advantage of any other inmates, I'll be transferred to DSEG."

Mad T snorted. "Man, that bitch is stupid. She spends like no time here and she gonna say something like that? Just because some crazy old woman wrote crazy shit in her suicide note?"

"She says I have twenty-four hours to appeal the report." Abby informed them.

"Girl, don't bother." Sheronda chimed in. "She hear the appeal herself. You think she goin' ta overturn herself? No way. You jus' be wastin' time."

Abby looked at the women she regarded as friends. If she was brutally honest, when she first arrived at the prison she saw these women as low and classless. And despite everything she'd been taught in church about loving one's fellow man, she saw them as less than her for having committed whatever atrocities that brought them here. What she found instead was a group of women who had tried to survive the circumstances of their place in life the only way they knew how. She found women who were struggling for sanity in a system that lacked the resources to deal with the profound issues surrounding mental illness or drug addiction. She watched as women created social microunits to substitute for the family they missed on the outside, or for family they never had. They were loyal and respectful of each other in ways the outside world wouldn't understand. In any way they could, these women were making the best of their current situation.

Abby hated herself for being a snob.

"Don't be beatin' yourself up, girl," Mad T warned. "Ain't nobody buyin' her shit."

"I can't help but feel like she has a point."

Mad T snorted. "Bitch ain't got no point. You ever ask for somethin' from someone you help? Or beat up someone for not payin' you back for a favor?"

Abby shook her head.

"Then bitch ain't got no point," Mad T declared with finality.

Abby didn't answer. She still wasn't convinced. Instead, she glanced out the suite door to see Quinn checking into the guard office. He and Big Ginger conferred for a few minutes. They each glanced in turn at Abby's door. Neither looked particularly happy. Abby turned and climbed into her bunk. She closed her eyes as she lay back and listened to the quiet sounds of the women discussing her situation. Soon she was asleep.

Chapter 19

DOWN BAD

As the days passed, Abby noticed a subtle shift in the dynamic of the unit. The COs stopped talking to her openly. Even Quinn, who spoke to her the least, seemed to avoid her altogether. There were no more gifts left on her bunk, although it had been only an assumption on her part that he was responsible for their appearance.

With more free time on her hands, Abby spent her time either sleeping or running. When it was time to report for cleaning crew, it was usually White and Ramirez escorting them. If Sheronda noticed the change she didn't say anything.

In support of their friend and roommate, Mad T and the ladies all kept themselves to themselves. Sheronda gathered her crew and joined Mad T's family to form a united front of cordial silence. The other women weren't quite so circumspect. Grandma's death had upset the balance in the unit. Her tactics had been harsh, but effective; and her absence removed any restraint some of the women might have exercised had she still been there to hold them accountable. Kelsey and Fred especially celebrated Grandma's death with more outrageous behavior than ever before. They preyed on unsuspecting incoming inmates, initiating the poor women to the seamier side of prison life. Where normally Abby would intervene on behalf of the women they targeted, she knew any attempt to help would be seen as bull dagging the weaker women. So she stayed out of it.

With the escalating violations came more shakedowns and body searches, which resulted in more visits to DSEG for some and unit-wide punishments for everyone. Phone, TV, and recreational privileges were taken away on a regular basis. Sleeping, eating, and working were all that remained.

Abby felt the change keenly, and took responsibility for the deteriorating conditions in the unit. She knew she wasn't directly responsible for Grandma's death, but she felt in her heart that if she'd only taken a moment to consider the impact of her last conversation with the older woman, Grandma would still be alive.

Things came to a head in November when Kelsey and Fred came to blows over the same girl. Originally Fred's, the girl undressed in the shower to reveal Kelsey's artwork permanently imprinted on parts of her body only seen in the most compromising positions. Once Fred saw Kelsey's name tattooed on the inside of the girl's upper thigh, she flew at her rival in a rage. Kelsey gave as good as she got, and by the time COs arrived in the showers, both women were bloodied and beaten.

Things quieted after Kelsey and Fred were sent to DSEG for a minimum thirty-day punishment. Abby resolved to enjoy the quiet while it lasted. She was happy that both troublemakers would still be in DSEG for Thanksgiving.

Unlike Halloween, nothing was really planned for the upcoming holiday other than an early special dinner and a day off from work. Since Abby was still denied the privilege of attending group sessions like Bible study, she met with Father Duncan privately for prayer and communion then went outside to the bitter cold to run.

She had resumed counting her steps to see if she could reach 30,000: the approximate number of steps in a marathon. It was difficult to keep count though, and Abby wished there was a way to get a pedometer. She resolved to ask Father Duncan if he could find one for her. If not, then Jane would probably send one if she requested it.

Abby stood at the perimeter fence trying to multiply the steps in her head when she heard a dull *thunk* like a large metal door closing. When she looked up she saw Quinn waving her in. Shivering, she crossed the yard and walked past him into the unit. Before she could take another step though, Quinn reached out and grabbed her hand in one of his. Abby didn't have on gloves, and she knew her hands were like icicles. His hand was warm and his body heat flowed into her stiff white fingers. Without a word he dropped her hand and walked away.

Later at dinner, Sylvia handed Abby a soft gray hat and mittens. "I see you coming in and you always look like you're freezing," she said by way of explanation. "I'm going to knit you a sweater next."

"Shit," Sheronda grumbled. "It's so cold outside, you need ta knit her a sleepin' bag wit legs."

Abby thanked Sylvia and made a mental note to get Sylvia something from the commissary as a thank you gift. She pulled on the hat and mittens. They fit perfectly and were so soft Abby thought she could sleep in them.

After dinner, Abby dropped off her gift and left with Sheronda for cleaning crew.

The days leading up to Thanksgiving were uneventful. There was the usual ebb and flow of old convicts finishing up their time and leaving, and new inmates coming in. Some were fearful and uncertain, while others were back for parole violations or repeat offenses.

Sheronda, Mad T, and their groups continued to keep a low profile. They operated under the assumption that if Abby was in jeopardy then they all were. Though she no longer assisted the other women with their GED studies or prison paperwork, Abby still donated commissary items to those women she knew weren't receiving outside assistance. Sheronda still served as her go-between, making sure no one was overlooked and that no one took advantage.

Despite Abby's efforts to remain anonymous, one of the new girls, a sweet, chubby blonde named Kendra, managed to track her down. Abby was watching the Food Network in the common room when Kendra tried to approach her. Abby sensed the girl hovering off to her left, too shy to speak to her directly. She turned to see the girl shuffling from side to side, obviously struggling with her words.

"Yes?" Abby asked.

"Um, can I ask you something?" Kendra's voice was quiet. Her speech was tinged with a slight southern accent.

"I guess," Abby sighed. From behind Kendra, Big Ginger came out of the guard office to stand nearby. Abby could tell she was monitoring the conversation.

Still timid, Kendra moved forward and sat across from Abby.

"I was hoping I could ask you a question about religious things," Kendra kept her voice down.

Abby was surprised. She had assumed Kendra needed instructional help or had a question about one of the prison's myriad forms.

Abby leaned forward to give Kendra her full attention. "Uh, OK. I'll answer as best as I can."

"I've been going to the Bible study group, and at first it was real nice because they were talking a lot about forgiveness." Kendra looked away as if she were uncertain about how to proceed. Abby waited and watched her struggle to find her resolve.

"But lately they've been saying terrible things about the women in here who have relationships with each other. You know, the lesbians?"

Abby nodded. The group's homophobia was a holdover from when Grandma led Bible study. Her opinions and influence in that area had been so strong as to be considered dictatorial. Jessica had taken over and, if anything, was more judgmental than Grandma had been.

"The thing is…well…I go to church. I mean, I went to church before I came here and…well….even though I didn't tell anybody…I'm one."

Abby listened to Kendra's stammering, not quite getting what the woman was saying. "One what?" she asked.

Kendra's face went an alarming shade of red. "A lesbian," she whispered.

Abby was still confused. "So?"

Kendra looked pained. "I just wanted to ask you…if….are they right?"

Finally Abby got it. "Oh…no. Of course not." She waited as the tension drained from Kendra's body. "Listen," she continued, "people like Jessica and her group take the laws of the Bible literally. Like the story of Lot in the book of Genesis, or the laws against homosexuality in the book of Leviticus. What they fail to understand is that even though the Bible condemns the act, the emphasis is on the behavior, not the condition. And they forget, or choose to forget, that the Bible itself says to hate the sin but love the sinner."

Kendra still looked conflicted. "What do *you* think?"

"I think the Bible is full of laws that made sense to the people of that time but would be considered ridiculous today. Like pretty much all of Leviticus. Did you know there was a law that says that any person who curses his mother or father should be put to death? Or how about Deuteronomy where it says that stubborn children should be stoned to death by their parents." Abby chuckled at that one, eliciting a small uncertain smile from Kendra. "They really seemed to like killing kids, didn't they?" Abby continued.

"And what about non-Christian homosexuals? They don't abide by biblical laws…are they still damned? Or what about cultures that acknowledge the differences in sexual preferences. The Bugis people of Indonesia recognize five genders. Simply put, they recognize male, female, a neutral gender, the masculine female, and the feminine male. To me that makes the most sense since no one is all one or the other, sometimes even biologically. All I can tell you is that you are as God made you. And if God made you a lesbian then God loves you as He made you."

Kendra still looked confused. "But what about the LURDs? Aren't they an abomination to God? Jessica says so."

Abby shook her head. "Jessica does not speak for God and it's blasphemy for her to presume to know what God thinks. Women cope in situations like this by creating support systems with the people available to them. They may not be gay on the outside, but they crave love and acceptance and will assume or assign roles that fulfill their emotional needs. And if you really pay attention, you'll see some women adopt more masculine roles while others remain feminine. In this way they surround themselves with women who love them and want to keep them safe or substitute spouses and children they want to protect. I can't imagine God condemning that. It goes against human nature."

Kendra seemed comforted. She looked at Abby curiously.

"What about you? You don't do either. You're not a bull or a Maytag."

Abby shrugged. "I don't know. I've never really thought about it. I'm not gay and the LURD thing doesn't really do anything for me. I guess I'm the neutral gender."

"Thank you," Kendra said. She seemed sincere. Abby hoped she had not overstepped her bounds again. She mentally kicked herself as the girl got up and walked away.

"That was really nice what you said," someone behind Abby said. She turned to see Big Ginger giving her a smile, something she hadn't seen in a long time.

"I just hope it helped," Abby shrugged.

"I'm sure it did," Big Ginger reassured her. "If there's anything a young gay needs, it's the unconditional support of someone they respect."

"I guess so." Abby still wasn't convinced. She'd missed the rest of the cooking show, so she got up and went into her suite to read.

Later that day, Abby left with Sheronda for cleaning crew. Quinn must have been off as it was White and Singh who escorted them to admin. Singh stayed with Abby and Sheronda while White took the others to their wing. Abby was halfway through one of the case manager's offices when she looked down and saw her file lying open on the desk in front of her. Abby noticed that there were several pages of meeting notes and reports documenting times that Emma Bronwin was supposedly monitoring Abby's behavior inside the unit. Abby picked up one of the reports and started to read.

"Inmate Blackwood's behavior appears to be obstructive and she is refusing to answer questions regarding her relationships with the other inmates," Abby read. She looked at the date in confusion. She had no recollection of the meeting. She'd only seen her case manager four times since the beginning of her incarceration at Maysville. She picked up the next report and checked the date on that one. Again, there was no meeting on that day. In fact, there were so many reports, Emma would have had to have been in the unit at least every other day to accomplish so much oversight. Abby checked through the content of the reports. They were all marginally negative, reporting behavior that was almost, but not quite, in violation of prison regulations.

Outside the door, Abby heard Sheronda turn off her vacuum. She quickly returned the papers to the folder and left the office without cleaning it. Abby was so lost in her thoughts as they returned to the unit, that she didn't hear Sheronda asking her what was wrong.

In a daze, Abby grabbed the hat and gloves Sylvia had made for her and went out to run.

For the rest of the evening, Abby ruminated over what she'd found and what to do about it. The reports were damaging and could result in a permanent transfer out of B Unit. But her only resource for personal issues was Emma herself. Abby tossed and turned all night as Emma's words ran through her head over and over.

By morning Abby was already awake and exhausted, but she knew what to do. After count, she went over to the guard office as Captain Dennis was stepping out. Abby approached him cautiously.

"Could I have a word with you, sir?" she asked respectfully.

Captain Dennis regarded her for a moment then nodded.

Abby described what she'd found the day before. "I know it was wrong to look, but the papers were out in the open on her desk. I usually just clean around them, but when I saw what she'd written about me, I couldn't help but read it." Abby paused, uncertain how to proceed. To his credit, Captain Dennis waited patiently.

"The problem isn't that she wrote marginally negative things about me. It's that she's documenting things for meetings that never occurred and recording events that never happened. She wrote a report that I was sexually predatory toward incoming inmates, and then a couple of reports later that I was being abusive and making homophobic remarks toward the gay inmates. That doesn't even make sense."

"Let me get this straight. You found a folder with your name on it with reports about you for case review meetings that you never attended?"

"Yes, sir. I know I shouldn't have looked at a confidential file but—" Abby began, but Captain Dennis interrupted her.

"Your file is confidential, but not to you," he said. "If someone outside the prison wanted to see it they'd have to make a formal request to the Board of Prisons, but you are allowed to review your own file. Kind of like your medical files." Captain Dennis paused to think for a moment then asked, "You're sure it was your file and not someone else's?"

Abby nodded. "Yes, sir."

"And you're sure these meetings didn't actually happen."

Abby nodded again. "Yes, sir. I've only met with her on four occasions: my first day in the unit, when Sergeant Redfern was attacked, when I started as an instructional leader, and after Grandma died. There are far more than four reports in the folder."

"Were your signatures on these reports?"

"I'm sorry, I didn't look. I was so taken aback by the reports themselves. Why? Would my signature be necessary?"

"Your signature is required on any meeting note your case manager generates, good or bad. Hasn't she had you sign paperwork during the meetings you did have with her?"

"Only twice. When I was censured for breaking Dana's arm and when she met with me about Grandma's suicide."

Captain Dennis stared off at nothing. His expression was pensive. "Let me think on this," he said finally.

"Thank you, sir." Even if nothing happened, Abby was grateful Captain Dennis had at least listened to her.

Sheronda and Mad T were furious when she told them what she'd found.

"That fuckin' bitch!" Mad T fumed. "Why she fuckin' with you like that?"

"I don't know. I've hardly seen or spoken to her since I've been here."

Sheronda sat on her bunk chewing her lip. "Why you go to Dennis and not Hannah? Why you wait a day?"

Abby thought about it for second before answering. "You know how Captain Hannah always seems so eager to help?" she began. Mad T and Sheronda nodded and Abby continued. "She seems to want to help the inmates but nothing actually happens. It seems really insincere to me. I knew she'd listen to me, but I doubted that she would actually do anything about it. Or worse, she could have gone to Emma and told her I'd read the file. I figured Captain Dennis would be more invested in righting a wrong…that it would matter to him that Emma's writing false reports. Also, all those meetings supposedly occurred during his shift. It probably affects him too."

Mad T and Sheronda conceded the point.

"You know what she's doin' right?" Sheronda asked. Abby shook her head.

"She's fuckin' with yer good time credit."

Mad T's mouth fell open. "Awwww dammnnnnn, you right."

Abby was confused. "What is that? I don't know what that is."

"You get good time credit toward yer sentence if you do good here. Like don't break rules, never get write-ups, do like extra stuff like get a degree or find Jesus or somethin'. Ever state's diffrnt. Some gives you a day fer a day, some five a month, some you get twenty days a month. Here it's one-third served. You finish a third of yer sentence and you can get early release 'cause you been good."

"I don't think I'm eligible for that because I served a third at county and my sentence was a mandatory minimum, which is five. Don't I have to serve five?"

Sheronda shook her head. "County time don't count here for good time. You gotta get here and serve yer third here."

Abby thought about that. "So in the spring when my third is done I could be eligible for release?"

"Yeah if that bitch hadn't fucked with it," Mad T fumed. "They go by her reports as much as the bosses."

"Wow," Abby mused. "I *am* fucked." Mad T and Sheronda silently nodded in agreement.

The next day was Thanksgiving, and other than the meal, it was nothing more than a day off from everything. Abby was so preoccupied with her troubles with Emma that she barely noted that Quinn was still away. Father Duncan had offered to come by for another small worship session, but Abby begged off, encouraging him to spend the day with his family. She knew from previous conversations that he had aging parents, as well as a new granddaughter, all living over an hour from the prison. She reassured him that Sunday worship would be fine and wished him a happy holiday.

Abby was in the common room watching the Macy's Thanksgiving Day Parade with the other ladies when Big Ginger came up beside her.

"I thought you'd have the day off," Abby commented.

Big Ginger snorted. "I'm here for Dennis. Montgomery's here. She's a Jehovah's Witness so she doesn't celebrate. Singh needs the money. Me and Hamilton took doubles so everyone else could spend time with their families. We're trying to buy a house, so we can use the double time pay too."

"You and Officer Hamilton are together? Married?" Abby asked, surprised that she hadn't figured that out before.

Big Ginger snorted. "Not in this state, no. Her parents live in Connecticut so we went there. Not that it matters here."

Abby felt badly for the woman. She wished the day when everyone would have the same rights and privileges would come sooner. She and Big Ginger shared a look and a headshake, and then they went back to watching the parade.

Dinner was a relatively quiet affair. The food in the cafeteria was usually pretty good and Thanksgiving dinner was no exception. There was actual roasted turkey, stuffing, cranberry sauce, and pumpkin pie. They even had apple cider to drink. Abby piled up and shared her tray with Sheronda.

The ladies enjoyed desultory conversation. Mad T had taken over Grandma's table, forcing the deceased leader's disciples to a table in the far corner. Abby felt better having a friend at her back. Plus, Mad T brought much needed comic relief when things got quiet.

After dinner everyone was so full that after count (and an unfortunately timed shakedown due to some inmates' fondness for hooch), most women took naps.

Abby reclined in her bunk. She was too tired to read or to go for a run. Instead she watched the small world of the common area just outside her door. Big Ginger and Hamilton chatted inside the guard office while the inmates sat and watched what sounded like HGTV. Kendra sat at one of the tables talking to one of the newer inmates, a young woman who, in Abby's opinion, was clearly transgendered. Her real name was Allison, but she called herself Brandon. Abby wondered if she took the name from the main character of the film *Boys Don't Cry*. Brandon was the youngest inmate in the unit. She had the look of a very young skater boy. Even her voice was masculine, which Abby assumed was from testosterone therapy. She didn't know what the prison's policy was regarding cross-sex treatment, but she found it interesting that it seemed easier for Brandon to get hormones than it was for other women to get antidepressants.

She turned her mind to the problem of Emma and the fake reports. Abby didn't hold out much hope that anything would come of her conversation with Captain Dennis. And since she'd had no clue about the good time credit, it wasn't much of a loss to find out about it, and then lose it within seconds. She had already reconciled herself to spending three and a half years at Maysville. With no home to go to, the prospect of leaving early was bittersweet at best.

Abby put her book aside and closed her eyes. She was tired of thinking.

Chapter 20

CATCH OUT

Since most of the admin staff was gone that Friday, Abby had another day off from cleaning crew. Still feeling sluggish, she forced herself outside into the cold to run. Abby was getting closer to her 30,000 mark, but she had to stop when it started to sleet. She trotted back into the unit to find Captain Dennis waiting at the guard office for her. He waved her over.

"You're wanted in admin," he said quietly.

"ADSEG?" Abby asked.

"No, I'm taking you to admin."

Abby was confused but followed him out of the unit. As Captain Dennis led her through the prison, Abby realized they were indeed going to admin though she couldn't imagine why. The offices were likely to be deserted.

Sure enough, all but one office was dark. Captain Dennis knocked on the warden's door and waited. He opened it after a moment and led Abby in. Abby was surprised to see Quinn and Big Ginger already there with another gentleman Abby didn't recognize. Warden Abellard sat at her desk with a pile of papers in front of her. The expression on her face was stern, and Abby wondered what kind of trouble she had found for herself.

"Have a seat, Miss Blackwood," the warden indicated the chair in front of her. Abby sat as Captain Dennis took a position next to Quinn. The warden introduced the man next to her as the legal counsel for the prison. Abby gave him a polite nod.

"Well, excitement certainly seems to follow you," the warden began.

K . W i l e y   S i d e r

"I'm so sorry that I snooped through the papers—" Abby began but the warden put up a hand to stop her.

"I'm sure Captain Dennis has explained why that's unnecessary. What is important is the veracity of the paperwork you found. Now, from what I understand you've met with your case manager only four times since you joined us."

Abby nodded.

"Yet there are more than forty reports here." The warden pulled out two reports and handed them to Abby. "Do you recall these meetings?"

Abby looked at the papers in front of her. One report was for the incident with Dana and the other was the meeting in which her privileges were removed following Grandma's suicide. Abby nodded as she handed the reports back to the warden.

"Yes, I remember these."

The warden handed her another report. Abby glanced at it then looked at it closer. It described an infraction for the holding of contraband, though it didn't describe what kind of contraband. It ended with a sentence recommending the removal of a portion of good time credit.

"Do you remember signing the reports for the meetings that you do recall?" the warden asked formally.

Abby nodded.

"Could you tell me if that's your signature at the bottom of the report you have there?"

Abby looked at bottom of the second page.

She looked up. "It's not my signature."

"They look very similar. Are you sure?"

Abby nodded. "I don't have the neatest handwriting. You see, I sign my name Abigail A. Blackwood but my middle initial always looks like an O. I usually don't finish the A before writing the B." Abby pointed to the signature at the bottom of the report. "This A is finished." She handed the forged report back to the warden who set all the signature pages side-by-side. She and the lawyer stared at them for a long time.

"I've compiled a list of the purported infractions and I'm going to ask you to confirm or deny them. Do you understand?"

Abby nodded, and the warden began.

"Insubordination to an officer?"

Abby shook her head. "Deny."

"Assault on a fellow inmate in the showers?"

"Deny."

"Intoxication?"

"Deny."

"Use of prohibited tobacco products?"

Abby snorted. "Deny."

"Receipt of contraband in exchange for protection?"

"Deny."

"Fraternization of a sexual nature with a guard?"

Abby kept her face stoic. "Deny."

"Abuse of a sexual nature with another inmate?"

"Deny."

"Harassment of another inmate for sexual orientation?"

"Deny."

"Distribution of commissary items for special favors?"

"Distribution of items, confirm. For special favors, deny."

"Please elaborate, Miss Blackwood," the lawyer asked.

"Before my father died he set aside a large amount of money for my attorney to deposit into my account," Abby answered. "It's more than I'll ever need the entire time I'm here. And since I don't eat the kind of food offered in the commissary, there's very little for me to spend it on. So when I found out that Sheronda didn't have any family helping her financially, I started to buy her things like shampoo and snacks. Then it seemed only fair to do that for anyone else who needed help. Sheronda seems to know who legitimately needs help and who's just looking for freebies, so she keeps it fair."

"And do you charge repayment for these items in some fashion? Or interest?" he asked.

"No. In fact, I don't exactly know who gets what. I trust Sheronda to do that."

The lawyer made a note on a pad in front of him and showed it to the warden. She nodded then turned to Abby.

"Captain Dennis and the other COs in your unit have already testified that the contents of these reports are false. That and the fact that there are no documented reports from your unit officers to support the dates and events leads me to believe that they are indeed falsified."

"I am restoring your privileges and your good time credit, both in full." The warden signed a paper in front of her and handed it to Abby to sign. "I want to formally apologize, Miss Blackwood. I assure you that I will be taking appropriate measures against Miss Bronwin."

Abby signed the form and handed it back to the warden. "What's going to happen to her?"

The warden sighed and suddenly looked very tired. "Her employment will be terminated immediately. Yours is not the only case file she's falsified, though yours is the worst."

"We'll also be pursuing fraud and forgery charges," the lawyer added. "If you wish to file a formal grievance, I can file the paperwork for you."

Abby shook her head. "I'm fine with what's happening. I don't wish to add to it. May I ask why she did it?"

The warden shrugged. "Our best guess is that she was covering for the fact that she wasn't providing the necessary oversight for her cases. From what I've found, she was filing counseling reports for inmates that you were assisting. If an inmate has an issue with paperwork, they are supposed to have access to their case manager. It's my belief that she was relying on you to do her job for her."

"But I like helping people," Abby protested.

The warden smiled at her. "Then you should continue to do so."

"May I ask another question?"

"Of course."

"Emma said in our last meeting that Grandma wrote that I was manipulative... that she thought I did things for people to curry favor. She implied that Grandma killed herself because of me."

The warden shook her head. "Agnes's letter only mentioned you in the context of your last conversation with her. She indicated that you showed her the truth of her actions, nothing more. Agnes stated in her letter that she could no longer live with what she'd done. She believed that as her crime ended a life, she no longer deserved to live. She essentially executed herself."

Abby felt the weight of Grandma's death lift from her body. "Thank you so much," she said sincerely.

The warden smiled. "You're welcome, Miss Blackwood. You may go now."

Abby thanked the lawyer as well, and then followed Captain Dennis back to the unit. She found Sheronda and MadT in the suite waiting to hear what happened. Abby told them in detail.

"Damn, you was right to go to Dennis," Sheronda mused. "He din't waste no time goin' to the warden."

"What they gonna do to her?" Mad T asked.

Abby pulled herself up into her bunk. "Well, she's fired for sure. And the lawyer said that she committed fraud when she filed the fake reports and forgery when she signed my name to them, so she's in more trouble than just losing her job."

Mad T laughed. "Bitch gonna end up in here with us. Serve her right. She a dumbass, think she can pull shit like that an no one gonna find out." Sheronda nodded in agreement then gave Abby the side-eye.

"What?" Abby asked.

"So's your boy Quinn been out a bit lately," Sheronda began slyly.

"He's not my boy, but so what?"

"*Soooo*, Gray tole me he been gettin' a divorce from his woman." Sheronda dropped that particular bombshell with great relish.

Abby was stunned. "He's married?"

"Not no more he ain't. Seems his woman made him marry her when she get knocked up. Then out popped a little brown baby." Mad T laughed as Sheronda stopped to shake her head at the stupidity of some men then continued. "But he stay and treat that baby like his own. Then a couple months ago she go an' pop out *another* little brown baby."

"Daaaaammmmnnn," Mad T said and laughed.

"So's it seem that his woman be fuckin' the same brother and havin' theys kids. But since they ain't got jobs, they be treatin' Quinn like a motherfuckin' ATM."

"That's terrible!" Abby exclaimed.

"You tellin' me. That be one cold bitch there. An' Quinn be a good man, a real good man takin' care of a kid that ain't even his." Sheronda was indignant. "Oh and get this, bitch file fer child support and everthin' still sayin' Quinn the daddy. Bitch even make a fake DNA report. Gray says Quinn did his own DNA test and the judge threw her shit out fast. Like nobody can look at those kids an' tell they ain't come from a white boy."

"Man, that's messed up," Mad T said and shook her head.

Abby silently agreed.

Chapter 21

PULL HER CARD

The ebb and flow of inmates continued in B Unit. It was considered a premium unit assignment since it had the lowest percentage of violent incidents and reported rapes. It also boasted the lowest inmate recidivism with its emphasis on rehabilitation, so incoming faces were rarely familiar.

As the days moved toward Christmas, the women prepared for the season as best they could. Those with attentive families saw an increase in visits and phone calls and more packages arrived during the month.

Abby enjoyed watching the other women celebrate, choosing to revel in their joy vicariously rather than dwell on her own lack of family. Father Duncan did his best to offer her support during the season and often spent time with Abby outside of worship services.

Even with her privileges returned, Abby never returned to Bible study. She'd heard from some of the other women that Grandma's old group had become more intolerant of people they perceived as "sinners," and she knew that she most likely wouldn't be welcomed back anyway. Emma had burned that bridge for her by deliberately misrepresenting Grandma's note when she conveyed her twisted interpretation of its contents to the women in the group. Abby knew it wouldn't help to speak with them directly. There was no reasoning with people like Jessica.

She was grateful to resume her teaching, however, and worked with the women daily. She was flattered that the attendance had gone way up, though it necessitated additional classes to accommodate the increasing numbers. She found that many women did not need GED assistance but were coming for the life skills portion of her instruction. So she added a third class just for them.

Working with the women gave Abby a chance to get to know almost everyone in her unit. Other than work detail, there was very little to do, and most women took advantage of the opportunity to improve themselves as a break in the monotony.

Captain Dennis and Big Ginger took to providing Abby with a short biography of the new inmates so that she would have a better idea of what she was up against. Abby was getting ready for her last morning class when Big Ginger pulled her aside.

"I need to give you a heads up about one of your new students," she whispered. It was odd that she was being so circumspect; most women in B Unit had fairly typical issues. "We just got a transfer in from the reformatory. She's a twenty-nine o'five."

Abby's eyes went wide. A 2905 was an inmate charged with a sex offense against a child she was not related to. It was extremely unusual for a 2905 to be admitted to B Unit. They were considered the lowest of the low and were likely to be the victims of vicious attacks by the other inmates. Of all the women on the unit, less than a handful were 2905s, and none had been admitted since Abby got there.

"Does anyone else know?" Abby asked.

"Not yet. We're trying to keep it quiet for as long as possible." Abby knew that as soon as Mad T had a name, she'd have the lowdown from one of her outside contacts in no time. The woman didn't stand a chance.

"If she's new, how is she being given class privilege?" Abby asked. New inmates typically had to earn the right to attend classes.

"Dennis and her case manager are trying to keep her out of general population as much as possible. ADSEG is full right now. She may have to go to DSEG."

"Great," Abby said under her breath.

"If you could just keep an eye on things in there, Dennis is trying to get her transferred as soon as possible."

"Sure," Abby consented though her tone was more sardonic than agreeable.

In her classroom, Abby stood collating papers as the women filed in. There were several she didn't recognize, so there was no way of knowing which one was the 2905. She launched into a quick introduction as she passed out worksheets on life skills and self-awareness. They were written for middle school students, but Abby found them useful for the women who came to the workshop. She was also using a program that taught the women how to identify feelings and reactions, appropriate conflict resolutions, as well as recognizing verbal and visual cues for different emotions.

As she went around the room answering questions, Abby couldn't tell which of the women was the sex offender. They all looked relatively benign, though one woman with the telltale sunken cheeks and skin lesions of a former meth addict could probably be ruled out. Abby put her radar up and found herself focusing on a plain, dumpy young woman sitting near the exit. She seemed nervous without the addict twitch, and Abby saw her check the door several times throughout the class. As she wrapped things up, she noticed the young woman idling behind until she was the last to leave. Abby watched her pause at the door then quickly dart to a table near the guard office. The girl put her head down and faked working on the papers Abby had given her. Abby exited the classroom then took a left into her suite.

Inside, Abby was not surprised to see Mad T watching the girl from inside their door. She nodded in her direction as Abby walked in to put her books in her locker.

"You see that girl?" Mad T asked.

"Yeah, she was in my last class."

Mad T stared at the girl. "Somethin' ain't right about her. See her bein' all twitchy like she comin' down from somethin'? But she ain't. I know tweakers, and she ain't one."

The two women watched as the girl sat and read the same piece of paper over and over again.

Finally, Abby gave up. She needed to get outside before the weather turned bad. She left Mad T to her watching and pulled the sweater Sylvia had knitted her over her head. It was a masterpiece of cables with alternating strand plaits and Celtic knots knitted all over. Abby had never seen anything like it. To show her thanks, Abby had asked Jane, her attorney, to ship several skeins of high quality wool to the prison. She was going to give them to Sylvia for Christmas. Abby planned to hit the yard for a run, and Sylvia's sweater was the warmest clothing she owned.

"You going to do that all day?" she asked Mad T at the door.

"If I have to," the woman answered, her eyes never leaving her suspect.

"You should have been a cop," Abby joked as she walked out of the suite.

"Fuck you, bitch," Mad T called after her. Abby turned to see Mad T smiling at her before turning back to her surveillance.

Outside it was bitterly cold. The sweater helped immensely, but Abby was still stuck with her thin blue scrub bottoms for pants with the prison's thin cotton thermals underneath. She didn't know if it was allowed, but she was going to ask Jane for cold gear next. She had forgotten to ask for a pedometer and made a mental note to request that as well.

The mid-December sky was a flat gray turning the colors of the yard dark and saturated. Gray turned grayer, black turned blacker, and the dark green of the evergreen trees on the other side of the fence seemed to glow. The week before had given them their first significant snow, and Abby had volunteered to help with shoveling the perimeter path. Other women joined her simply to have something to do. There were still icy patches though, and Abby had to pay more attention to her steps to avoid them.

She ran for a little more than an hour before she was forced in by the cold. When she got back to the suite, she found Mad T and Sheronda in conference. Mad T's "nephew," who went by the abbreviated moniker "D," was casually leaning outside the door.

Sheronda waved Abby in and indicated the space next to her.

"Sheronda got her tag," Mad T told her. Abby wasn't surprised. If Mad T should have been a cop, Sheronda should have been in the FBI. She was the most skillful interrogator Abby had ever met.

"So she tell me she be Jennifer Hamilton an' she three for ten for sexual misconduct. That's all she say to me." Sheronda told her. Mad T snorted. "Bitch be scared shitless."

"So I get my girl outside to look her up," Mad T said. She had a teenage daughter who would do Internet searches for her mother whenever she needed it. "She been all over the news 'cause she kidnapped a neighbor girl from her house and this bitch give the girl to her boyfriend so he can mess with her. Baby was only seven-years-old. She watch him fuck with the little girl then she take her back and leave her at her house."

Abby instantly felt sick. The thought of such a young child being subjected to such horrors was unimaginable.

"Get this," Mad T continued, "dumb bitch says her boyfriend told her if she did it he was gonna marry her 'cause it proved she really love him. She got caught tryin' to take another girl from her school. She pretended to be the girl's momma, but the teacher know she ain't an' she calls the cops. They arrest her an' the boyfriend at the school. That baby was only in kindergarten. Cops be lookin' at them for other stuff now too. Like one baby still missin' where they used to live."

"Time to cut that bitch's knot," Sheronda intoned. Mad T nodded silently. All three women turned to stare at the unsuspecting girl.

Abby hated to admit it, but deep in her heart she almost agreed. There was a peculiar form of justice in prison, with punishments harsher than any found on the outside. And the abuse of a small child guaranteed the worst. Abby was surprised at the nature of the young woman's crime. Most of the women who were in Maysville for sex crimes were either teachers or neighbors who'd been caught with teenagers fifteen-or sixteen-years-old. So far the worst they'd seen was a special education teacher who'd performed oral sex on her twelve-year-old developmentally disabled student. She'd been badly beaten over a year ago and was now a permanent resident of Maysville's infirmary until her sentence was up.

Most of the other women who'd assaulted older students were pretty much ignored. They were not invited to join any families, and did not typically mingle with the general population opting instead to sequester themselves for their own safety. Abby never saw any of them in her classes, either because they were all educated or not in need of any life skills training.

"We cool, right?" Mad T broke through Abby's thoughts. She knew what Mad T was asking.

"Always," she answered then pulled herself up into her bunk to pretend to read.

Over the next few days, things were tense in the unit as news of Jennifer's crime quietly spread among the women. The COs were especially on edge, sensing trouble brewing. Abby noticed the girl always placed herself in full view of the guard office or near the door in Abby's classes. By midweek, Big Ginger admitted to Abby that Captain Dennis was frantically trying to get the young woman out of B Unit before things turned ugly, but both ADSEG and DSEG were still full. Even the Hole was at capacity. Abby asked her why they didn't just transfer some lesser problem out to make space.

"They've got four suicide watches going," she replied. "They can't move them until they've been released by the psychologist. Kelsey's still in DSEG for fighting, so Dennis is trying to get her back early and make the switch."

By the end of the week though, he needn't have bothered. When she didn't show at afternoon count, the COs called a lockdown and swept the unit. They finally found her, beaten within an inch of her life and shoved between the last half wall and toilet in the community bathroom. She was transported to the infirmary, and then taken to the hospital where they determined she'd been kicked so hard one of her ribs had broken off and pierced her lung. After treatment, Jennifer was going back to the ODRC medical center to serve the rest of her sentence in rehabilitation.

After lockdown, Captain Dennis called a toss and body search. Abby glanced a question at Mad T as their doors unlocked, but the other woman shook her head. They remained mum as they stepped out of their suite. It didn't take long for the COs to find evidence of the assault. Shakedowns were never exactly the same, but they ran in sort of a pattern and always started at the ends of the units.

For the first time, first and second shift combined for the toss so it was both Big Ginger and Quinn who found blood on clothes and shoes in what used to be Grandma's suite. None of the women in the suite struggled as Gray and Martinez cuffed them. Jessica, who had been Grandma's protégé and taken over the Bible study group, was defiant while her suitemates stood by their leader with their heads down like supplicants.

Abby watched as Quinn carried out an elongated sock that was dripping wet but still stained pink. As he placed it in a ziplock evidence bag that Captain Dennis held open, Abby realized what they'd used to beat the girl. It was not uncommon for the women to place a heavy padlock in a prison issue sock to use as a weapon. She bet that if they examined the lock they would find telltale white cotton caught in the rubber grip around the shackle.

Sure enough, Gray handed Quinn a key ring of master keys. A moment later, Quinn reappeared with the same lock Abby used to secure her things. It too was dropped into an evidence bag. Then the women from the suite were ushered out of the unit by Quinn, Ramirez, and the SRT team.

Captain Dennis continued the rest of the shakedown without incident. Rather than completing full body searches, Big Ginger examined the hands of the rest of the women. When it was Abby's turn, she murmured, "Jess and her group all had blood on them." Abby nodded but remained silent. Big Ginger moved on to the next suite of women.

When toss was done, Abby went into the suite and sat down with Mad T and Sheronda. Sylvia and some of Mad T's family lingered in the doorway.

"Damn," Mad T began. "Who woulda thought it be Gramma's girls?"

"They're big on eye for an eye," Abby answered. "They probably convinced themselves they were doing God's work."

"Saved me the trouble," Mad T said quietly. Her family nodded in agreement. "God squad be in some deep shit now. They's too stupid to do it right."

"What do you mean?" Abby asked.

It was D who answered. "You gotta wear kitchen trash bags so you don't get nothin' on you. An' you make knuckles with paper—like you do with shanks—so you don't get blood on your hands and you don't break nothing. You can take the knuckles apart and flush 'em when it's done, and nobody be lookin' fer blood on black trash bags."

Abby admired the ingenuity of these women as much as she feared their ability to exact brutal justice without a shred of sympathy or conscience or mercy.

"So what happens to them?" she asked.

Mad T and Sheronda both shrugged. "They's be charged here and will get more time added. They's gonna be transferred out too. If not to DSEG then to the reformatory. COs ain't gonna let them back here," Sheronda answered. "Either way they fucked if she die. They can get life then."

By the next morning, the whole unit knew every detail of what had happened. And by the afternoon Sheronda's network of ears reported that the girl had died. The news spread like wildfire. Jessica and her group would be charged with murder.

Abby sat with Sylvia vainly trying to learn a simple crochet stitch when the news reached her in the common area. Sylvia got up to let the rest of her group know the news.

Abby put her yarn down and sat quietly analyzing her feelings about the fate of the young woman. She'd never given a lot of thought about death as a punishment. Her church did not take a formal position on the death penalty. Abby suspected that her clergy silently supported it for the most severe of crimes. She found she bore very little feeling for the girl's fate other than a certain acceptance that on some level it was appropriate. Abby wondered if she should administer the Levenson Self-Report Psychopathy Scale on herself to see what her level of psychopathic behavior was. Though it didn't necessarily indicate criminality, the test was a research tool that worked well to determine an individual's level of psychopathic tendencies in areas of behavior and empathy. Or she could just assume that prison had hardened her to the realities of human failure and leave it at that.

Chapter 22

ON THE LEG

Christmas was only a few days away and the women on the unit were preparing for the holiday with an excitement not seen since Halloween. Jessica and her group had cast such a disapproving atmosphere across the unit that it wasn't until the God Squad was gone that Abby noticed an easing of the tension among the women.

Christmas cards had been arriving in a steady flow, and the women loved nothing more than taping them to the walls of their suites. Mad T had a considerable family network on the outside, so she easily outdistanced everyone else in terms of incoming mail. Abby helped her tape her cards all around, papering the inside wall of her bunk and up the side toward Marianna's bunk above. There were so many cards that Abby stacked them up their only fully blank wall in the shape of a Christmas tree. Mad T even had a Christmas star card for the top. When she was done, several of Mad T's family came by to admire her handiwork.

Even Abby had a few cards from Jane, the Abbots, and even Father Duncan to hang over her bunk. A meager display next to Mad T's, but they made her feel like someone was thinking about her. She was grateful that Jane had come through for her, sending the cold gear she needed for running as well as items to give to her closest friends in the unit. She was happy to see that almost everything made it through inspection, including a small gift for Big Ginger. She wasn't sure how she was going to present it since inmates were forbidden from giving COs gifts and vice versa. She had asked Jane to send "hers" and "hers" pillowcases for Big Ginger and her wife. Since Sheronda and Mad T both loved borrowing the CD player, Abby ordered each of them one from the commissary and had Jane send CDs for each of them. *The Best of Girl*

Groups for Sheronda and *The Bomb Shelter Sessions* for Mad T. She also sent *A Motown Christmas* for all of them. For Marianna, Abby had a tube of Chanel lipstick. And Jane had come through in the yarn department. In fact she had sent so much yarn, Abby decided to divide it among all of Sheronda's knitting ladies with the lion's share going to Sylvia. Even Rita and Rosita had gifts coming as Abby had ordered Spanish spices not available in the commissary.

She'd also ordered her favorite book, a copy of Edward Gorey's *Gashleycrumb Tinies* for Quinn, but struggled with whether or not to give it to him.

The only thing missing was the pedometer. Abby didn't know if Jane hadn't sent it or if it had been confiscated. She assumed the latter, but she couldn't do anything about that. She was happy to see that Jane even thought to use decorative tissue paper as packing material, which gave Abby something pretty to wrap the presents in. Despite her lack of family, Abby was really looking forward to the holiday.

With the suite to herself, Abby quickly wrapped everything, including Quinn's book, and locked it up in her locker. She'd just snapped the lock shut when Sheronda showed up to fetch her for cleaning crew.

With Christmas only a couple of days away, the admin offices were mostly deserted as staff rotated vacation days. Quinn had accompanied them but remained in the wide hallway just outside. Abby had finished all the other offices. She had just started dusting the warden's plants when he appeared in the doorway. Abby could hear Sheronda's vacuum go on down the hall. She paused in her dusting and gave him her attention.

Never one to say much, Quinn simply stared at her as if waiting for her to speak first. Abby decided to be polite.

"Will you be going home for the holiday?" she asked.

Quinn shook his head. "I volunteered to pull a double so that Captain Dennis can go see his family. Singh and Hamilton are coming in and Montgomery has offered to pull a double also, since…well, you know…and she needs to make up for the extra maternity leave she took."

Abby nodded. Jehovah's Witnesses did not recognize December 25 as Jesus's birthday, so it was just another day to Montgomery.

"I'm not sure if I'm standing in for Hannah or not. I think so, but I'm here either way," he finished.

It was one of those weird conversations you had with someone you spent a lot of time with but barely knew. Abby was searching for something to say when Quinn turned and left the doorway. She stared at the empty space for another moment then resumed her dusting.

After they checked in their carts, Abby moved over to the double doors that opened onto the yard and looked out. As it was winter, night had already fallen and a new layer of snow covered the walkway. Abby's running shoes were already showing significant wear and tear on the soles. So much so, that to preserve what use they had left for running, she'd switched to the prison issued tennis shoes, called bobos, to wear around the unit. They were supremely uncomfortable compared to her running shoes. Abby knew they'd kill her feet if she didn't ask Jane to send another pair of running shoes soon.

Rather than risk a fall on the unshoveled path, Abby went back to her suite to turn in early.

The next day Christmas Eve dawned. Everyone was up and excited even as the doors unlocked for the morning.

With families coming in to visit, Abby canceled her classes for the next couple of days so the women would have more time with their loved ones. Though more snow had fallen, the storm had passed. Abby went out to the yard to shovel. Under orders from Mad T, D came out to help, bringing with her the lower ranking members of the family. Many hands made light work, and together they cleared the path in no time. Abby thanked them as they went back into the unit then set off for her run.

The cold gear was so successful that, instead of the weather, the time brought Abby in. There was a scheduled count then lunch, followed by Christmas movies in the common room. Abby found a spot near the back with Sylvia and Sheronda who, like Abby, did not have visitors coming for the holiday. Big Ginger put in the DVD then came out to stand near their table. Abby wondered when she'd have the opportunity to give Big Ginger her present without incurring any trouble for either of them. She gave it up when the movie started. Abby noted that Big Ginger had made a great choice as *Elf* started to play.

The Christmas movie marathon served as an effective means of distraction for the women without families. Big Ginger had taken it upon herself to make the selections and Abby could state definitively that her efforts were a resounding success. Along with *Elf* they watched *Love Actually*, *Home Alone*, *A Christmas Story*, and *Planes, Trains, and Automobiles*. The marathon ended for afternoon count and dinner. As the ladies got up to report to their suites, Big Ginger hinted at another set of classics for after dinner.

Dinner was a noisy affair as some families were permitted to come in and dine with their loved ones. Abby enjoyed watching the kids reunite with their mothers, but the noise eventually drove her out into the quiet of the yard for her run. When she was done, she stepped into the unit and made her way to her suite to change for cleaning crew.

Marianna was the only one in the room as her family had left for their long drive home. Abby pulled off her layers and hung them up in her locker. Abby pulled on her hoodie then closed her locker. She was looking for a ponytail holder near her bed when she saw a small wrapped box tucked under her pillow. She glanced a question at Marianna who feigned innocence then winked. Abby turned back and opened the box. It was a Garmin Foot Pod. A much nicer pedometer than Abby had asked Jane to send. With it was a Forerunner GPS Fitness watch that took Abby's breath away. The watch was insanely expensive, but it was the top of the line product for runners. It was programmable and tracked heart rate, distance, pace, and calories while plotting fitness goals. There was no way she could accept it. Abby put both items in her pocket then left for crew.

Sheronda and Quinn were already there with the others waiting for her. Abby apologized for being late and the group set off. Quinn stayed with Sheronda and Abby as the others went off to the other section of offices. Abby was finishing up dusting the warden's books when she turned to see Quinn appear in the doorway.

Abby stepped off her ladder. "I have something to give you," she said as she pulled the pedometer and watch from her pocket. "I can't accept these. I know how expensive they are, and I just can't, in good conscience, keep them."

Quinn glanced at the watch and pedometer. "Your attorney sent those. They were confiscated in the mail center. Dennis approved them for you."

Abby looked down at the watch and pedometer. She felt stupid for assuming they were a gift. For all she knew none of the things that had shown up on her bunk had been from Quinn. Maybe all of it had been sent by Jane and confiscated.

"Thanks for letting it come through," she said embarrassed. Quinn just shrugged.

Sheronda appeared in the doorway. "Man you ain't my boyfrien' no more. You ain't bring me nothin'."

Abby's face flamed red with shame as Quinn's also turned beet red. Sheronda huffed then pushed her cart out of the doorway. Quinn turned to follow her, but Abby put a hand out to stop him.

"I have a gift for Big...Sergeant Redfern but I don't know how to give it to her."

Quinn frowned for a second. "Where is it?"

"It's in my locker. It's wrapped in red tissue paper."

"I can grab it during the next toss," he offered. "I'll make sure she gets it."

Abby smiled. "Thanks."

Quinn looked like he wanted to say something else, but he hesitated. Instead he returned her smile with a brisk nod then left the office.

By the time they returned to the unit, the second marathon was in full swing. *Fred Claus* was on. It was not one of Abby's favorites so she decided to get a shower in before the next movie. She finished in time for *The Polar Express*, which she loved. Abby settled in to watch.

By the end of the evening her backside was sore and she was ready for bed.

Chapter 23

COLD TRAILING

Abby opened her eyes just as the locks disengaged for the morning. As a courtesy for the holiday, the inmates were allowed to sleep in, so the morning buzzer remained silent. Abby sat up and looked around. She was surprised at how dark it still was. A tall slit of a window was their only source of natural light in the suite, and though it only afforded a view of mere inches of the world outside, she could see dark clouds hovering over the prison and a thick layer of snow on the ground.

Abby slid off her bunk and quietly padded over to her locker. The other women snored softly as she pulled her gifts out and placed them under the makeshift tree on the wall. Then she closed her locker as quietly as possible before stepping out of the suite.

Big Ginger was in the guard office as Abby passed by. Abby paused to motion scrubbing her armpit. Big Ginger gave her the thumbs up and turned back to her monitor.

It was a luxury to have the showers to herself. Despite the newer construction, the prison was still a huge concrete building, so it never really got warm, even in the summer. Abby had taken to wearing her cold gear on a regular basis and doubling up her socks inside her bobos. Even so, her core temperature remained low and she found herself shivering often. Abby took her time letting the hot water pour over her.

It didn't take long for the heat of the water to warm her fully. She turned to let the water run down her back exposing her breasts to the cold air. Her nipples instantly hardened at the change. Abby put her hands over them, idly soaping them. As her nipples began to ache, she began to pull at them to satisfy the itch that was growing. In her mind's eye she saw Quinn as he had approached her that day months ago. She moved her right hand down to the cleft between her legs. Her middle finger moved along the center. She leaned against the wall and closed her eyes. Her finger furiously worked her sex as her imagination put Quinn between her legs in place of her hand. Abby began to moan quietly as the itch built, and her fingers worked even more furiously. Her body shuddered with orgasm as the water sluiced over her body. Spent, she slid to the floor and let the shower rain on her as her sex continued to throb against her fingers. Each drop of water that fell between her legs sent another wave of pleasure through her.

Mindful of the time, Abby reluctantly pushed herself off the floor and rinsed off. When she was done, she pulled the thin prison issue towel inside her stall and dried off. As she finished drying her hair, she spied movement out of the corner of her eye. Abby wrapped the towel around her body and watched the doorway. When nothing appeared, she quickly finished drying and got dressed.

Women were just beginning to stir as she made her way back to her suite. The morning buzzer still had not gone off and the women of Abby's suite were all in varying stages of wakefulness. Marianna was already up. Sheronda sat on her bunk and stared off as if still on the sleep side of consciousness. Abby put her things away then pulled herself up into her bunk as the other women began to rouse.

Mad T rolled over and perched at the edge of her bunk. She rubbed the sleep from her eyes, yawned hugely, and then gave Abby a smile.

"Hey girl," she said through another yawn. "Merry Christmas."

Abby smiled back, "Merry Christmas."

Marianna stretched then smiled. "Santa's been here."

Mad T looked over at their makeshift tree and smiled. "Damn girl, you been busy! What time you get up?"

Abby shrugged and said nothing.

"Well, you ain't the only Santa," Mad T continued then lightly punched the underside of Marianna's bunk. "Girl, get yourself up and fetch the presents."

Marianna jumped down and opened her locker. Inside were parcels wrapped in plain white paper on which holly and Christmas trees had been drawn in what looked like marker.

Marianna pulled out the gifts and placed them under the tree next to Abby's.

"Who's gonna play Santa?" Mad T asked.

Sheronda raised her hand. "I ain't got nothin' to give so I'll do it." She moved over to the pile of presents under their Christmas card tree as Rita and Rosita came over to sit on Sheronda's bunk with their own Christmas offerings in their laps.

There was much joy and exclamation as the ladies opened Abby's presents. Rita and Rosita chattered at Abby about the spices in broken English. Abby was touched as Rosita handed her a gift wrapped in the pages of a magazine. She tore at the paper and found a small hand painted statue of La Santa Muerte, the unofficial patron saint of outcasts. Abby loved it and jumped down to hug the two women who returned her affection with their own.

Marianna interrupted with squeals as she opened her Chanel lipstick, and then began to laugh hysterically at Abby's unintentional joke. Abby got it right away and laughed so hard she almost fell out of her bunk but Mad T remained mystified.

"Why y'all dyin' over lipstick?" she demanded to know.

Marianna wiped the tears from her eyes. "Abby's calling me out for being a lipstick lesbian."

Mad T shook her head. "You all is crazy," she remarked as Sheronda pushed over her gifts from Abby.

The two women opened their CD players with enthusiasm then went crazy for their CDs. Both got up to hug Abby and when they pulled away, Abby was touched to see tears in Sheronda's eyes.

"Ain't nobody ever been so nice as you been," Sheronda said as she wiped her hand across her face

Mad T stared at her CD. "I ain't never heard of them."

"They're called Vintage Trouble," Abby told her. "They're like old school blues rock bands from the 50s and 60s but they're current."

Mad T plugged in her new CD player and put the CD in. Abby selected "Blues Hand Me Down" then sat back. Mad T stared at Abby. Her expression was skeptical until the music started to play. It soon turned to surprise as sounds reminiscent of early James Brown filled the suite. Then, laughing, she got up and started to dance. Mad T was one of those very large women who happened to be very light on her feet. Sheronda got up too and started her own little shuffle in the small space remaining. The women were fully enjoying themselves until a cough at the door interrupted their revelry. Quinn stood there with a barely concealed smile on his face.

"Too early ladies," he said then turned away.

Mad T shook her not inconsiderable bottom in his direction, but she turned off the music.

"Girl, you done good," she said when she sat back down. Marianna handed her a flat wrapped box, which Mad T in turn handed to Abby.

"Since we can't get you the kind of things you deserve, we all put together somethin' we hope you like."

Abby tore the paper off and opened the box. Inside were dozens of photos and kids drawings. She pulled some of them out and saw that they were the same faces she saw over her suitemates bunks.

"Me, Sheronda, and the other girls saw you ain't got no pictures of family to hang over your bed," Mad T said by way of explanation. "So we goin' ta make you part of our families."

Tears formed in Abby's eyes as she looked at the smiling faces of her friends' children and parents, and in some, even grandparents. Marianna pulled herself up onto Abby's bunk and started taping them to the wall. Abby turned to watch as her empty white wall filled with her newly adopted family. Sheronda's parents smiled next to Mad T's kids, while Marianna's grandparents posed formally in front of a bright stucco house. Since Sheronda and Mad T's kids were grown, Marianna had her daughter and two sons draw pictures for Abby, which went up alongside their school photos. Even Rita and Rosita had added a big family photo that looked like it had been taken at a family reunion.

By far it was the best present Abby had ever received. To be given a place in the world was better than anything else she could think of. She slid off her bunk and gave each woman a fierce hug. By the time she was done, even Mad T had tears in her eyes.

Outside the suite the buzzer went off, calling the women to start the day. Abby and the other ladies put their gifts away and set off for breakfast.

The rest of the day was filled with phone calls and visits for the ladies. Abby sat back and enjoyed the women's time with their families. Quinn continued Big Ginger's movie marathon for those women who did not have family to phone or visit with. His selections veered toward films that were set during Christmas, but weren't necessarily about Christmas like *Trading Places*, *Just Friends*, and *The Holiday*. Abby sat with Sylvia and watched until lunchtime. Then she came back for *Edward Scissorhands*, *While You Were Sleeping*, and *Scrooged*. She had to wonder at Quinn's choices. They were all more comedic than sentimental. Abby turned to look at Quinn as the others stared at the screen. He looked tired. His expression was unreadable as usual, but there was tension around his eyes that hadn't been there before. If she had to describe it, Abby would say Quinn looked stressed and irritated. She watched him a bit longer then turned back to the TV when he glanced in her direction.

Her backside was numb by the time afternoon count rolled around. Abby stood up and stretched as the rest of the unit came in from the visitor center. Then she walked over to her suite for count.

Though most rules were somewhat relaxed for the holiday, Quinn still called a toss, earning him more than a few dirty looks. Abby felt terrible until the COs started pulling out more contraband than usual. Though their suite was usually free of any prohibited items, Quinn came out with Abby's tissue wrapped packages earning her a dirty look from Mad T.

Abby leaned over. "They're guard gifts," she whispered. Mad T's face relaxed as she nodded her understanding.

When toss was done, they were spared body searches and allowed to go into their suites. Abby was first in, and she was surprised to find a box on her bunk. It hadn't been there earlier but then again, neither she nor the other ladies had been in the suite since morning. The other women watched as she opened the box. Inside was a new pair of gel New Balance running shoes. Abby pulled them out and looked at her friends.

"Who left these here?" she asked as the other women looked at each other in surprise. Abby had been sitting just outside for most of the day, and she hadn't seen anyone go into the suite. And Quinn certainly hadn't had a standard shoebox with him during toss.

Mad T fell heavily into her bunk. "We musta had a ghost."

Abby glanced out the door, but Quinn was nowhere to be seen. It was likely he'd left at shift change so she wouldn't be able to ask him until he returned. She was only assuming he'd left them. For all she knew, Big Ginger could have given them to her. Or they were from Jane and had just passed inspection. And since gifts between inmates and COs were strictly prohibited, she might never know.

Abby ruminated on the gift of the shoes until dinner, and then gave it up to enjoy the ladies' impromptu Christmas show in the common room. Her gift of the Motown Christmas CD was put to use as Mad T and several of the women of the unit performed the songs. As talented as she was funny, Mad T had an amazing voice as did many of the other ladies. Sheronda was invited to join them, but Abby knew from experience that Sheronda couldn't sing at all so she wasn't surprised when Sheronda demurred.

By bedtime, the day could be counted as successful, with most women enjoying time with their families while others enjoyed time with each other. There had been no fights, no work, and no grief from the COs.

Chapter 24

BOOGIE MAN

The days following Christmas were a time of transition for the inmates at the prison. Though sentences began at any time during the year, New Year's Day served as an unofficial anniversary for the women, marking the completion of another year of their incarcerations. And for some, it brought the day of their release that much closer.

It also brought two new faces to the unit. Staff was always short at the prison, guard staff in particular. Quinn, Big Ginger, and the others were often pulling double shifts to ensure appropriate staff to inmate ratios. Abby suspected most of the blame could go to Captain Dennis who was hesitant to bring in anyone new after the Pike debacle. Unfortunately, his officers were getting tired, so he caved and brought in help. One was almost an exact replica of Mad T with a voice that was either dead silent or loud and hectoring. The other was every warm-blooded inmate's dream.

His arrival was met with a great deal of unofficial fanfare. Like Quinn and Pike, the new guy was strikingly good-looking. By the time Abby saw him, Mad T and Sheronda already had the 411 on him.

She had finished her last morning class and was returning to her suite to put on her running gear when she came up behind Big Ginger and the new guard touring the unit. Abby followed at a discreet distance, not wanting to dart in front of them as they passed the doorway to her suite. She could hear Big Ginger giving him the same brief bios she gave Abby when someone new came into her classes. She slid behind them into her suite to find the ladies watching the new guy closely.

"You see him?" Mad T called over to her as Abby changed her shoes and layered her hoodie and sweaters over her scrubs and cold gear. The prison issue coat was too bulky and stiff to run in so she left it off.

"Who?"

"The new guy. Damn but he is one fine lookin' young man."

"His name Julien Tobin," Sheronda began. "He ain't never work in corrections, but he be a cop before here. He get shot and go out on disability. But it don't pay nothin' so he come work here. He from Loosianna but he move here for the job. His momma was mostly white, like French and Spanish, and his daddy was from Trinidad so mostly black, but pretty. He calls hisself creole. Ain't got no wife, no kids, no nothin'."

Mad T turned away as the new guard and Big Ginger moved out of sight.

"My girl checked him out online," she said to the room. "He get shot bein' a hero savin' some girl. He pulled over a car for speedin'. It had a girl in the back that say she was bein' kidnapped, so he pull his gun, and when the driver try to get away, our boy shoot him. But he didn't know the guy in the other seat pull his gun first so our boy get his own bullet. Then, even though he been shot, he pull the girl out of the car before they drive away."

"Wow," Abby was impressed.

"Now he's here makin' the place look real pretty," Mad T finished. "Those mixed boys look fine."

"Damn. He look just like that boy, what's his name? Jessie Williams, from that doctor show," Sheronda remarked.

Mad T shook her head. "No way. You's crazy. He look like Gary Dourdan from CSI."

"I think he looks like DeAndre Brackensick," Marianna commented from her bunk.

Mad T and Sheronda both looked at her like she was crazy.

"Girl, you just sayin' shit now. He don't look nothin' like that little kid." Mad T turned her back on Marianna, dismissing her opinion altogether.

"Well, I have no idea who any of those people are so I'll have to take your word for it." Abby put on her pedometer. "I'm off."

Out in the yard, the snow had melted from the path but remained in all the grassy areas. It was still extremely cold, so Abby started to jog as soon as she hit the pavement.

She was warmed up and almost out of breath from the cold when she heard the door to the unit bang open. She was still on the far side of the yard and slowed to a jog as she made her way back to the entrance. The new guy stood there waiting for her.

Abby had to admit the ladies were right: he was very striking looking. He had light skin, the color of coffee with a little bit of cream in it and curly light brown hair. His cheekbones and chin were chiseled. But his eyes were the most noticeable. They were a light gray-green that almost didn't look real. He was taller than Abby by a few inches, and he was lean but not skinny. Broad shoulders and a thin waist indicated a body well-kept by its owner. He smiled at her as she slowed to a walk.

"Sergeant Redfern says you're to come in," he said. His voice was low with a pleasant grit to it.

Abby returned his smile. "Thanks."

She moved past him into the unit and was surprised when he took up next to her.

"You're really fast," he began.

Abby gave him a sidelong glance. She couldn't tell if she had another Pike on her hands. Though she didn't want to jump to conclusions, she really wanted to avoid being involved in another situation.

"I ran in college," she offered, more out of politeness than a desire to continue the conversation.

"Sergeant Redfern told me a little about you," he continued. "You should have been a cop."

Abby smirked. "So I could get shot too?"

Tobin stopped in his tracks. There was a look of surprise on his face.

Abby paused and looked back at him. "No offense, but you should know that most of the ladies here know everything about you already," she said as kindly as she could then left him to enter the unit.

Quinn stared at her as she passed the guard station. Abby wondered about it for a second then ignored him as she went into her suite.

For the next week it was the Tobin show. The ladies in the unit took greater care with their appearance than usual like they had for Pike. Abby enjoyed the fact that everyone was on their best behavior for Tobin who, unlike Pike, seemed oblivious to their efforts. From her few encounters with him, she found him to be a genuinely nice person and not the peacocking frat boy Pike had been. The only person who didn't seem to appreciate Tobin's presence was Quinn. Abby noticed him scowling more whenever Tobin was around.

She also noticed Quinn was around more than usual. Typically, officers were rotated through all tasks and positions to prevent fraternization with the inmates, but with the smaller size of the guard staff, familiarity was inevitable.

Abby found Quinn routinely taking position near her; whether it was in the cafeteria or in the common area. The only times she didn't see him were during the shifts and days he had off.

On the other hand, Tobin seemed to be everywhere. The unit wasn't huge, but it was large enough that days would go by before Abby saw some of the other officers. But when Tobin was on shift, she'd no sooner leave him in one section to find him in the next area she was entering. She had to wonder if it was the crowd of ladies that he seemed to have around him at all times. He was extremely nice, which really worked to his advantage with the inmates. Morgan, the female guard Dennis had brought in, used bullying and threats to manage the inmates. When she wasn't yelling, she was silent and brooding. Tobin used far more sugar than salt with the ladies. He innocently flirted his way into their good graces and by turn, received a measure of compliance from them. In Abby's opinion, both approaches were wrong. Morgan's approach bred hostility and Tobin's a false sense of friendship that could inevitably result in defiance. Most of the other COs followed Captain Dennis's example of a benevolent dictatorship, neither cruel nor friendly, that left the inmates knowing exactly what was going to happen if they stepped out of line.

To his credit, though, Tobin was a good guard and seemed to be a really good guy. Abby might not agree with his approach, but she certainly appreciated his kindnesses.

She wasn't surprised when he stepped up to volunteer for cleaning escort. Quinn had no choice but to acquiesce as White willingly stepped aside. Nor could he object when Tobin offered to take Abby and Sheronda to admin. Abby watched as Quinn stalked off after the group parted. He seemed royally pissed.

For his part, Tobin seemed oblivious to Quinn's hostility and smilingly led them down the hall.

As they cleaned, Tobin split his time between Sheronda and Abby, wandering the hallway as they moved from office to office. Abby learned more about him within the first hour of their shift than she'd ever learned from Quinn in months. He seemed to be sincere, if a little too talkative. He kept up a running narrative as they went about their tasks, a complete departure from the taciturn Quinn. Abby found it a little distracting after a while, and she could tell Sheronda was getting irritated. Their normal speedy work slowed considerably. They were still finishing up when the other crew stopped at the end of the hall to wait for them. Abby pulled her cart out of the last office to find Tobin standing there still talking. She felt bad because she hadn't been listening at all. Abby gave him a polite smile and pushed her cart past him to join the rest of their group. She stopped next to Quinn. Abby was unsurprised to find him glowering at Tobin who seemed oblivious that no one was listening to him. As they left admin, Tobin took up next to Abby and continued a conversation that she had no idea she was part of. By the time they checked in her carts, Quinn was no longer glowering at Tobin but looked concerned at the other man's constant running dialogue.

"Damn, that boy don't shut up," Sheronda remarked as she and Abby walked back to their suite. "He 'bout give me a headache with all that talkin'. Someone need to tell him to be quiet and just look pretty."

Abby silently agreed.

Chapter 25

HARD CANDY

New Year's Day came and went without incident. Unlike Halloween and Christmas, there weren't any planned celebrations or formal activities, but there was a certain air of festivity as most of the woman marked off another unofficial anniversary.

For Abby it meant she was closer to earning her full good time credit. She hadn't pursued it any further, and she wasn't sure whom to ask about it. She'd been assigned another case manager, an older woman named Paula, who'd been with the prison forever. Abby hadn't seen her since their initial introduction. She assumed Paula would find her if there was anything she needed to know or do. She wasn't sure exactly how long one-third of her time was supposed to be either. Was it a third of her remaining three- and-a-half years or a third of the full five years of her sentence? One meant she might be eligible for release in late spring, while the other meant she was eligible for release in the fall. Either way, this could be her last year of incarceration. Her feelings were surprisingly mixed about that.

She wasn't sure if it was her lack of family and friends on the outside, or the fact that she'd grown so close to both the COs and inmates in her unit that they were like family to her, but Abby seriously wondered if she even wanted to be released. She cared deeply for Big Ginger and Captain Dennis, and despite the confusing and indefinable nature of her relationship with Quinn, she knew she didn't want to leave him either.

Quinn had resumed his place near her, despite Tobin's overtures at friendship. Abby knew Tobin was just being nice, even if Quinn didn't. But as an inmate, there was nothing she could do or say that wouldn't get either of them in any trouble.

Abby's concerns were forgotten when things came to a head between Kendra and Brandon.

Though one wouldn't know it to look at her, or him, as the case may be, Brandon had turned into somewhat of a player in the unit. For the last couple of months, she'd been playing one girl against the other. Harmlessly at first, until one of the newer inmates, a small but tough girl named Maya, decided to put a stop to it.

It was drama straight out of a high school cafeteria when Maya confronted Kendra, accusing her of stealing her "boyfriend." The other ladies watched as the two women started screaming at each other about who had dated Brandon first. Abby knew that it was Kendra, but she wasn't interested in entering into the fray. Morgan broke up the screaming match sending Kendra to her suite and Maya to DSEG for starting it. Abby was impressed at her fairness. She'd always thought Morgan to be a bit of a bully.

Brandon did her best to reconcile with Kendra, promising that it was nothing more than flirtation. Kendra eventually calmed down and the two could be seen surreptitiously holding hands again. But a stint in DSEG did very little to improve Maya's mood. By the time she got back she was fuming.

Things were quiet for a week, though Abby knew violence was simmering just below the false calm. Maya was still a powder keg of anger just waiting for a spark.

It was during dinner that Maya finally blew. Abby sat listening to the desultory conversation around her. Quinn was leaning against the wall beside her. Tobin was on the opposite side of the room laughing at something one of the ladies was saying to him. Kendra and Brandon sat at the next table, their heads together as they shared a quiet conversation. Maya stared at them from the other side of the room. Abby happened to be looking in her direction and watched as Maya jumped up and stalked over, making a beeline for Kendra. Before anyone could do anything, she wrapped a cord around Kendra's neck and pulled her off the bench. Abby was shocked to see blood coming out from under the cord and stood up to intervene. Quinn pulled Abby back and shook his head as he placed himself in front of her. Abby turned to see Tobin and White running over to pull Maya off Kendra. The other women scattered as alarms went off. SRT would be there any second and no one wanted to get in the way.

Abby was shocked at Maya's inhuman strength as two grown men attempted to pull her off Kendra. Tobin sprayed her with pepper spray to no avail as Maya maintained her hold on the now limp girl. At the sight of all the blood, Abby knew Kendra was seriously hurt.

As the SRT team arrived, one pulled a Taser from his belt and aimed it at Maya's back, sending 50,000 volts to her nervous system. Maya's body began to shudder and her hands fell away from the cord around Kendra's neck.

As the SRT team pulled Maya away, Abby pulled her scrub shirt over her head as she ran to Kendra. She fell to her knees next to the bleeding girl and ripped a long strip from her shirt. The cord around Kendra's neck fell away to reveal a row of razor blades embedded in the plastic. Though they were short and could only make shallow cuts, Maya's strength had driven them deep into Kendra's throat. Abby made a quick assessment and determined that Maya hadn't had time to perforate either the jugular or the carotid, though Kendra was bleeding badly. She made a pack with the rest of her shirt and pressed it against Kendra's throat then secured it with the strip she'd torn off.

Quinn and Tobin were doing crowd control trying to force the rest of the women back to the unit for lockdown while White delicately placed the cord in a plastic bag.

SRT had already removed Maya, making room for the prison's EMTs. One pulled Abby aside and quickly examined her as the other examined the wounds under her make-shift bandage. They left it in place, put Kendra up on the gurney, and rushed her out.

Both Quinn and Tobin turned to Abby. Quinn reached her first. Wordlessly he lifted her hands and searched for cuts or other injuries. His expression was tense. Tobin came up behind him.

"You OK?" he asked, looking where Quinn had already looked. "Are you hurt?"

Abby shook her head. Quinn held her bloody hand a little bit longer then let it drop.

Tobin picked the same hand up and looked at it himself. Abby and Quinn both looked at him oddly, wondering at his proprietary gesture.

"I'm fine," Abby said, pulling her hand out of his. Tobin stepped back.

"That was insane," he remarked. "Does that happen often?"

"No," Quinn answered then turned and took Abby by the elbow to escort her from the cafeteria.

In the unit, all the suite doors remained closed and secured as lockdown was still in place. White went into the guard office to open Abby's suite and Quinn led her to her door.

"It shouldn't be much longer," he said quietly. "Can you give a witness statement?"

"Yes," Abby replied then stepped into her suite. Quinn pulled the door closed behind her and the lock engaged with an audible *thunk*.

Abby turned and faced her suitemates who were all looking at her expectantly.

"It was razors in a plastic cord, like the ones on headphones," she said in answer to their unasked question. "The cuts are serious but not life-threatening."

"All over a man…and not even a real man!" Mad T shook her head in disgust. "Y'all see how strong that girl was?"

Sheronda smirked. "Y'all see how fast our boy Quinn move to protect our girl here?"

"I think he knew I was going to try to pull her off," Abby said in answer, and then moved to the sink to wash off Kendra's blood.

Marianna pushed herself up and smiled at Abby. "Your boy didn't want you getting any cuts on your pretty little hands, did he?"

Abby ignored their jibes and pulled herself up into her bunk where she pulled out her ponytail and began to brush her hair. She was glad they weren't witness to Tobin's gestures of concern. She knew she'd never live it down.

Lockdown lasted only a few more minutes then the doors opened. Captain Hannah stood in the center of the common and called for toss and search. White pulled Abby aside and handed her over to Ramirez who would be escorting her to ADSEG for her statement. As Abby's involvement was minimal, she was only there long enough to give her version of the events that occurred leading up to and during the attack, the response of the staff and SRT team, and a description of the weapon used and the wounds they had caused. Since her testimony was identical to that of the prison staff on the scene, she was asked to sign her statement then dismissed. Quinn had already finished his statement so he escorted her back. They were halfway to the unit when Quinn pulled Abby into a dark corner and wrapped his arms around her. Abby stiffened in surprise then closed her eyes and relaxed against him.

"I need you to stop chasing trouble," he said quietly into the space at the base of her neck.

He tightened his hold on her and seemed to struggle with his words.

Abby held her breath and waited for him to speak again. It was the most he'd ever said to her about his feelings, yet it still wasn't enough.

Unable to articulate his thoughts fully, Quinn resumed his usual stoicism and pulled away. Though he'd dropped his arms, he'd kept her hand. Instead of speaking, Quinn lifted it up and pressed his lips into the center of her palm then looked at her. His expression of sadness and longing was a mirror of Abby's. Then he dropped her hand as well and the two walked silently back to the unit.

Chapter 26

BEAUTIMOUS

Things returned to a relative normal in the aftermath of Maya's attack on Kendra. Maya was charged with attempted murder and transferred to the reformatory. Brandon was also transferred, but to a prison out of state. Kendra spent several weeks in the infirmary and returned to the unit with a lifelong reminder of her ill-fated romance marked upon her neck.

To get their minds off the recent troubles, Captains Dennis and Hannah arranged for a group of church volunteers to come into the unit. They were hair stylists who would be spending the week donating haircuts, coloring, and perms to the inmates of B Unit. One of the church ladies was also an aesthetician who would give makeovers to anyone who asked.

Abby had visions of tight curly hair helmets and bright blue eye shadow taking over the unit, but since her hair hadn't been cut since she'd arrived at the prison, she figured there was very little damage they could do to her. Already long, her hair had grown several more inches. When out of its usual topknot, it hung past her waist. After lunch she put her name on the list and sat down.

She watched as the women before her got haircuts and perms. Several opted to have their hair colored and a fresh layer of makeup applied. Abby had to admit, the results were usually very flattering.

When it was her turn, Abby got up and sat in front of the stylist. Several of the ladies gasped as she pulled out her ponytail holder and a sheet of brown-black hair fell past the seat of the chair. Few in the unit had seen Abby without her hair up.

As their clients sat under dryers or waited for their highlights to take, the church ladies gathered around Abby and remarked on her bounty.

"This color is natural, isn't it?" one of them asked and Abby nodded.

"There's so much of it," said another. "How much do you want to have off?"

Abby glanced behind her. "I know the ends are split. I was hoping just to get a trim."

The eldest beautician stepped in front of her. "I hope I'm not being too forward, but, since it's so long and it's never been processed, would you consider donating some of it?"

"What do you mean?" Abby asked.

"Well, we accept donations for Locks of Love. It's a group that makes hairpieces for children who've lost their hair and can't afford wigs. Sometimes it's because of chemo, sometimes it's from alopecia. Whenever we find someone with long, unprocessed hair we usually ask."

Abby looked concerned. "How much do you take off?"

The older woman smiled. "Only ten inches, which on you is still the middle of your back. And as a thank you, Maggie here will do your makeup."

Abby smiled. "You can have my hair, but I don't wear a lot of makeup. In here you don't really need it."

"Oh honey," the older woman laughed, "everyone needs makeup."

Abby gave herself up to the ministrations of the church ladies, and by the time she was done, her hair felt healthy and her face looked the same only better. She thanked the ladies and left feeling better than she had in a long time.

Quinn, Tobin, and the other women of the cleaning crew were waiting for her when she walked back into the unit. Sheronda chuckled as Tobin stared and Quinn's eyebrows went up in surprise. Abby suddenly felt shy and awkward. None of them had ever seen her with makeup, and if any of them had seen her hair down, it was usually wet.

She was silent as Quinn led them to pick up their carts and escorted them to admin. As they arrived at the juncture in the hallway, Quinn took advantage of Tobin's speechlessness to guide Sheronda and Abby to their section, leaving Tobin to get himself together and escort the rest down the other hallway.

Abby started in the warden's office and worked her way down her side of the suite of rooms. Sheronda worked in the opposite direction to finish at the top of the hallway. Abby had just started the last office, which was still empty after Emma's departure, when Quinn walked in.

When Sheronda's vacuum went on, Quinn crossed the room and pulled Abby against him. Abby's breath caught as he pressed his lips against hers, one hand moving up her neck to twine his fingers in her hair while the other moved around her waist to press against the small of her back. His lips searched hers. His tongue moved between them. Abby responded timidly at first with her arms crushed against his chest, and then more assertively as he pulled her collar aside and began kissing her down the space from her ear to her collarbone.

Abby's breath caught in her throat as his hand moved from her waist, traveled under the elastic of her panties, and cupped the bare skin of her backside. His fingers caressed the sensitive skin near the part in her legs. Quinn's other hand moved under her shirt to cup her breast. His thumb moved across her hardening nipple.

As his fingers moved to enter her from behind, Abby moved her hands down the front of his chest. With a deftness that surprised her, she pulled his belt open and slid her hand down to clasp his erection at the base. She was surprised at its thickness and length.

Quinn groaned at her touch then shuddered as she moved her hand up and down its length. As her lips sought his, he moved his hand from her breast and plunged it down the front of her panties. His fingers stroked the length of her cleft as the fingers of his other hand entered her. It was Abby's turn to shudder and a second later her body exploded as the force of her orgasm ripped through her. Abby's head went back and she fought the moan that threatened to escape her throat. She could feel Quinn's body thrust against her and in moments they were both shaking as they came together.

Quinn held her close, his breath still fast and hard in her ear. Abby opened her heart and let it fill with the moment as she lingered in the aftermath of her orgasm. When Quinn pulled away, his face was flushed. Whether from the force of his own orgasm or embarrassment, Abby didn't know. She turned and grabbed the roll of paper towels from her cart and handed them to Quinn then turned away to give him some privacy.

In the distance, Sheronda's vacuum continued its roar and Abby had to wonder at the time. A quick glance at her watch showed that only minutes had passed. She turned when Quinn cleared his throat. He had put himself back together so well that one would ever know what had occurred between them. He reached over and combed his fingers through Abby's hair, straightening the mess he'd made.

As she retied the front of her scrubs, Quinn leaned over and kissed her gently then turned and left the room.

Abby stared after him for a second, and then, still in a daze, looked around the office. There was nothing left to do in there, so she pulled her cart out and went down the hall to wait for Sheronda.

Only Sheronda seemed to sense a change as the group moved to check in their carts. Abby avoided her smiling gaze as Tobin took up step beside her, chatting as if continuing a conversation already in progress. Abby tuned him out for the remainder of the short distance back to the unit. Her eyes were glued to the curve of Quinn's ear as he walked in front of her.

As they passed the door to the yard, Abby glanced out the thin strip of window to see icy rain falling steadily and realized she would be missing her run for the day. For once she didn't mind. All she really wanted to do was curl up in her bed and daydream about Quinn. Without realizing it, Abby walked away from Tobin in midsentence and went into her suite.

Chapter 27

AIN'T FITTIN' TO BUST A GRAPE

The next morning Abby had to drag herself out of bed as the doors opened. Though it was morning, the unit was still dark as the skies overhead hung low with gray swollen clouds. She'd tossed and turned all night, aching with the need to feel Quinn's arms wrapped around her. Her hunger for him was so insatiable, not even her fingers could satisfy her.

Sheronda's knowing smirk didn't help either. Abby ignored her as best she could, but Mad T immediately caught sight of it.

"What?" she demanded.

Sheronda feigned innocence. "What do you mean 'what?' I got nothin'."

Mad T looked from Abby to Sheronda and back. "I ain't askin' again."

Sheronda knew better than to try to dodge Mad T's demand. "It ain't nothin' big. Our girl just got some. Thass all."

"What do you mean 'got some'?" Mad T asked. She was quickly losing patience.

"*I mean*, our girl here finally got some lovin'. Am I right?" All the women of the suite were awake now and turned to stare at Abby who started blushing furiously.

"I hope it ain't from that Tobin boy," Mad T joked. "He be followin' you like a puppy."

"Can't be him," Marianna laughed. "Boy can't shut up long enough."

"I'm thinkin' our girl finally steal my boyfrin'," Sheronda said slyly.

Abby slid off her bunk and straightened her blanket. "I don't know what you're talking about," she said to the wall in front of her, and the ladies all started to laugh.

"Don't worry, baby," Mad T got up and gave Abby a rare hug. "We got yer back."

Abby returned the hug, then, without admitting anything, went to get cleaned up before breakfast.

The day passed in a blur. Abby couldn't even remember teaching her classes that morning let alone anything she might have said. All her thoughts were consumed by images of Quinn.

Sleet and rain poured steadily throughout the day eliminating any possibility for a run. Unable to sit still long enough to read, Abby sat in the common area watching hours of mindless home and cooking shows, her foot tapping out her restlessness.

Captain Dennis sat in the guard office behind her watching Abby's foot go up and down in a frenetic staccato until he just couldn't take it anymore.

Out of the corner of her eye, Abby saw him cross the common to a small closet tucked in the corner. He pulled a broom from it and stalked back to where Abby was sitting.

"You ever see *One Flew Over the Cuckoo's Nest?*" he asked her.

Abby sat up. "I read the book in high school."

"Good," Captain Dennis said then thrust the broom into her hands. "Then make like Chief and clean this place up."

Though inmates were often given cleaning tasks as punishment for minor infractions, Abby saw his order for what it was intended. He might not know the reason, but Captain Dennis recognized that if Abby couldn't run, she needed some other way to work off her energy.

Abby stood and started in the farthest corner of the unit and began to clean. By the time she reached the opposite corner it was nearly lunchtime, and she had gathered a considerable pile of hair, bits of trash, as well as other things humans shed throughout their day. Captain Dennis handed her a dustpan and Abby finished her task.

"I'm done," she said as she handed back the dustpan and broom.

"My momma always said, 'There's always somethin' to do.' You need that broom again, you just ask."

"Thank you."

"You're welcome, Chief."

Lunch was less awkward than Abby thought it would be. Sheronda and the ladies deliberately stayed away from any conversation about Quinn, opting to talk about some of the new inmates instead.

Abby listened but had nothing to add since she hadn't met any of them yet. By the time lunch was done, the weather had cleared and Abby layered on almost everything she had to go for a run.

It felt good to be outside, despite the cold. With her pedometer, she was able to keep track of how far she was going and how close she was to making her marathon distance. As she ran, she ruminated on the irony that if she'd never gone to prison, she most likely wouldn't have had the time to train. Her class and work schedule would have taken precedence over running, leaving her no time to put in enough training to make a whole marathon distance. Abby had run almost every day since her incarceration. She was only eight miles shy of her twenty-six point two mile goal.

Time got the best of her and she worried that she might never reach her goal; not because of her conditioning or speed, but because she simply didn't have enough time to run the entire distance. Elite marathon runners could finish in a little over two hours while the average runner could complete the race in about four hours. Abby put herself somewhere in the middle and estimated a finish time of three- to three-and-a-half hours. Unfortunately, she never had that long of a block of time inside the prison's regimented schedule.

The break in the weather was over and the clouds gathering over the prison were already sending arrows of sleet down into the yard. It was definitely time to go inside.

Abby changed into dry clothes then crawled into her bunk to try to read before count. Since it was Saturday, she had two whole days to agonize over Quinn before she would see him again.

Chapter 28

KICK ROCKS

By the time Monday rolled around, Abby had convinced herself that her encounter with Quinn had been an isolated incident. It was the only way to cope with what would otherwise be an untenable situation. The bottom line was that Abby was an inmate and Quinn was a guard. To continue a physical relationship was inviting trouble, especially for Quinn. And for Abby to hope that he had actual feelings for her was borderline delusional.

Her suitemates continued their subtle teasing throughout the day as the start of Quinn's shift approached. Abby didn't have the heart to tell them how mistaken they were. They seemed to be genuinely happy for her.

On the outside, Abby would have been eagerly awaiting her next encounter with Quinn, planning every word she'd say, and searching for any and every moment that afforded the opportunity to touch him, even innocently. But she felt the reality of her incarceration more keenly now that he'd taken her over the already blurred line of propriety. She awaited his arrival with something more like dread.

The shifts changed after the 3:00 p.m. count, and Abby did everything she could think of to keep her mind off the time. After breakfast, she ran her classes longer than usual, went for a long run despite the weather, and then swept the entirety of the unit just to keep herself from thinking about him.

She was almost grateful when the 3:00 p.m. count was off and Captain Dennis declared lockdown so that a recount could be done and the missing inmate located. Her relief was short-lived, however, when Morgan returned with one of Sheronda's ladies in tow, having neglected to log the inmates trip to the infirmary with the guard office.

When the doors opened for recount, Abby stepped out to see both Quinn and Tobin standing at the entrance to the guard office. Tobin was smiling amiably while Quinn looked at her with his usual mask of stoicism.

This time the count was accurate and Captain Dennis decided to forgo a toss in favor of going home. Captain Hannah could always call a toss if issues arose during the evening shift.

Though she'd gone for a run earlier, Abby put on her damp clothes and went back out, just to have something to do other than stare at Quinn. She'd forgotten her pedometer so she counted instead, not caring how accurate it was.

By the time the door banged open, she was shivering as her sweat froze on her skin. She jogged over to see Tobin waiting for her.

"Dinnertime," he almost sang as she approached.

Abby smiled politely in response, but didn't slow her pace until she was inside the unit.

Sheronda was waiting for her in the suite, so Abby changed quickly, and then the two walked into dinner.

Inmates were creatures of habit, out of both necessity and compliance. Though there were no assigned seats anywhere, the women typically sat in the exact same seats at all mealtimes. Abby occasionally switched sides of the table, but it was always the same table and always the end of the table. Sheronda always sat next to her.

COs, however, unofficially rotated their positions in the cafeteria with the exception of Quinn who usually took up a spot on the wall nearest to Abby. This was allowed for the simple reason that he and Abby never spoke. If they had been chatty, Captains Dennis and Hannah would have assigned him to a post outside of the cafeteria. She was so used to Quinn standing nearby that she was taken aback to see Tobin parked near her table when she sat down. Quinn stood on the opposite side of the room, his face in a scowl. He was clearly angry that Tobin had usurped his position. Abby knew Quinn outranked Tobin but doubted he'd do anything that would arouse suspicion.

Halfway through the meal, though, she wished he had. Tobin kept a running dialogue with the air in front of him to such an extent that Abby wanted to put her fingers in her ears. It wasn't until then that she realized how much she appreciated Quinn's silence.

Sheronda was also reeling from the verbal barrage. She slouched in her seat, apparently hoping that Abby's body would block the sound waves.

"Damn, don't that motherfucker ever shut up?" she mumbled into her food.

Sylvia gave Tobin a long side-glance. "I'm going to knit us all some earmuffs before we all go crazy."

"Knit me a gun so's I can blow my brains out," Sheronda muttered and the women at the table all tittered. Tobin, for his part, was oblivious of the conversation in front of him.

"Girl, you actually listening to him?" Sheronda asked Abby.

"God no," Abby replied quietly. "I'm not even sure who he's talking to."

"Are you done?" Sheronda pushed herself up from the table. "I'm goin'."

Abby got up and followed Sheronda over to drop off her tray then the two ladies left. Abby wasn't surprised to see the rest of their table right behind them.

They had a few minutes before they had to leave for crew, so Abby went into the bathroom to stick her head under the hand blowers to dry the rest of her hair. She'd spent too long outside and she was still cold.

When she was done, the crew was ready to go and she was dismayed to find both Tobin and Quinn waiting to escort them. She didn't know which was worse: Tobin's chatter or Quinn's silence. Tobin continued his running dialogue, this time about his new neighbors at his new apartment, as they checked out their carts then traveled down the halls to the admin wing.

At the juncture, Tobin looked like he was going to take Sheronda and Abby when Sheronda spoke up.

"Uh uh," she said. Sheronda had planted herself in the middle of the entrance to the executive offices and faced him squarely. "I can't get shit done with this one runnin' his mouth the whole time. I ain't got time to be polite and clean at the same damn time." She pointed at Tobin then at the other hallway. "You go that way."

Abby's mouth fell open. No inmate spoke to a guard like that without consequence. Everyone stared at Sheronda, including Tobin who looked like he'd been slapped. Quinn stepped forward to pull Sheronda and her cart down to the end of the hallway. Tobin had no choice but to take the others.

Abby followed Sheronda's cart, still stunned at the little woman's nerve. She pulled her cart into the warden's office and started to clean.

As Abby made her way down the hall, she wondered if Sheronda was going to get into any trouble for her outburst. As she pulled her cart into the last office, Quinn stepped out of the conference room where Sheronda was cleaning. Abby hoped he'd at least been fair.

The office was still unoccupied, but it was starting to collect dust from its lack of use. She was wiping down the last of the empty shelves when Quinn stepped in and closed the door behind him. Abby turned to find he'd crossed the room already, and before she could put down her rag, he'd pulled her close and started kissing her. She hesitated at first, as if she considered stopping him. Then she gave herself up, dropping her rag on the floor and returning his kisses with equal ardor.

Quinn's hands were everywhere. His lips traced the line of her jaw to a spot just behind her ear that immediately sent chills all over her body. In no time her scrubs and panties were down around her knees, and his belt was off and pants undone as if his erection couldn't be contained by mere leather and cloth. Abby gasped as he pressed himself into her, filling her fully. Quinn groaned into her neck as he thrust against her, the edge of the desk pressing into the backs of her thighs. To fill her more deeply, Quinn pushed her clothes down to her ankles and lifted her knees. Abby held herself at the edge of the desk and let her head fall back, relishing the ache that was growing between her legs. Quinn leaned over and pushed her shirt up to press his lips against her rock hard nipple. This time Abby moaned as Quinn drew circles around her nipple with his tongue and then sucked it in his mouth making it harder. She thought she would explode as his teeth gently nipped her. Between her legs she could feel his urgency building as his thrusting grew stronger. She was bracing for his climax when she felt his hand move between them to the center of her cleft. Waves of pleasure coursed through her body as his thumb moved against her. The combination of his hardness inside her and his thumb caressing her was too much to bear. Abby's body arched as a massive orgasm coursed through her entirety. She stifled a cry and heard Quinn do the same as his body shuddered against her.

In the distance, Abby heard Sheronda's vacuum go on. The sound brought Quinn back to the present and he slowly pulled himself off her. As he pulled himself out, Abby was surprised to see he had put a condom on at some point. She was belatedly grateful. The last thing she needed was a pregnancy. Quinn kissed her, and then turned away to clean himself up and dispose of the condom in the waste bag attached to her cart.

Abby pulled her clothes back into place and redid her ponytail, turning away slightly to hide the fact that she was on the verge of tears. She wanted him to say something to her, to tell her he loved her, or needed her…anything but his usual silence.

As if he could sense her struggle, Quinn turned her face to his and looked at her. Abby drowned in the blue water of his eyes then closed her own before she started sobbing. She could feel Quinn's lips against hers as he kissed her long and hard. In another moment, Abby was returning the kiss as Quinn wrapped his arms around her.

Their time was cut short when Sheronda's vacuum turned off. Quinn broke off the kiss and stepped back, listening. When the vacuum turned back on, he gave Abby one last kiss then left the room.

Abby gave the rest of the room a quick swipe then dragged her cart to the conference room where Sheronda was still vacuuming. Inside she could see Sheronda struggling to get what looked like cake crumbs out of the commercial carpet.

"Damn if these people didn't have some kind of food fight in here," she grumbled when she saw Abby come in. "This shit ain't comin' up at all."

Abby grabbed a small bristle brush from her cart, and on hands and knees, scrubbed at the food mess to loosen it from the carpet fibers. Then she moved so Sheronda could vacuum them up behind her. Working in tandem, they were able to get the rest of the conference room clean in no time.

Exhausted, Sheronda turned off her vacuum and pulled the plug from the wall. "Thanks, hon," she panted as she clipped the machine back onto the cart. "You good?"

Abby smiled. "I'm fine."

"Mmhmm, I bet you are." Sheronda smirked as she pushed her cart into the hallway. "Let's get the fuck outta here."

Everyone was waiting for them. This time the trip back to the unit was mercifully quiet as Tobin trailed Abby silently.

Abby watched Quinn go into the guard office then went to get her shower things.

It was a good time to shower since it was mostly deserted. The small group of women already there were quickly drying themselves in the cold room. Abby took the stall on the far end and entered the spray of hot water. She moved carefully. The ache between her legs was acute from years of disuse. It was a pain she relished. As she gently soaped herself, her thoughts turned to Quinn and the feel of his body in hers.

She finished as another group of women entered. The cold was bracing as she stepped out and dressed quickly.

Quinn was nowhere to be seen when she returned to her unit. Only Tobin sat in the guard office. He looked up and gave her a hopeful smile. Abby turned away and entered her suite to turn in early.

Chapter 29

RUNNING YOUR NECK

The next few weeks were a blur for Abby. Whenever he could, Quinn served as escort for cleaning crew and spent as much time with her as possible. Abby enjoyed their intimate moments immensely, but chafed at his lack of communication. The ever-present self-doubt grew to the point that Abby had herself convinced she was nothing more than a guard groupie. She struggled with that, at times vowing to cut Quinn off, until she saw him and her resolve melted. But more than anything, she didn't want to become one of those women who insisted that their man define their relationship. She'd never done it before and she was definitely not going to start now.

Oddly, Tobin was infinitely more tolerable and, at times, even enjoyable. Sheronda's outburst seemed to flip a switch in him. He was far less talkative than he'd been before that fateful day. He still seemed to be following Abby throughout the unit, but his presence was more companionable now rather than irritating, and she never lacked for compliments when he was around. If only Abby could combine Tobin and Quinn, she'd have the perfect man.

Abby was sitting in the common area listening to Sheronda and her ladies discuss the merits of the COs they had known over the years. Sheronda was complimenting Captain Hannah's leadership when Tobin offered up a bombshell of gossip.

"You know she's leaving soon," he broke in. Sheronda paused in her comment and the ladies all stared at him.

"What you mean, she's leaving?" she asked.

Tobin stepped closer and lowered his voice as if realizing that he was being less than circumspect in sharing Captain Hannah's news with inmates.

"She's retiring in a couple of weeks," he said quietly. "They're promoting one of the sergeants to her position but I don't know which one."

"You mean Redfern or Quinn's gonna become captain?" Sheronda asked.

"I don't know," Tobin shrugged. "It could be a sergeant from anywhere in the prison, I guess."

Abby was about to ask about guard seniority when Paula, her new case manager, appeared behind Tobin.

"Abby," she said as she gave Tobin a brief smile, "can we have a quick meeting?"

Abby nodded and stood up to follow her as the ladies catcalled behind her.

Paula led Abby to one of the four vacant rooms located at the end of the common area. Two were classrooms, one was the small exam room where Abby had been treated for her exposure to Captain Dennis's pepper spray, and the last was a small hearing room she'd never been in before. Paula led her into the hearing room as it afforded more privacy than the tables in the common area.

Abby noticed Paula carried a file with her, presumably Abby's, and some blank paperwork. She set them down on the table then indicated for Abby to sit.

"I'm sorry it's taken this long for me to speak with you," she began. "With Emma's unfortunate indiscretion and termination, we are woefully short staffed."

"It's OK," Abby said with a smile. "I understand."

Paula looked grateful. "Well, hopefully you'll be happy to see me then. I've been going through your file...your corrected file, and I noticed that you haven't filed for parole consideration."

"I thought I was required to serve the full five years under the mandatory minimum sentencing laws," Abby said. "I didn't think I was eligible for parole consideration."

Paula shook her head. "I've read through your file several times, and from what I can tell, since you had no felony priors, the prosecutor exercised his discretion to not file for a mandatory minimum. They may not have explained that to you fully since your attorney filed a guilty plea." Abby watched her as she shuffled through the file to find Abby's sentencing report. "Nope, nothing here, which means you can submit for parole based on your earned good time credit."

"So when am I eligible?" Abby asked. Her feelings were still conflicted on the subject of leaving.

"Well, typically it would be after one-third was served at the federal or state prison level, but you spent an extraordinary amount of time in the county jail, and for the life of me, I can't see why."

"It was part of my plea agreement," Abby offered. "My attorney negotiated that part of my guilty plea to ensure that I wouldn't be sent to the reformatory. At that time there wasn't any room here and since my father was sick, the judge ruled that I could stay in the county jail until space opened. So I was there a total of eighteen months."

Paula looked stricken. "Wow. That must have been awful."

Abby shrugged. "It wasn't great."

"Well, county time isn't typically applied toward your parole consideration since it's usually served during your trial, but I'm pretty sure the hearing officer will take it into consideration since its technically time served following your conviction. If you want to apply, I'll discuss it with him. We go way back." Paula pushed the forms across the table. "They don't typically review parole requests on such short notice, but given the fact that you were never informed by your previous case manager, they will definitely make an exception. And if he accepts your county time, your one-third will end in late March, early April at the latest. You could go home." Paula smiled.

Abby mirrored her smile, but it wasn't sincere. Paula wouldn't know, but Abby didn't have a home to go to. She took the papers then offered her hand, which Paula didn't hesitate to shake.

"Let me know what you want to do, OK?" Paula stood and escorted Abby to the door. "I'll make time if you have any additional questions."

"Thank you so much," Abby said, and this time she was sincere.

Abby slowly walked back to the tables, staring at the forms in her hands while Sheronda and the other ladies stared at her.

"You in trouble or somethin'?" Sheronda asked as Abby sat down next to her.

"No, just the opposite. Paula just gave me my paperwork to file for parole consideration. She said my one-third is up at the end of next month."

The group erupted as the ladies moved to hug her and offer their congratulations. Though it was highly inappropriate, Tobin stepped over and gave Abby a big hug.

"That's awesome," he said sincerely. "Congratulations." When he stepped back, Abby saw Quinn standing behind Tobin, his face a mask of anger. She watched as he turned around and stalked into the guard office, closing the door behind him. Abby stared after him for a long moment then got up and went to her suite to fill out her paperwork.

Chapter 30

SKIN BEEF

Since Tobin would put on a big show and Quinn was inexplicably angry with her, Abby waited until after dinner to ask Ramirez to call her case manager once her paperwork was completed. To her credit, Paula arrived only a few minutes later, pleased to see Abby had decided to file for parole.

"I'll get this in today and let you know when they schedule you with the hearing officer," she said as Abby handed her the forms. "I've already spoken with the guard staff and I'll have their recommendations by tomorrow."

Abby was grateful. "Thank you so much."

Paula smiled at her. "You are more than welcome. I'd wish you good luck, but I don't think you're going to need it!"

"You don't know the half of it," Abby thought to herself as she watched Paula leave with her future.

Abby walked back into the common area where she met Sheronda and the two set off to report for cleaning crew.

She was less than thrilled to see both Tobin and Quinn waiting to escort them. As they checked out their carts, Tobin questioned Abby further on her parole application. Abby responded politely, but more than anything, she just wanted Tobin to shut up. Every answer she gave made Quinn's scowl deepen, and by the time they reached the juncture between the wings, he looked murderous.

Quinn stalked to the set of double doors that separated the executive hallway from the rest of the admin wing, effectively eliminating any discussion about which guard would be taking which group. Abby pushed her cart past him, both fearful and angry in equal measure.

Sheronda paused and glanced a question at Abby who just shook her head. Sheronda gave Quinn her own scowl then moved down to the end of the hallway as usual.

Abby started in the warden's office with one eye on the door in case Quinn came in, but she needn't have bothered. Quinn remained planted at the top of the hall, not even looking in her direction as she made her way down to each office.

By the time she started dusting the shelves in the last office, she figured she was home free, but then he appeared in the doorway. Abby turned to find him scowling at her. Her initial fear gave way to anger as he continued to stare. She wanted to scream at him but knew it would be pointless to do so. Love her or hate her, Quinn refused to speak to her.

"Fine, let him stand there all day," she told herself as she climbed down from the stepladder. She was poised to tell him exactly what she thought of him when she realized he was standing right behind her.

Loving, passionate Quinn was gone. This Quinn was angry—worse—he was enraged. Abby gasped as he grabbed her and kissed her furiously. His hands moved over her in a frenzy of need, as if by touching all of her he could possess her fully. Abby's nerves were vibrating, her body responded to every touch. This was hate sex, and even though she should have put a stop to it, she didn't want to.

Abby's fingers moved to his shirt, hastily undoing the buttons to reveal a plain white T-shirt. In her frenzy to touch him, she ripped it down the front baring his chest. Her breath caught at the sight of him, toned and tan. Quinn groaned as she ran her fingers up his skin, stopping to pinch his nipples. He returned the favor by pulling her shirt up and pressing his lips against her, his teeth biting at her nipple then pulling it further into his mouth. As he pulled her scrub pants down, his other hand pulled his belt off. Abby reached down to pull open his uniform, freeing his erection.

As Quinn moved from her nipple to her lips, Abby pulled her scrub pants down and let them fall to her ankles. Quinn fumbled with the condom for a moment then pressed himself against her. She could feel him pushing into her, and she spread her knees to open herself wide. Once inside of her, Quinn pounded into her as if he could expel his anger with each thrust. Abby could feel that delicious ache building. Quinn groaned as he reached the precipice of his need for her and his thrusting grew more frenzied. Abby knew she was close to orgasm when she felt a snap like a rubber band deep inside of her.

She moved to push against his chest but Quinn was past the point of no return. His body shuddered with pleasure, Abby's orgasm following on the heels of his. Quinn held her close for a moment, panting with the effort of expelling his demons then pulled away.

Abby looked down to see a small amount of his seed leaking down her leg. His condom had broken.

Quinn followed her gaze, his expression stricken. Acting quickly, Abby pushed him away and stood up to grab the paper towels from her cart. She handed him a handful then took a wad to clean herself up.

Quinn turned away from her and attended to the broken condom. She could see that it had captured most of his emission and hoped it was enough. Not much was leaking from her, so chances were she would be fine.

Abby pulled her clothes back on and fixed her ponytail. She watched as Quinn pulled his uniform shirt off and tore the remains of his T-shirt off, throwing it in her trash bag.

His shoulders and back were as toned as his chest, and his waist was trim without an ounce of fat. Abby felt her nipples harden again and she desired to grab him and kiss him all over. She started to reach for him, but when he turned back to her, his expression stayed her hand. If anything, he looked even angrier than before. All desire fled when he gave her the coldest look she'd ever seen then turned and left the room.

Abby knew she loved him, and in that single moment, she knew he didn't love her.

Chapter 31

ROOKIE LOOKIN' FOR A COOKIE

After their last encounter, Quinn dropped Abby cold. He didn't speak to her, look at her, or even acknowledge her in any way. Abby was hurt and angry, but given her situation, there was nothing she could do about it. She felt adrift, soiled even, and more than anything, she needed to find her way back to her faith. Father Duncan had accepted the position of the prison's chaplain, so Abby spent as much time with him as was allowed. His kindness was a balm for her damaged heart.

Then a week later, everything changed for the worse. Captain Hannah's retirement was moved up so that she could exhaust personal time that she'd banked over the years. The day after she left, Quinn showed up to the unit with captain's bars on his shirt. He'd been promoted. He would no longer be mixing with the inmate population in the same manner as a guard. Then the new girl arrived.

COs were short on the ground, but it didn't take any time for Quinn to find someone to take his place in the unit. As the most senior guard on the unit, White was promoted to sergeant and a new officer was brought in. She looked younger than the other COs, and was remarkably pretty. As if to compensate for her looks, she was harsh with the inmates, and quick to give them a tongue lashing if they didn't perform to her standards.

It wasn't until designated free time that Abby personally felt the sting of her hostility. Without Quinn to distract her, Abby concentrated all her mental and physical energy to fulfilling her twenty-six-mile goal. She had three hours outside and she resolved to make the best of them. She put her Garmin to good use, programming it to show how close she was to her distance goal. Despite the freezing rain, Abby had hit the twenty-mile mark when the door banged open. It was thrown open with such force that the sound resounded throughout the yard startling Abby into stopping suddenly, her feet sliding on the icy wet pavement.

The new guard stood at the door waving Abby in. Abby jogged over to see the young woman scowling at her.

"You're time is up," she barked, affecting a tone much like Captain Dennis's when he was using his drill sergeant voice. Abby looked for her name tag. It said V. Stephens. She was shorter than Abby by a few inches but definitely curvier. Her brown uniform shirt had been altered to show those curves to her advantage. She had straight brown hair pulled back in a tight bun and large brown eyes fringed with long dark lashes. She wore just enough makeup to play up her features. If she smiled, she'd be truly pretty.

Abby looked at her watch. "I have twenty more minutes."

"I don't care what you think you have." Stephens sneered, her pretty face turning ugly as her lip curled up. "I'm not standing out here till you're done. Yard is closed. Now get inside."

"Yard time is mandatory privilege. You can't revoke it unless there's a disciplinary reason," Abby said as politely as she could manage.

Stephens put her hand to the spray on her belt and gave Abby a stony look. "Are you giving me a disciplinary reason?"

Abby stared at her for a second and wondered if this was the standard in prison guard behavior. If it was, then they'd been really lucky in B Unit. Abby shook her head and went inside.

She briefly considered complaining, but she knew Quinn wouldn't listen to her. As she was so close to her release date, she didn't want to do anything to jeopardize it.

As she walked into the common area, Abby saw Sheronda go into their suite so she followed her.

When she entered, Mad T and Sheronda looked up in surprise. "What you doin' here so soon?" Sheronda asked.

"The new guard canceled the rest of my yard time," Abby said as she crawled up into her bunk and wrapped her blanket around her. She pulled her ponytail out and towel dried her hair as best she could, and then pulled her hairbrush through it. Even after her haircut, it hung in long sheets around her shoulders. It was shiny and so dark from the rain it looked black.

"Man, that chick a bitch," Sheronda remarked. "She be in DSEG before here and be thinkin' we all in the Hole. Someone gonna pull her card if she keep it up."

Mad T simply scowled at the guard office. Abby found her silence scarier than any comment she might make. She figured, if someone as nice as Big Ginger could be attacked, Stephens was in trouble.

She was spared from answering when Ramirez showed up at the door to the suite.

"Your CM wants you," she said and smiled at Abby. Unlike Stephens, Ramirez was a consummate professional.

"Thanks," Abby responded as she slid off her bunk.

"She's in the unit hearing room," Ramirez said and stepped aside to let Abby pass.

Abby crossed the unit, glancing in the guard office as she walked by. Stephens was leaning against the desk where Quinn sat in front of the computer. He was laughing at something she was saying and responding with more words than Abby had ever heard from him at one time.

She put her chin up and straightened to her full height. As much as her heart ached, she was not going to let Quinn know how much he had hurt her.

Paula was smiling when Abby walked into the hearing room. She had a huge pile of papers in front of her.

"You're attorney is a real firecracker," she began. Abby sat down in front of her.

"What do you mean?"

Paula sorted through the pile. "An application for parole consideration must include recommendations from your trial judge, the state's attorney who prosecuted you, and your defense attorney. Was this Jane Howerton your defense attorney?"

Abby nodded. "She's kind of a jack-of-all-trades where I'm from."

"Well, she's been looking out for you." Paula was impressed. "She already had the outside recommendations that were required and overnighted them. I have reports from Captain Dennis, Captain Hannah, Sergeant Redfern, and, I guess he's a captain now, but I just got Sergeant Quinn's as well. They all gave glowing recommendations and even without Captain Quinn's, the Parole Commission set your hearing date for February twenty-first. I'm not supposed to tell you, but your projected release date is March fourteenth."

Abby was surprised. It was all happening so soon. She could be out of there in only six weeks.

"But Quinn's report could change that, right?"

Paula looked confused. "Why would it change the commission's decision? His reports are the most complimentary."

Abby was surprised. "No reason, it's just that he isn't the most talkative person. In fact, he doesn't really say anything."

Paula shrugged. "Be that as it may, he had a lot to say about you that was extremely flattering. One would wonder how you were ever sent to prison."

"Even Jesus went to prison," Abby thought, but held her tongue.

"I should warn you that you still have one small hurdle," Paula continued. "There are two issues standing in front of you that are critical to your release. The first issue is that you must have a living plan in place. The second is that you must have some form of employment waiting for you upon release. Your attorney has assured me that she is finalizing your employment situation, but she has not yet secured appropriate housing for you. This means you may be released to a detainer, or a transitional housing situation. It's what most people call a halfway house. The location will be determined by your employment. If your job is in central state, you'll most likely be sent to one in Columbus unless your housing situation can be resolved sooner."

"Does that affect my parole negatively?" Suddenly Abby very much wanted to leave.

Paula shook her head. "As long as you have employment, the housing situation won't be a deal breaker. You'll be fine. And to be honest, the executive staff is extremely embarrassed about what happened with Emma. I think they'd like to get rid of you before you change your mind about filing a suit against the prison. That gives you some leverage."

Abby thought about her leverage but kept quiet. There was no reason to play her hand unless she needed to.

This time Paula held out her hand. Abby took it, thanking her for all her help.

"You are more than welcome, Abby."

Abby and Paula parted ways just outside the office. It was time for cleaning crew, and Sheronda was already waiting for her.

With Quinn now a captain, it was Tobin and Stephens escorting them to their shift. Tobin fell in beside Abby once they picked up their carts, but maintained a companionable silence rather than the constant chatter of before.

When they arrived in admin, Stephens acted as if she was going to take Abby and Sheronda, but was trumped when Tobin unlocked the double doors and waved them into the suite.

Abby was glad. The last thing she wanted was another minute in Stephen's presence.

Without Quinn to distract her, Abby made quick work of her side of the suite and finished long before Sheronda. She quickly vacuumed the hallway then reassembled her cart to wait with Tobin.

"So, you looking forward to finally getting out of here?"

"Sure," Abby answered politely. "I think anyone would be."

"What's the first thing you're going to do?" He smiled with amusement. Looking at him, Abby realized that he was the nicest person she'd ever met.

"I don't know," she answered honestly. "I really haven't given it any thought."

Tobin looked thoughtful. "Say the first thing that comes to your mind. What do you miss more than anything?"

"Bookstores," Abby answered. "I miss bookstores."

Tobin nodded appreciatively. "That's a good answer. Most people would say a good steak or alcohol. But, bookstores...that's a good one."

Sheronda appeared in the conference room doorway and dragged her cart into the hallway.

"Damn if they didn't have another party," she grumbled.

Abby felt badly. She should have gone in there to help and said as much when Sheronda pulled up next to her.

"Nah, you got more rooms than me and you did the hallway," she answered as she waved away Abby's apology. "Hey, Pretty Boy. Why don't you push my cart for me? This girl is tired."

Tobin moved to do as she asked, but Sheronda put up her hand. "Jesus kid, don't you know when someone's kidding? I got it. Let's go." Sheronda pushed past him to return to the unit without the rest of the crew.

Abby shrugged then followed.

Chapter 32

BROKE WEAK

Despite her deteriorating situation with Quinn, Abby resolved to keep her head down for the rest of her time there. She finished her classes, and gave her replacement, a volunteer from the outside, all her teaching materials, and an overview of what to expect from the inmates.

Valentine's Day arrived with very little fanfare. Inmates in relationships with each other might have exchanged tokens of their affection, but it was an overall depressing holiday and primarily ignored by the general population.

Without classes in the morning, Abby spent most of her time running when the weather permitted and reading when it didn't. She was glad to have the morning free time since Stephens had put an inconsistent moratorium on her access to the yard in the afternoon. Abby recognized it for what it was—a petty power play—and chose to ignore it. Mad T took offense though and began demanding that she too be allowed to go outside during the afternoon. Abby appreciated the effort but did not want her friend to fall under any scrutiny. It was to no avail anyway. Stephens denied Mad T yard privilege as well, and she made the mistake of doing it in the nastiest way possible.

But Mad T had an ace up her sleeve: the ACLU National Prison Project. Stephens had underestimated the amount of influence Mad T had over the inmate population and her ability to invoke the ACLU to ensure that every inmate's rights were protected.

Abby had dressed for her run, but she was disappointed to find the yard doors locked. She walked into the common area to find Sylvia at one of the tables with her Christmas yarn. She sat down next to her and took up one of the needles to practice her crochet stitch. She was still trying to get the hang of it when D walked up to the guard office. Stephens opened the door and leaned out. Just past the guard office, Abby saw Quinn approaching from the cafeteria hallway. He stopped just inside the common area and appeared to be assessing the situation.

"What." It was more a demand than a question.

D's tone echoed Stephens's. "We need the yard unlocked. We want to go play some basketball."

"It's February. Yard is closed."

Abby turned to watch, as did most of the ladies. Mad T strolled in and took the seat next to Abby and watched in amusement as D tilted her head and regarded Stephens then stated, "Ain't snowin'…ain't rainin'. We need the yard unlocked so we can play some basketball."

"Are you deaf? I said it's freaking February and the yard is closed." Stephens's teeth were clenched, her jaw muscles working overtime.

D's eyes narrowed as a slight smile played across her face. "Yard is open during the first shift. You sayin' it ain't February during the first shift?"

Stephens's face tightened. "I don't care what they do during the first shift. It's closed now."

As D stood regarding Stephens silently, another member of Mad T's family walked up. She went by the ironic name of Tiny. She was taller than D, but a mirror image of the woman.

Tiny put her chin up and narrowed her eyes at Stephens. "I need to go out to the yard for some fresh air. Who's gonna unlock it?"

Abby watched as Stephens struggled with her temper. "Yard is closed."

Tiny tilted her head and stared daggers at Stephens. "Yard open in the morning. Why's it closed now?"

"Because I said so," Stephens said through thin white lips, a flush creeping up her neck.

Abby could see Quinn frowning at Stephens from his spot along the wall. She understood that COs would always back each other up, but Stephens was clearly in the wrong. She wondered when he was going to intervene.

Tiny's eyes went wide in mock surprise. "You said so? You did?"

Before Stephens could answer, Kendra, Kelsey, and a handful of Kelsey's girls walked up and stopped next to Tiny. Tobin had wandered in behind them and stood a short distance away, his hand on his pepper canister. So far none of the guards had thought to call the SRT.

"Hey," Kelsey called out, "why is the door to the yard locked? We want to go for a walk."

By now Stephens looked like she was ready to explode. "I'm going to say this one more time. THE YARD IS CLOSED!"

Ramirez and White had come in and positioned themselves along the perimeter of the common area. Their faces were a mixture of concern and fear. By this time, most of B Unit's inmates were either standing in the doorways to their suites or had joined the silent crowd standing in front of Stephens. It was an eerie sight, like standing in the eye of a very small hurricane. No one said a word, and every single woman stared at Stephens.

Abby watched Quinn pull his radio from his shoulder as a woman dressed in street clothes came in from the admin hallway to make her way through the crowd. Abby recognized her as one of the case managers, a woman named Ellen, whose office she cleaned every day. The director of security services followed her and stopped just outside the group of women. He looked surprised and a little alarmed to be in the middle of almost an entire unit of silent but angry inmates.

"Excuse me," Ellen called out as she reached the guard office. "Officer...?"

Stephens managed to look simultaneously angry and uncertain. "Officer Stephens."

"Officer Stephens, may I have a word with you in the office?" Ellen was firm but polite.

"I can hear you just fine out here," Stephens answered mulishly.

"I think it would be better if we stepped inside the office," Ellen insisted but Stephens wasn't budging.

"I said I can hear you."

Ellen regarded the woman with concern and a little irritation. "Fine then. Officer Stephens, why are the doors to the recreational yard locked?"

Stephens looked over at Quinn, as if seeking help, and then turned back to Ellen. "Yard privileges were...suspended...for disciplinary reasons."

"For whom?" Ellen asked.

Stephens looked again at Quinn who'd turned away. She was on her own.

"For...everyone," she stammered. Despite the number of inmates who'd crowded into the room, you could hear a pin drop. No one coughed or mumbled or even fidgeted. Everyone was dead still and dead silent, waiting to see Stephens hang herself.

Ellen looked around the room. "You're telling me that every single inmate in B Unit had their yard privileges suspended, but only for the afternoon for an undocumented rule infraction?"

Abby watched as Stephens struggled to find an answer that would make sense. The tension in the room was growing, and Abby knew it needed to be diffused quickly. She wasn't surprised to see the director move through the crowd to push Stephens through the door and into the guard office. Ellen and Quinn were right behind him.

Though they'd made their point, the ladies stayed put to bear witness to Stephens's temporary downfall. SRT had arrived but didn't know what to do with the group as the women stood silent and motionless.

With the door closed, no one could hear what was being said, but through the wide-open windows everyone could see both Ellen and the director reading Stephens the riot act. It looked like Stephens had nothing to say, but her face went alarmingly red as she stood there. Then the director opened the door and pointed toward the hall to the yard. Stephens exited the common area with her head down and stalked to the double doors with the director following her, and the large group of inmates following him.

Abby and Mad T smiled as Stephens was made to unlock the doors and step aside to allow the women to go outside. She turned to Mad T who had a satisfied smile on her face.

"That was genius," Abby told her friend.

Mad T snorted. "Go on, girl, before that bitch change her mind."

Abby jumped up and made her way through the onlookers to go out to the yard herself. She pulled herself up to her full height and looked down on Stephens, giving her a withering look. Humiliated and furious, Stephens kept her head down as long as the director stood next to her.

It was surprisingly warm outside and the ladies who braved the weather sat at the benches while D, Tiny, and the others decided their teams for basketball. Abby walked up to D.

"Thank you," she said and gave D a hug.

"Don't thank me," D joked. "Thank Mad T. I wanted to cut the bitch."

Abby laughed, but reluctantly. She knew D wasn't joking.

Chapter 33

PULLED UP

Stephens might have been foiled in her attempt to take away the yard, but she got her revenge in other ways, usually by venting her full rage on anyone who committed the least infraction. Fred and Kelsey got the worst of it. By the end of the day of "Doorgate" both were sent to DSEG for an extended period of time. Abby knew she wouldn't see them again before she left, which was just fine with her.

Everyone else was on their best behavior, which meant Stephens had to look hard for reasons to enact punishments. She was so harsh, even the other COs stayed away from her.

Abby opted to ignore her until even that wasn't possible. Stephens had maneuvered things so that she was escorting Sheronda and Abby to admin for cleaning crew. Tobin gave Abby an apologetic look then turned and followed the rest into the other wing.

Even though they'd never had a complaint about their work before, Stephens seized the opportunity to point out minute flaws in their work, forcing them to go over areas they'd already cleaned. Their job had already taken twice as long when she demanded they vacuum the entire floor again.

"Girl, there ain't nothin' left to suck up. We done clean the whole damn thing." Sheronda sighed, her voice betraying her exhaustion.

Stephens took a step toward Sheronda. "What did you just say?"

Sheronda looked at her like she was crazy. "I said there ain't nothin' left to clean and you can't keep tellin' us to clean somethin' that ain't dirty."

Stephens looked incredulous. "I can tell you to do whatever I want. And you're going to do it or I will make you do it!" Abby watched as Stephens put her hand on her pepper spray and unsnapped it.

Abby put herself between Sheronda and Stephens and looked down into the guard's face. "And I can tell Father Duncan how troubled I am that you forced your hands down my pants and molested me. And he'll go to my CM because she's a mandatory reporter. And she'll go to the warden. And I'll sit and cry in front of the warden because a guard raped me and I'm just...so.....ashamed."

Stephens stared up at Abby, stunned into silence. Abby stared back, her expression stony.

"You can't do that," she said with a sneer, but it was halfhearted. "Nobody would believe you."

Abby held her stare, waiting for the other woman to get it.

Stephens was spared from getting it when the other crew pulled up behind her.

"I'm not done with you," she growled through clenched teeth then turned and stalked back to the unit.

The next day went by without incident. With her parole hearing so close, Abby didn't want to inadvertently do or say anything to jeopardize it, so she kept out of sight as much as possible. Tobin made it difficult, taking every opportunity to chat with her. Abby tried to be polite, but more than anything she just wanted him to go away. It didn't help that every time Tobin walked up, Quinn would turn and stare. Sometimes she caught him staring at her when no one was near. During both instances, she gave him the back of her head to stare at.

Tobin was in the common room pestering her as usual, when dinnertime was called over the loudspeaker. She was grateful he left before she did so she could enjoy a few moments of blessed silence.

She waited for Sheronda at the door to their suite then the two women walked to the cafeteria.

Inside they grabbed their trays and made their way to their usual table. Abby was dismayed to see Stephens holding up the wall next to them, but she ignored her.

Mad T had already filled her tray. She was walking up with Tyana when Stephens stepped over to the table.

"You sit there," Stephens said to her pointing to the seat across from Abby.

Mad T stopped and stared at her as if she'd just grown another head.

182

"I love my girl, but I don't sit there," she replied then nodded to the table behind Abby. "I sit there."

"Well, now you sit there," Stephens kept her tone even but Abby knew better.

Mad T shook her head and spoke loudly enough that the other women in the room all turned to watch.

"You ain't tellin' me where to sit," Mad T warned.

"You think you can do whatever you want, don't you?" Stephens sneered. "You think you're a big shot convict. Like you've got any power here."

Mad T regarded the smaller woman. "You think we don't got power? We got our yard back didn't we?"

Stephens stared daggers at Mad T. "Who knew a gorilla could be so smart?"

Mad T's face went red as she threw down her tray, food splattering everywhere.

"The fuck you just say?" she yelled and moved toward the smaller woman. Abby jumped up and put herself between them. Her hands were on Mad T's shoulders

"Stop," Abby said quietly. "She isn't worth it."

"You heard me," Stephens said behind her.

Mad T surged forward. "Say it to my face."

Abby pushed back, putting all her slight weight against Mad T's considerable size. Luckily the food on the floor helped her effort as Mad T slid backward.

"Fucking gorilla," Stephens said quietly and the room erupted.

By now it seemed like everyone was shouting and alarms were blaring, but Abby was so focused on Mad T she couldn't see or hear anything else. She could only hear what sounded like a thousand voices punctuated by the peal of the siren under Mad T's shouts. Tobin and Ramirez had tried to move closer, but the crowd of women them blocked their path. Everyone was so angry at Stephens's oppressive rule; they were hungry to see some payback. Quinn ran in and tried to work his way along the wall behind Stephens, but he was jammed up there, too.

"Stand down." Abby heard someone shout.

"STAND DOWN!"

"I'm warning you. Stand down or I'm gonna make you stand down."

"WHAT? YOU GON MAKE ME? WHO GON CHECK ME, BITCH. HUH? WHO GON CHECK ME?" Mad T was shouting now, sending Abby's ears ringing.

Abby pushed Mad T back further and kept her voice soothing. "It's not worth it. Stop. It's not worth it."

Abby couldn't see, but Stephens had pulled out and opened her baton.

"WHAT THE FUCK YOU GON DO WIT DAT? HUH, BITCH? YOU GON HIT ME? I WILL FUCK YOU UP."

Despite Abby's efforts, Mad T lunged toward Stephens who took a batter's stance and swung hard, hitting Abby in the elbow. Abby cried out as her arm went numb and Stephens swung again, this time breaking her rib. As Abby slid to the floor, Stephens went for the home run, striking her in the head. Abby's world went dark.

Abby opened her eyes. The world was still a little bit blurry and she was confused at first. It didn't look like the cafeteria. When her vision cleared she realized she was in the exam room in the unit. The nurse who'd treated her burns stared down at her with a worried expression.

"How are you feeling?"

Abby shifted slightly, and then caught her breath as a bolt of pain shot up her side. Her shirt felt damp and her hair was sticking to her neck.

"Hurts...to breathe," she whispered. "Rib."

The nurse nodded. "I think it might be broken. The EMT's are coming to take you to the hospital for x-rays and a head CT."

"What happened?" Abby's memory was foggy. She remembered lots of yelling in the cafeteria...Mad T fighting with Stephens.

The nurse smiled. "Once again you were in the wrong place at the wrong time."

Abby closed her eyes as another wave of pain moved through her. She heard the nurse leave the room then return a moment later.

She opened her eyes and saw the EMTs rolling in a gurney. Through her pain she worried that they would ask her to stand, but instead they picked her up and placed her on the gurney without incident. She tried to look down, but she couldn't raise her head. At some point she'd been secured to a backboard. When they turned her, she saw blood covering the table she'd been lying on.

Abby closed her eyes and didn't open them again. She didn't see Quinn standing in the corner as they rolled her out.

Abby spent the night under observation at the local hospital. The nerve in her arm was damaged, but otherwise, her arm was fine. She did have one broken rib and a crack in another, as well as a serious concussion under an inch long head laceration. Once the hospital determined that she hadn't suffered any more serious head trauma, they sent her back to the prison heavily taped with a sling for her arm and five staples holding her scalp closed.

Abby was admitted to the infirmary for the duration of her recovery. For the first day, she did nothing but sleep in a fog of painkillers.

Several of the staff came to see her, but it wasn't until the next day that she awoke to see Paula sitting next to her. The lawyer from legal and the director of security were standing behind her.

"Hey there." Paula smiled. "How are you feeling?"

Abby shifted slightly. "Sore, but better."

Paula's smile was strained. "I've been waiting for your pain dosage to go down to get a statement from you. How much do you remember about what happened?"

"Pretty much everything until I got hit. It was Stephens who hit me, wasn't it?"

Paula nodded. "Your attorney has been informed of the incident. Officer Stephens has been placed under suspension pending the investigation. We've taken everyone else's statement, so yours is just a formality. You feel like giving it now?"

Abby nodded then gave her version of the events. Paula recorded it with a small digital video camera. When she was done, the lawyer put a paper in front of her to sign. Then he and the director left. Paula remained behind.

"What's going to happen?" she asked.

"I honestly don't know on this one," Paula admitted. "It will be up to the warden. I can tell you she's not in trouble for pulling her baton, but in serious trouble for beating you with it."

"Did Mad T get hit?" Abby asked out of curiosity.

Paula shook her head. "No, and that's where her troubles begin. Tanya Grant was the aggressor, but Officer Stephens struck you. On the tape it looks very personal."

"It was," Abby thought.

"Not to change the subject, but your parole hearing is tomorrow. Do you feel up to it? Or I can ask for a postponement if you're not."

Abby carefully shook her head. "No, I can go. I'm not in the best shape, but I can go."

Paula smiled. "Great. I'll be here tomorrow to pick you up. Get some rest."

Abby smiled then closed her eyes.

The next morning Abby was awake before her scheduled pain pill, which was a good sign. With the nurse's help, she was able to get cleaned up and wait for Paula. Since there was nothing wrong with her legs, Abby declined the offer of a wheelchair and left the infirmary with Paula on her own two feet.

She was less than happy to see Quinn waiting to escort them to the hearing room, but she couldn't do anything about it. She chose to take the high road and ignored him as she followed Paula.

It was a short walk as the hearing room was located in the section of the admin wing that Abby didn't clean. When they arrived, she was happy to see her attorney there. Jane, on the other hand, was shocked at Abby's appearance.

"What is this?" she demanded. "Why didn't anyone tell me the extent of her injuries? I was told she was 'accidently' struck during a fight. This is far worse than what was communicated to me yesterday. I want to know exactly what happened."

Abby decided that Quinn should be the one to explain what had happened. Paula seemed to feel the same way and gave him a pointed look.

Quinn looked uncomfortable. He cleared his throat and seemed to search for a reasonable explanation where there wasn't one. So he told the truth.

"She was assaulted while trying to defuse an altercation between an inmate and a guard."

"Who assaulted her?" Jane asked looking like *she* was about to assault someone.

Quinn glanced toward Abby and fell far short of meeting her eyes. "The guard involved in the altercation."

Jane stared at him then looked to Paula for some kind of clarification, but Paula refused to help Quinn out.

"And what is happening to the guard involved in the altercation?"

"It is currently under investigation," Quinn answered, his voice quiet.

"My ass 'under investigation,'" Jane muttered. "And who's going to explain this to the hearing examiner?" Jane indicated the bandages on Abby's head. "This is highly prejudicial. You're asking Abby to beg for parole looking like she's been in a fight."

Paula finally stepped up. "I have. It was made very clear to him when I presented the incident report."

"It had better be," Jane warned. "This smells like a huge civil lawsuit to me."

Both Quinn and Paula winced at that. Anyone could be named in a civil suit, including them. Behind them the door opened and a young woman Abby recognized as one of the administrative assistants poked her head out. She startled at the sight of Abby's bandages.

"Abby Blackwood?" she asked hesitantly. Abby nodded. "They're ready for you."

Abby followed the young woman through the door. Jane, Paula, and Quinn followed behind her.

The hearing examination room was slightly larger than a conference room. A long wooden table sat at the end of the room for the hearing examiner and any other representatives of the Prison Commission's office. There were chairs set up in front of the table for anyone speaking on behalf of or against the inmate, with a single chair behind a small wood table in the front row for the inmate. A large flat screen TV was located behind the table flanked by video cameras.

As Abby made her way to her chair, the assistant who'd brought them in sat at the end of the table in front of a laptop and an overhead projector to both run the video recording equipment and take notes. The hearing examiner, a largish man in his forties, and someone Abby assumed was a commission representative, an older man who looked like a high school principal, were already seated behind the table. Their nameplates identified them as George Heman, and Louis Baker respectively. They sat behind laptops, and were surrounded by papers.

The hearing examiner startled at the sight of Abby's appearance but said nothing.

When everyone was seated, he turned to the assistant and indicated that she begin recording. She flipped a switch on the console and a quiet hum filled the room.

The high school principal cleared his throat then looked up.

"Abigail Blackwood?" he asked.

"Yes, sir," Abby answered.

"And for the record, your Department of Corrections number is two eight seven two five six?"

"Yes, sir."

"I am Parole Commissioner Louis Baker and next to me is hearing representative, Mr. George Heman."

Abby smiled politely. "Good morning." Both men returned her smile politely before continuing.

"We are here today to hear your first request for parole for case number D 78503 for a single count sentence of sixty months for conspiracy to traffic one hundred kilos or less of marijuana. You are eligible for parole on the fourteenth of March two thousand fourteen, and your projected completion date is the first of April two thousand sixteen. Is that your understanding?"

"Yes, sir."

"About a month ago you received notice of this hearing and were advised of your rights by your case worker. Please review the document on the screen and verify your signature."

Abby glanced at the screen above them as it lit up with an enlarged view of her parole application.

"Yes, sir. That's my signature."

"Your acknowledgment indicates to our panel that you were appropriately notified of these proceedings. We will now continue. Is there a statement you would like to make to the panel today?"

"Yes, sir, thank you." Abby paused to collect her thoughts. Her brain was still fuzzy from the medication. "I arrived here at Maysville in May of two thousand thirteen after having spent eighteen months of my sentence at the Clark County Jail. I was incarcerated after pleading guilty to a conspiracy charge. My crime was that I agreed to introduce an undercover police officer to a drug dealer, knowing that he wanted to purchase marijuana. I didn't know that was a crime, but I broke the law and my punishment was deserved. During my time here I've tried to contribute to the success of not just my own incarceration, but that of my fellow inmates as well. Many of them are troubled, misunderstood women who need someone to guide them through the developmental stages they missed in childhood. I've grown to deeply respect the majority of the guard staff, and have made efforts to ensure that, at least as far as I'm concerned, their performance on the unit is successful, and that they are safe. I have spent as much time with Father Duncan as is allowed, asking God for strength during those times when it's difficult to be here. The rest of the time, when I wasn't teaching, I was running. It's a solitary activity that afforded me the opportunity to reflect on my time…and my purpose here."

"Thank you for your statement. We are now going to look at your risk assessment. It is a statistical instrument to determine your level of risk and potential for success. We will now go over it, factor by factor. OK?"

"Yes, sir."

"What was your age at the time of your arrest?"

"Twenty-two, sir."

"And you have no prior juvenile convictions?"

"No, sir."

"Your employment prior to incarceration was graduate student, graduated teaching assistant?"

"Yes, sir."

"What about alcohol or substance abuse? Was it a contributing factor in this offense?"

"No, sir. I was training for a marathon, so I avoided illegal substances and had only had less than two alcoholic drinks within the three hours prior to my arrest. It was my poor judgment that led to my crime."

"And you are currently twenty-five years of age?"

"Yes, sir."

"I'm going to assume no gang affiliations."

"No, sir."

"Have you completed any of the long-term prison programs?"

Abby was confused for a moment. "I participated in the group faith foundation program, and I continue to work with Father Duncan on an individual basis. I also taught the GED program and conducted foundation preparation for the restorative justice dialogue, victim impact, and commitment to change programs."

"For clarification, you completed them?" Both men frowned at the computer monitors in front of them.

"No, sir. I served as the institutional instructor for them."

Mr. Baker looked at her over his reading glasses. "You were the instructor?"

"Yes, sir."

Abby waited as they made notes on the tablets in front of them.

"It is the expectation of the board that you have received no disciplinary write-ups and the board appreciates that you do not have any disciplinary write-ups at this time. You are currently assigned to B Unit at the medium security level. Your score is a three, which is a low risk score that, combined with your offense, necessitates the consideration of factors. Your aggravating factor is your known association with the illegal drug trade minus victim impact, minus financial impact. Your mitigating factors are that you have a single sentence with good time credit earned and you have no conviction history. So if we were to parole you, what is your living and employment plan?"

Jane stood up at that point. "May I make a statement as to Miss Blackwood's plan?"

Louis Baker waved Jane forward.

"Please state your name and relationship to Miss Blackwood."

Jane moved up next to Abby. "Jane Howerton. I'm the legal counsel for Miss Blackwood."

"And you have Miss Blackwood's living plan?"

"Yes, sir. I have an employment agreement from St. Mary's Episcopal Church in Grayson. Miss Blackwood has been offered a position as sexton, which also provides a living situation on the campus of the church. Her supervisor will be the head rector, the Reverend Dorothy Buckman." Jane approached the assistant and handed her a copy of the employment agreement.

"Thank you, Miss Howerton."

Jane nodded and sat down.

This time it was the hearing officer, George Heman, who spoke.

"At this time we would like to hear about your work assignment. What contribution did you make during the time you've been here?"

"Other than my work as an instructional leader, which was not a paid position, I also worked on the cleaning crew. I had a daily assignment to clean the executive offices here. I also accepted a nonpaying assignment from Captain Dennis to sweep the floors of the unit."

George Heman smiled at her. "Thank you, Miss Blackwood."

Louis Baker resumed the hearing. "At this time, Miss Blackwood, we will introduce your letters of support. Only two are required, however your case manager has submitted several. They are from the Reverend John Abbot, Mrs. Margaret Abbot, Deputy Mark Stone, Father Miles Duncan, and several of our own correctional officers. I have letters from Captain Dennis, Captain Hannah, Sergeant Redfern, and Captain Quinn here."

"Yes, sir."

"Is there anything else you would like to say today?"

"No, sir. I don't want to take up any more of your time."

Abby sat politely as the two men tapped on their computers. It was only a handful of minutes but felt like hours.

"Miss Blackwood, you have met the requirements for good conduct, and it is the recommendation of Mr. Heman and myself that you be granted parole. Our recommendation will go before the Parole Commission for consideration and the final decision will be forwarded to your case manager. Your pending release date is the seventeenth of March of this year. Congratulations, young lady."

Abby's smile was huge and genuine. "Thank you so much."

"You are most welcome, and the best of luck to you."

Abby turned and hugged Jane, and then Paula. They were more than thrilled for her. Quinn stood up, and for a moment, Abby thought he too was going to hug her. Instead he opened the door leading to the hallway and pulled in a wheelchair. Abby sank into it gratefully and let him push her into the hallway.

Jane's smiles turned serious as soon as the door closed behind them.

"So what happens next in the investigation on Abby's assault?"

Quinn had the good grace to look uncomfortable. "She's to meet with the warden on Monday."

"I'm going to be there," Jane said. It wasn't a request.

Quinn nodded then moved to push Abby down the hall. Paula and Jane followed until they reached the entrance to the executive suite.

Paula turned to Jane. "If you'll come with me, I'll get the paperwork in for your visit Monday."

Jane nodded then turned to Abby. "I'll see you then, OK?"

Abby was exhausted, so she simply nodded. She closed her eyes and prayed for a pain pill as Quinn silently pushed her back to the infirmary.

At the end of the short trip, Abby opened her eyes to find they'd stopped just short of the infirmary doors. Quinn came around and stood in front of Abby, his expression unreadable. Abby kept her silence as she watched him struggle with his words.

"I'm glad they're recommending you for parole," he began then paused.

Abby stared at him, her chest filled with pain as her heart split in two. "I'm sure you are. Now you can go find another fuck buddy for your girlfriend to beat up."

Quinn winced at that. Abby suddenly realized she had hit him close to home. Her face burned with rage and humiliation.

"It's not like that," Quinn stammered. "I never expected…and when she told me about you and Tobin—"

"Me and Tobin what?" Abby demanded.

Quinn looked uncertain for a second then shook his head. "Nevermind. It's none of my business. I really just wanted to ask you if you're OK."

"No, I'm not OK. I have an arm that won't work, broken ribs that make it impossible to breathe, and a literally splitting headache."

Quinn blushed a furious red. "No, I understand that. I mean if you're OK since the last time…when we…when the…"

"Are you fucking kidding me?" Abby thought, and then in her haste practically fell out of the wheelchair trying to get away from him. She regained her feet as Quinn reached out to steady her. Abby pulled her hand away, knowing if he touched her she'd completely fall apart.

"Don't worry about it," she said, on the verge of tears, "That part of me never worked normally. In three weeks your little mistake will be long gone."

Quinn moved to speak again, but Abby was done. She pushed past him into the infirmary and let the door slam behind her.

Chapter 34

OUT OF POCKET

Abby spent the weekend working through her feelings for Quinn. By Monday she'd resolved to cut out that part of her heart that wouldn't let him go. She was tired of thinking about it, and she was relieved when Paula finally came to get her for her meeting with the warden. Abby eschewed the wheelchair, choosing to walk. She didn't want anyone to see her weakness. This time Big Ginger escorted them to the admin wing. Abby gave her a genuine smile.

"Congrats on the parole decision!" Big Ginger beamed. "I'd hug you, but I don't know which part of you doesn't hurt."

Abby laughed carefully. "All of me hurts."

Big Ginger's smile turned sober. "I'm so sorry about what happened to you. I just can't wrap my brain around it."

"Thanks, but it's not like there was anything you could do about it."

"Still…" Big Ginger shook her head. "Well, let's get you going."

Abby moved slowly but managed to get to admin without incident. Big Ginger led them to the conference room attached to the warden's office. Abby wondered about it until they entered and she saw the sheer number of people in there. Besides Warden Abellard and her ever-present legal counsel, there was Jane, Quinn, the director of security, Stephens and a handful of people Abby didn't recognize. Some were in the black uniforms of the prison's SRT team. Most were seated on the far side of the conference table with the warden seated in the center and the uniforms standing behind them. Only Jane and Abby sat on the other side. Quinn stood in the corner. Paula moved along the wall to stand next to him. Big Ginger remained standing behind Abby.

Jane pulled out a chair for Abby and helped her into it, more for show than anything else.

"Well, Miss Blackwood, we meet again," Warden Abellard said by way of greeting. Abby smiled ruefully but politely and the warden continued. "The purpose of this meeting today is to resolve the matters surrounding the events of February eighteenth of this year. I understand your attorney, Miss Howerton, is present today?"

"Yes, ma'am," Abby replied.

"And I understand Miss Howerton has a request for us?" The warden did not look happy.

Jane leveled a look at the warden. "I believe it's only fair that Miss Blackwood be permitted to view the video footage of the assault by Officer Stephens. We respectfully request that it be provided prior to any decision made today."

Abby was taken aback. She wasn't sure she really wanted to see it.

Warden Abellard shook her head. "I'm sorry, but the video footage is considered evidence and is not available for public viewing."

"So, if I'm to understand you correctly, you are denying the right of my client and I to review evidence submitted on her behalf?"

"Correct."

Jane pulled open her briefcase and pulled out an envelope. "I have a subpoena from Judge Horner ordering the immediate release of any and all items of evidentiary value to the case against Officer Victoria Stephens for the assault on my client, Abigail Blackwood, which may directly or indirectly impact the content of her victim's impact statement."

Jane slid the paperwork across the table. Warden Abellard accepted it reluctantly. Her lips were pressed into a thin line. She had been royally trumped. It took a couple of minutes for the warden and the prison's lawyer to review the subpoena. The lawyer nodded slightly then the warden gestured to one of the women seated in the corner. She turned and activated the video equipment mounted on the wall. Everyone turned to watch.

The screen showed snow at first but then an overhead view of the cafeteria popped into view. The picture quality was very good but the sound was less so. The video began with the view of Abby sitting down at the table with Sheronda. It was pretty much as Abby remembered it: Mad T entering the picture with her tray, Stephens pointing to the table, the beginning of their argument when Mad T slammed her food tray on the floor. Abby watched herself jump up to prevent Mad T from assaulting Stephens. She saw Stephens pulling her baton from her belt. The audio picked up the shouting and caught Mad T's words perfectly. Then Mad T lunged and Stephens started swinging.

Abby's face was stony as she watched Stephens hit her as she went down. It was clear that Stephens never intended to hit Mad T who was still standing despite trying to catch Abby as she fell. After the third strike, Stephens had raised the baton over her head to hit the an unconscious Abby a fourth time when the screen showed Quinn shoving inmates aside to throw himself in front of Abby as Tobin grabbed Stephens in a full nelson wrestling hold, forcing her to drop the baton. Tobin dragged Stephens off camera as Quinn turned to examine Abby. Everyone watched as he turned her head to one side to view the damage to her scalp, which had started bleeding profusely, and then gently pulled her arms across her chest as Ramirez came into view with a backboard. As Ramirez turned away and tried to move the inmates back, Quinn gently put his arms under Abby and lifted her into his arms. There were too many inmates to put her safely on the backboard, so Quinn stood and carried Abby out of view of the camera.

Then the screen went blank.

"Jesus Christ," Jane muttered under her breath.

Abby's eyes were hot with tears or anger. She didn't know or care. She turned back to face the warden fully.

"We seem to spend an inordinate amount of time apologizing to you," the warden said, having the good grace not to smile. "On behalf of this institution, I am deeply, deeply sorry."

"Thank you," Abby responded quietly. She didn't trust herself to say anything more.

"Officer Stephens is also here to offer an official apology." During the video Stephens had kept her head down and stared sullenly at the table in front of her. At the warden's words she looked up and stared at Abby, whether in anger or regret, Abby couldn't tell and didn't care.

"I mean no disrespect to you, Warden, but I will not accept an apology from Officer Stephens because I know it is not sincere. Given her conduct and her inability to understand her shortcomings as a human being, I strongly suspect at some point she'll be in here, and not as a guard. Any apology would be completely meaningless." Abby stared at Stephens as she spoke. The other woman glared daggers at her, not realizing that the warden was looking at her.

Warden Abellard cleared her throat then turned to Abby.

"Given the severity of the assault and the video evidence to support that you were beaten despite not having been the aggressor, it is the decision of this institution to charge Officer Stephens with federal civil rights offenses, aggravated battery, and violating her oath of office. Do you support these charges?"

Abby stared at Stephens. "Yes."

"Very well." The warden turned back to address the uniform behind her. "Please return Miss Stephens to custody." Abby noticed the warden had already dropped 'officer' from Stephens's name.

The warden looked tired when she turned back to Abby.

"Again, I am very sorry, Abby. I understand why you won't accept an apology from Miss Stephens, but I hope that you will accept mine."

Abby nodded. "Yes, ma'am."

"Thank you. Now we have another item to discuss. I have made my recommendation to the Parole Commission, and the decision has been handed down to approve your parole request."

Abby was not surprised. "Thank you, ma'am."

"Also, your release date has been expedited. You will be released on March fifth."

That surprised her. In a little more than a week, Abby would be leaving Maysville forever.

"Thank you, ma'am. Thank you so much." Her gratitude was heartfelt.

"You're welcome, Abby." Warden Abellard gave Abby a tired smile. "If there isn't anything further, you are free to go."

"No, ma'am, there's nothing else. Thank you again."

Jane helped Abby up, and a beaming Big Ginger opened the door for them. Paula walked up and the women left together.

Just outside the door, Abby gave the women careful hugs all around.

"Congratulations, Abby," Paula said as she gently put her arms around Abby. "I'm so happy for you."

Jane smiled and took her turn. "I'll be here on the fifth to pick you up. St. Mary's wasn't expecting you so early, but I'm sure they'll be happy to have you."

"Thank you for setting all of this up. I don't know what I would have done otherwise."

"Well, don't be too impressed. I had help from Father Duncan and Father Abbot. Apparently, Reverend Buckman went to seminary with them, and is a staunch women's rights activist. We lucked out."

Abby laughed then waved as Big Ginger led her back to the infirmary.

Chapter 35

SWINGING ON MY NUTS

Abby spent one more day in the infirmary so the visiting doctor could check her over before releasing her. She still hurt, but she only needed to rest and heal at that point. The doctor declared her fit enough to return to her unit, but excused her from her work assignment for the remainder of her time at Maysville. Abby thanked him then went back to her friends.

She was glad that she was spending her last week in the suite. It gave her a chance to say goodbye to the people who mattered to her the most.

It felt good to see everyone's faces light up when she walked in the door. Marianna slid down from her bed as Sheronda and Mad T carefully hugged her. Then Marianna helped Abby to her bunk, pulling one of the short storage lockers over so Abby could get up there and rest.

While still in the infirmary, Abby had transferred the bulk of her book to Sheronda who had used part of it to buy food so that Abby wouldn't have to travel back and forth to the cafeteria. She was grateful when Sheronda passed a bowl of soup up to her, and pleased that it wasn't horrible.

After giving them a brief rundown of the last few days, the women left so that Abby could rest.

An urgent need to pee woke Abby up. She looked around, confused and disoriented. The suite was empty as was the common area. A glance at the guard office revealed Ramirez behind the computer, which meant she'd slept through the shift change. Everyone must have been at dinner.

With great effort, Abby pushed herself up and stared down at the floor. There was no way she was going to be able to get down without help. She looked out the door again, hoping someone might have come back who could help her or at least find someone to help her. There was no way Ramirez would be able to hear her through the glass.

Her need to pee was growing dire, so Abby decided to try to get down by herself. She dangled her legs off the side of the bunk and tried to slide on her right side to protect her broken ribs, but she panicked and rolled onto her stomach. The pain was so intense she worried she might have reinjured herself. She quickly rolled back onto her uninjured side. She didn't realize she'd cried out until Tobin appeared in the doorway.

"Oh my God, Abby." Tobin rushed over and picked her up off the bunk then set her on the floor. "Are you all right?"

Abby sank to her knees and shook her head, unable to talk through the pain.

"Do you need medical?" He asked as he helped her onto Sheronda's bunk.

Abby nodded, more out of need to get rid of him than anything else. Abby pushed herself up as Tobin rushed from the suit. She put her feet on the floor and carefully pulled herself to standing with her good arm. As she regained her feet, she saw Quinn framed in the doorway.

She moved slowly through the door, stumbling a bit as she passed him. Quinn put his hand out to steady her, but Abby slapped it away.

"Abby—"

"Get away from me," she snapped then slowly hobbled to the community lavatory. Even though they had a commode in the suite, it was mostly exposed, and the last thing she was going to do was pee in front of him.

Abby had cleaned herself up as best she could when Sarah, the infirmary nurse, appeared in the entryway to the showers.

"Are you OK, Abby? Officer Tobin told me he thinks you've reinjured yourself trying to get out of bed."

Abby shook her head. "I compressed it slightly sliding out of my bunk, but I think I'm fine. I can breathe freely and it doesn't hurt to cough."

"I brought you some ibuprofen. You haven't had any today, have you?"

Abby shook her head and accepted the small red pills. Sarah had even thought to bring a cup so she wouldn't have to take them dry.

"Thank you."

Sarah smiled and shook her head. "Let's get you back to your suite and see if we can come up with a better plan."

Abby had lied about the pain and did need Sarah's help back through the unit. They came up on the ladies returning from dinner and Mad T was less than pleased that Abby was hurting.

"You gon take my bunk and Sheronda gon go up in yours till you go home," she decided. Sarah thought that was an excellent idea and the two women got Abby back to the suite. Mad T had sent Tyana and D ahead to change the sheets and get her space cleaned up. They were done by the time they got there, and Abby gratefully sank onto the bottom bunk, warning the women that she might not be able to get back up again.

Marianna snorted. "You ain't weigh but nothin'. I can get you up."

"And if she can't then I can," D offered.

"I'm glad you have so much help," Sarah said as she checked Abby's bandages. "I'll be back in the morning with more meds, OK?"

Abby nodded then thanked her. Sarah gave her a gentle smile then left the suite.

The ladies were making adjustments to accommodate Abby's injuries when Quinn appeared in the doorway. He held a stepladder that had more than likely come off one of the cleaning carts.

"We done moved Abby to the bottom," Mad T told him, but Sheronda interrupted.

"Yeah, but if I'm bein' on the top I'm gonna need that." Sheronda marched over and took the stepladder out of Quinn's hands. "Thank you, sir."

Quinn nodded then glanced back at Abby as he left.

Sheronda opened the stepladder and used it to climb up into Abby's old bunk. Tyana sat at the end of Mad T's bunk as D took a seat at the end of Abby's.

"Damn girl, what you do to that boy?" Sheronda asked as she settled in. "He be mopin' round here like you die or somethin'. Boy be missing his girlfriend."

Abby shook her head. "Stephens was his girlfriend, not me. He's probably upset that she's gone."

Mad T snorted. "Him and that bitch? Maybe a million years ago."

"They be a thing when I first got here," D said. "But when she was in D Unit, she be messin' with one of the other COs in there and Quinn find out. They get into a fight in the guard office there and then Quinn transfer here to B Unit."

Mad T nodded. "Then he get married. Then he meet you. That Stephens bitch ain't got nothin' on you. Plus that bitch lie like anything. She make shit up just to fuck with people."

"Well, she's gone now, too, so he can go find someone else. Maybe she'll give him little Asian babies." Abby knew it was mean but he deserved it.

As the other women chuckled, Tobin appeared in the doorway. The women stopped and stared.

"It's time for count," he announced to the room. "Abby, you're excused from count if you stay in here."

Abby shook her head. "I can get up."

D jumped up, and with no effort, lifted Abby to her feet. Abby shuffled to the door, surfing the furniture on the way out. D was right behind her in case she fell.

D had to go back to her own suite, so Abby leaned against the wall. She regretted not taking up Tobin's offer to stay in her bunk. Mad T did her best to keep Abby up, but she wouldn't be able to do it much longer if there was a toss. Quinn seemed to have the same worry, so since all of the chairs in the unit were fixed, he brought out a desk chair from the guard office and rolled it over. Abby sank into it gratefully, though her thanks was grudging.

"Next time, stay in your bunk," he said. Abby stared after him then looked away when he turned around.

The count was completed without incident, so Mad T rolled Abby back into the suite and Marianna helped her into her bunk. Sheronda gave her one of her books, but between the pain of her injury and the stress of being back in the unit and unable to care for herself, it was too much. Abby soon fell asleep.

She awoke the next morning feeling much better. As the doors unlocked, Big Ginger stepped in with four more ibuprofen and a cup of water.

"Sarah said to give this to you before you try to get up," she said as she handed them over to Abby. "She also said you need to eat right away so they don't upset your stomach…but you probably already knew that."

Abby smiled and nodded. "Thank you." She took the pills and drank the water. Big Ginger put her hand down and helped Abby up. It didn't hurt as much to move, so Abby was hopeful the day would go better than the day before.

"You going to be OK for now?" Big Ginger asked. Abby nodded. "Call out if you need me, OK? I'll be nearby."

"Thanks," Abby said then her smile faltered as Big Ginger left the suite.

"They's a lot of people you gon miss, ain't there?" Mad T said from her bunk.

Abby nodded then shuffled off to the bathroom.

The rest of the day and the days that followed were bittersweet for Abby. With no classes to teach or cleaning crew to report to, Abby sat in the common area and watched the ebb and flow of day-to-day life in B Unit. She spent most of her time on a pillow in the common area, enjoying the opportunity to be still. She was surprised that she wasn't chomping at the bit to go out for a run, but she figured it was her body's way of telling her it still needed to heal. When she felt up to it, D walked with her outside, though nowhere near the distance she could cover when she was able bodied. When she wasn't up to going outside, D and the other members of Mad T's family sat with her and taught her the meanings of urban slang and gang signs. They would laugh as Abby's fingers twisted into pretzels trying to copy them. To them there was nothing funnier than a preppy white girl flashing gang signs.

"This is the only one I know," Abby joked as she held up the sign for "I love you" then laughed as they tried to "gangify" it.

"What is it?" Tyana asked.

"It's sign language. It means 'I love you.'" Abby smiled.

Tyana stared at her hand in wonder. "Y'all think that maybe deaf people really ain't talkin' but be like one really big gang?" D, Tiny, and the others all stared at her then everyone fell over each other laughing. Abby glanced up and caught Quinn smiling at them. She turned away quickly before her heart could remind her of his betrayal.

When all the women left for their various jobs around the prison, Paula came by with Abby's formal parole paperwork for her to sign and instructions on her release. Paul vowed to return on Abby's release date. Sarah stopped by to check on her, and Abby was happy to report that she no longer needed the meds to bear the pain.

The only downside to being so sedentary was it afforded Tobin the opportunity to pester her more than ever. When she could walk unassisted, Abby took to her bunk whenever he appeared.

Even Sheronda was irritated. She had brought Abby some dinner when Tobin walked up and started chatting.

"Boy, ain't you got guardin' to do?" she interrupted. Tobin looked surprised but took the hint and wandered away.

"Man, he get on my nerves sometimes," Sheronda muttered.

Abby nodded then made her way into the suite to rest.

Later, Abby awoke to Tobin talking to Sheronda. She had missed the first part of their conversation, but caught the rest as he finished his sentence.

"…and I feel like I either made her mad or offended her in some way."

"Boy, I ain't yer motherfuckin' therapist. What's wrong with you? You a *guard*, you ain't her boyfrien'. You wanna fuck her? You gon get fired…or worse you go to jail. You feelin' me?"

"I don't want to fu…I mean have sex with her. I mean I do…eventually, when she doesn't have to be in here anymore. I just want her to care about me the way I care about her."

"Boy…the girl is in *PRISON*. You get that? This ain't no dating game. What the fuck's wrong with you?"

"I'm not trying to be her boyfriend. Not now. I just don't want her to be mad at me. You're her friend. Could you ask her?"

"Ask her what?"

"Ask her if she might eventually care about me."

"Oh Lord." Abby could hear the frustration in Sheronda's voice. "Boy, I'm gonna tell it to you straight. She don't care about you. Not like that. She a good person and she care if you live or die, but she ain't gonna love you like you her man."

Abby waited out the pause, hopeful that she'd finally be free of Tobin's attention.

"But could you ask her?"

Abby waited out another long pause. She could picture Sheronda's expression of exasperation.

Sheronda caved. "Oh, fine. I'll ask her," she surrendered then stalked into the suite and climbed up into Abby's old bunk.

"Something you need to ask me?" Abby called up quietly.

Sheronda turned and glared at her. "No." Then her face softened. "That boy got it bad, but he ain't the right boy for you. He jus' a boy an' you need a man. Quinn was spose to be that man an' he gone an' fucked it up. Now he sad and you sad and ain't nothin' I can do to fix it."

"It's not your responsibility to fix this," Abby replied. "If this is what Quinn wanted then all he needed to do was say so. But he couldn't, or more likely didn't want to."

Sheronda shook her head. "That boy love you. He get poisoned somehow, but he still love you. You so busy turnin' away when he look at you that you can't see it. He die a lil' bit ever time you walk away."

Abby didn't know what to say. Her heart hurt too much to say anything.

Chapter 36

SPRUNG

Finally, it was the morning of Abby's release. Big Ginger had advised her to pack early so that she wouldn't be rushing on release day, but Abby knew she wouldn't be taking much home, or wherever she was going. Big Ginger handed her a pair of gray sweatpants that were standard issue on release, and Abby wore her own gray hoodie. The blue scrubs would be staying at the prison. She no longer needed her arm sling, so it would stay as well.

Her blue duffel was large enough to hold everything she wanted to keep. She put in the clothes she wouldn't need, her pedometer and running shoes, the things that Sylvia had knitted for her, the La Santa Muerte statue, and the books she'd brought with her. She left the mysteriously appearing books and CDs in her locker knowing the anonymous donor would retrieve them after she left. Or if Quinn hadn't left them, someone else could use them.

She gave her CD player and headphones to Marianna and made sure Sheronda understood that the fridge and hot plate were hers to keep. The only things she wanted other than what she had packed were hanging over her bunk. Marianna and Sheronda carefully took down the pictures and drawings and placed them in a large yellow envelope Paula had donated.

Mad T moved her things back to her original bunk and Sheronda moved back down.

When everything was packed, they looked around the suite. Abby's bunk was a bare mattress next to a bare wall. The suite looked as it had when Abby walked in for the first time. She was surprised that she was going to miss it. But as she looked at the women gathered around her, she realized why. Big Ginger had appeared in the doorway, indicating that it was time to go. Marianna stepped up and gave Abby a warm hug, then Mad T, and then Rita and Rosita. Sheronda moved to Abby last and wrapped her arms around her waist.

"You is the best white girl I ever knew," she said quietly. "You is my best frien'."

The tears that had been threatening started to fall down Abby's cheeks. "You're my best friend, too, Sheronda," she said quietly, hoping Sheronda could hear the love in her heart. "And you always will be."

Sheronda pushed away. She wiped her eyes and nodded at Big Ginger. "You better go on, girl, 'fore they change they minds."

Abby laughed and wiped her cheeks. She picked up her duffel and followed Big Ginger out.

As they made their way through the unit, Abby stopped as several more women wanted to say goodbye. Kendra gave her a warm hug then passed her on to several of the ladies Abby taught in her classes. They were followed by Sylvia and the knitting ladies, and then the majority of Mad T's family who'd grown to become her family too. Tiny hugged her a little too hard, making Abby wince. D punched Tiny then showed her how to hug gently. The ladies stood and waved as Abby followed Big Ginger down the last hallway.

She was surprised to see Captain Dennis waiting at the main exit to the unit. He held out his arms and Abby gladly walked into them.

"You're a good girl," he said quietly. "You go on and be a good girl out there. OK, Chief?"

Abby laughed and nodded. Captain Dennis gave her a rare smile then let her go.

Big Ginger led Abby back the way she'd come almost two years ago and they ended where she began. The hallway for release ran alongside the intake center but was much smaller. Big Ginger handed her over to Hamilton but waited as was required by the prison. Hamilton beamed when she saw it was Abby.

"I always wonder when we do releases if I'm going to be seeing the prisoner back in here, but I *know* this is the last we'll be seeing of you!"

Abby laughed then stepped aside as Paula walked up to hand over her paperwork. Hamilton paged through the papers and signed each one as verified. Then she escorted Abby into a small room to take her photograph and do a cursory body inspection. It was quick since they were less concerned about what left the prison than with what might be brought in.

"Sorry, but I've got to ask you to pee in a cup," Hamilton apologized then gave the speech as she pulled on her gloves. "It is an institutional requirement that you are to be given a mandatory urine test to determine the presence of illegal substances. If your test results are negative then you may proceed with your release. However, if your test results are positive, your release will be canceled and you will be remanded to Administrative Segregation for the duration of the investigation and pending charges. Your parole offer will be revoked. Do you understand?"

"Yes, ma'am," Abby said seriously then smiled as she took the cup.

There was an exposed commode in the corner. Abby was required to urinate in full view of the guard. It wasn't the first time, but Abby still felt weird. Hamilton tried to lighten the mood by thanking her for the "hers" and "hers" pillowcases she'd given them. She told Abby they'd inspired her to put "hers" on everything.

"It gets really confusing when people come over and they see salt and pepper shakers with 'hers' on them." Hamilton joked as Big Ginger shook her head behind her.

Abby laughed then cleaned herself up and handed over the cup. As expected the test was negative.

When that was done, Abby was led to the window that accessed the storage room for inmates' personal property. She pushed her forms through and the guard on the other side went in search of her bin. He returned in just a few minutes. He pulled each item out and checked it off the list. Other than the clothes she'd brought in after her father's funeral, there were a few items that did not make it through inspection. Jane had sent her iPod, the shampoo that she preferred to use, and a pair of spiked running shoes for use on snow and ice that had been in her closet. Jane must have sent them not realizing they wouldn't be allowed. Abby signed the property release form and placed the items in her duffel. Since she'd transferred most of the money on her book to Sheronda, the guard handed her a balance of $35 and another $200 in "gate money."

Paula stepped up and gave her a warm hug then Hamilton took her turn. Abby's tears returned as Big Ginger enveloped her.

"I'm really going to miss you," Big Ginger said. Abby nodded, unable to speak. "Promise me you'll keep in touch, OK?" Abby nodded again and smiled as Big Ginger let her go and turned to unlock the last door.

She was finally done. Abby said one last goodbye then stepped out into the sunlight.

She could feel the weight of the prison lifting from her. She'd made lifelong friends, loved a man with an intensity she'd never felt before, lost that man, and still managed to hold on to most of her heart. She'd been hurt badly and had hurt others badly. And she'd survived.

Abby walked to where Jane waited just outside the perimeter fence. She heard a shout from the far end of the building and saw her friends standing at the interior perimeter fence. Sheronda was dwarfed by Mad T, D, Tiny, and all the others who began to cheer as Abby made her way to the last fence. They were waving, and when Abby looked closer she realized they were all signing, "I love you." She paused and signed back to them. Then with tears streaming down her face, Abby stepped through the last gate.

She was officially free.

At the end of an unused hallway, Quinn stood at a window quilted with wire. His face was a mask of desolation as he watched Abby drive away. His fingers pressed to the glass, signing with the rest of them.

Chapter 37

SOMEWHERE HOME

Jane drove Abby's car a short distance to a motel that catered to families visiting the prison. Abby took Jane's room key and went inside to change into civilian clothes then met Jane outside. Jane handed her the keys to the car. Abby stashed her duffel and pulled out the old, gray Longchamp bag she'd been using for a purse before her arrest. Together they walked the short distance to the motel's office so Jane could check out, and then they went over to a small diner that attached to the motel.

There was only one patron seated at the counter, so Jane and Abby had their pick of seats. A pleasingly plump waitress brought them coffee then left them alone so they could talk.

"Thank you for bringing my car," Abby said. "But how are you going to get back to Springfield?"

Jane waved her thanks away. "Don't worry about it. You're going to need a car where you're going and my boyfriend took time off from his fellowship so he could drive behind me." Jane nodded toward the young man seated at the counter. He waved without turning around. Abby smiled and Jane chuckled. "He's good about client confidentiality."

Jane pulled a pack of papers from her briefcase and sorted through them. "You have your first meeting with the adult probation officer on Monday at 11:00 a.m. His office is in Medford, so you won't have too far to go. Here's the information and directions from the church. Be prepared to take a drug test. He may ask for one then, or anytime really. You'll need to have your parole paperwork, proof of your residence at the church, a paystub, and your ID with you at all your visits after your initial meeting. Also, know that your probation officer can show up anywhere at any time if he so chooses."

Abby accepted the papers, and then set them to one side knowing there would be more.

"Your probation officer will tell you at that first meeting how often he'll expect to see you. Since you are low risk, it'll probably be biweekly or even monthly. That will continue until the end of your original sentence. In a few months I'll petition the court to have the remainder of your sentence discharged, and we'll see if we can't shorten that time considerably. Then we can try to have your record expunged altogether."

Abby nodded.

"I have an accounting of the distribution of your father's estate and the monies spent during your incarceration. You didn't ask for much, so the money he put aside is pretty much intact—"

"What about your fee?" Abby interrupted.

Jane shook her head. "Your dad paid me a considerable retainer that was to last through the end of your release date in two thousand sixteen. You'll be getting a good portion of that back."

This time Abby shook her head. "Not now and maybe not ever. You've already done so much for me. It feels good to know you've got my back."

Jane smiled. "How about we revisit the issue in a few months?"

Abby returned her smile. "Agreed."

Jane pulled over another set of papers. "Going back to the accounting...I have good news to report. Once your father's estate was probated and some of the contents sold, you were left with a very nice nest egg of $327,600.00."

"Oh my gosh," Abby was shocked. "I didn't think there would be anything."

Jane smiled. "Well the Abbots were certainly looking out for you. Two of the books from your dad's collection were signed first editions. One sold for $15,000 and the other for $30,000. And even though your mom didn't exactly go crazy with decorating, that giant black cabinet with the cracked finish sold for $165,000."

"That's insane," Abby remarked. "That thing was so ugly."

Jane nodded. "Uh huh. Ugly and valuable. Apparently it was built in the late eighteen century, and since it had never been refinished it was worth a fortune. Congratulations."

Jane pushed over the accounting paperwork. "Everything has been deposited into the trust. This way, if anyone wants to sue you for anything, like that Dana girl's family, you personally are outside judgment. They can't touch the trust at all. I do need you to go to the bank and set up your account access. You have an appointment with the Medford location's bank manager on Monday also, but you can go any time before 5:00 p.m. I'm still listed as the trust administrator, but I'm not going to object to anything you do with the money since all of it is yours. I put $500 into the wallet in your purse, so you're good to go for a little while. You also have a debit card that draws from the trust. Just use it like a credit card if you need to buy anything." Jane passed over the debit card across the table.

"Finally, I took the liberty of buying you a new GPS. Yours crapped out on the way here and you're going to need it to get to Grayson."

Abby looked up. "You're not going with me to the church?"

Jane smiled and shook her head. "Father Duncan will meet you there. They don't expect you until late this afternoon, so you have plenty of time. You drive right through the city so you can even stop at the mall downtown and buy yourself some new clothes. I'm warning you, though; your trunk is packed with stuff Margaret Abbot thought you might still want."

Abby's thanks were heartfelt. "You've done so much for me. I really appreciate all of it."

Jane took Abby's hand. "You got a raw deal. Your life should be something entirely different right now. I just want to help you get it back on track."

"I really appreciate that," Abby said.

"You're more than welcome." Jane replied then stood and pulled her briefcase on. Abby grabbed her paperwork and zipped it up.

After a quick introduction to Jane's boyfriend, Matt, the two women parted ways.

Abby got into her car and took a few minutes to program the church address into the unfamiliar GPS, and then pulled out of the motel parking lot and drove off. She only got as far as a small gas station that served as the last stop before the highway that ran alongside of it. Abby pulled her car into a spot farthest away from the building and stared at the cars speeding down the highway in front of her. She was suddenly afraid to go any further.

Intellectually she knew she was feeling the effects of institutional syndrome: her emotional need for control and institutional hypervigilance were at war with her newfound freedom. She sat and waited for the shaking to abate. Abby didn't trust herself behind the wheel until she was calm again.

She startled as someone tapped on her window. Abby looked over and saw an older man in a sheriff's uniform leaning over and looking into her window.

Abby pushed the button and smiled wanly as the window went down.

"You OK, miss?" he asked, not unkindly. She knew she looked benign. After all, she was a white, attractive girl in a newer, well-kept BMW.

She nodded. "Just feeling a little bit sick is all."

The sheriff tilted his head toward the service station. "They got fountain drinks inside," he offered. "You should get yourself something to settle your stomach."

Abby smiled and nodded then rolled up her window and got out.

The sheriff followed her in and stopped to speak to the older gentleman at the counter as Abby walked up to the soda machine. She didn't really drink soda, but she knew the sugar and carbonation would help. She filled a small cup with root beer, grabbed bags of turkey jerky, fruit and dried nut mix, and a bottle of water.

She carried them over to the register where the elderly cashier was already smiling at her. The sheriff was still there leaning against the counter.

"You got far to go?" the cashier asked politely.

Abby nodded. "I took a job at a church outside Medford, so I think I have at least a couple of hours," she replied thinking a church job sounded much better than "newly released inmate" did. She knew she was taking advantage of inherent prejudices, but at that point, Abby didn't think it mattered.

"Yeah, you got yourself at least two hours driving but you should be fine. It's all highway to Medford," the sheriff said. "You know where you're going, right?"

Abby smiled. "I do. Thank you so much."

The sheriff tipped his hat. "No problem. Safe travels."

"Thank you," she replied then pushed her way through the door.

She'd finished half of the root beer by the time she made it back to her car. The sugar hit her with a jolt and did much to take the edge off her anxiety.

Abby got in and settled herself then started the car and pulled off.

The drive *was* all highway and extremely boring, so Abby stopped at the mall Jane had suggested. It was a high-end mall in the middle of downtown. As Abby made her way through the throng of shoppers, she realized that the mall itself was like a prison. Like inmates, some shoppers were polite while others were aggressive. Some kept their heads down in an effort to avoid the allure of overpriced temptations. But no one got out without paying some kind of price.

Abby turned around and walked out.

She made her way north for another hour then left the highway to take smaller and smaller rural roads to Grayson. She'd pulled into a small but picturesque town when her GPS told her she was close.

She was pleased to see that St. Mary's was a smaller version of her own church back home. Set back off the road in its own park, the small stone church was surrounded by trees with an old cemetery beyond. A matching stone building that had a stucco addition added at one point stood nearby. There was a small parking lot alongside it. The building was definitely newer, but its architecture was in keeping with the church. A third building sat in the back, almost in the cemetery. It was a large stone and siding house. Abby assumed it was the rectory. The buildings were spread out enough that a long blacktop driveway wound around the trees connecting them in a way that didn't detract from the beauty of the campus.

Abby assumed the office of the rector was located in the stone building and drove there.

She was more than an hour early, but Abby was relieved to see Father Duncan walking outside to greet her. He had an older woman with him. She looked to be in her midsixties with a thin frame and light brown hair pulled to a short ponytail at the back of her head. She wore her collar, so Abby assumed she was Reverend Dorothy.

"You made it!" Father Duncan cried out then gave Abby a big hug. "I was worried you might not be able to find the church. I hope you didn't have any trouble."

Abby shook her head. "None at all. It's very beautiful here."

"I agree," Reverend Dorothy held out her hand and shook Abby's warmly. "I'm Dorothy Buckman. I'm so happy to have you join us."

"Thank you so much for the opportunity," Abby replied with great sincerity. "I just hope I can live up to your expectations."

Reverend Dorothy waived Abby's concerns aside. "Let's go inside and get acquainted."

Though it was a newer building, great thought had gone into keeping both the exterior and interior of the church offices consistent with the look of the church itself. Large double doors opened onto a small foyer with a reception area on one side and a sitting area on the other. The furniture in both the reception area and the waiting area looked like high quality early American in the Chippendale and Windsor styles. The floors were wide plank hardwood stained a dark rich brown. They led to another set of glassed double doors. Reverend Dorothy led them through the doors and past several offices to the last set of doors at the end of the long hallway. There were only two rooms: one was a large library that held a huge ancient table and the other was the rector's office. That is where they stopped. The room was also a library with walls filled with books. It was decorated in the warm rich brown of the hardwood floors and furniture, but to keep it light, the walls had been painted in a bright white and the windows were dressed with curtains made of a bright white fabric printed with a repeating pattern of blue French fleur, the symbol for Mary, the Mother of God. A large desk sat to the left while a small sitting area sat to the right. Reverend Dorothy invited them to sit.

Abby perched at the edge of the soft gray velvet sofa. In her mind it was still a job interview, and the opportunity could go away at any time.

Reverend Dorothy offered drinks, which both Abby and Father Duncan declined, and then she began.

"St. Mary's is an old parish serving an aging community. Grayson calls itself a city but is really more a village surrounded by small-scale agriculture. Some of our younger families commute to Akron or work at the college in Gambier while our older families are mostly retired couples. We have just under a hundred families evenly divided between those with children and those whose children have grown and left the area. However, for such a small church, we have a committed volunteer base of both older and younger parishioners, so we are very lucky."

"We have a small staff here. Other than myself, there's Father Tom Laird who's our assistant rector, Ella Smithson, our parish administrator who also serves as our comptroller, Allison Brickson who is the director for our children and youth faith education program, and finally, Blaine Henke who is our parish administrative assistant."

As if on cue a young man entered bearing a tea tray.

"Thank you, Blaine." She smiled as he set the tray down on the coffee table. Reverend Dorothy continued as the door closed behind him.

"Technically, the sexton is a volunteer church official who oversees buildings and grounds. But it's been my experience over the last fifteen years here that if you want consistency, you have to pay for it. Unfortunately, the job doesn't pay well. Our previous sexton left us to care for his ailing wife. Until Margaret Abbot called, I was at a loss as to what to do for a replacement. I'm hoping you're OK with the situation."

Abby nodded. "This is perfect for me; especially since it affords me a living situation as well as employment. I can't tell you enough how much I appreciate this opportunity."

Reverend Dorothy smiled. "Let's call a duck a duck, shall we? I'm sure it wasn't your lifelong dream to accept a position normally held by a septuagenarian with handyman skills and marginal organizational abilities. You need this situation, at least for the interim, and we need help. So, it's more of a mutually beneficial arrangement, don't you think?"

Abby smiled slightly and nodded. Reverend Dorothy reminded her of Margaret Abbot who had gone to seminary and wrote curriculums for adult and youth faith educational programs. She wondered if pragmatism was a prerequisite for the Episcopal Church.

"Miles here and I have had extensive conversations about your previous situation, but I'd like to hear it from you."

Abby took a deep breath. "I was twenty-two. I had gone to meet friends at a local pub…well it's more a bar that calls itself a pub but…my friends were already there. There was also a guy that I'd grown up with, Mark. Our mothers were very close friends, and Mark and I had attended kindergarten through high school together. He was sort of infamous for being a drug dealer because his dad was the local judge. It was one of those barely kept secrets that everyone knew about."

Abby paused before continuing. She'd told her story so many times that it shouldn't have bothered her, but she found herself embarrassed to share it yet again. "That night, I had gone up to Mark to say hello and give him a hug. He was my friend, after all. I didn't know it, but there were undercover narcotics officers there who had been trying to get introduced to Mark because he didn't sell to people he didn't know. And he knew almost everyone on some level. Because they saw me hug him, they asked me to make the introduction. And since I knew why they wanted to meet him, the introduction was a criminal act."

"And did you participate in his activities?" Reverend Dorothy asked tactfully.

Abby shook her head. "No. I've never been interested in that kind of thing. It seems like a waste of time…and money."

"And what about your time in prison?"

"I was very lucky in some respects. Maysville is a newer prison and mostly progressive in its approach to incarceration. There were wonderful people there that I grew to love very much. But some were a challenge. It was an interesting experience, and I came away from it with a better understanding of what lies underneath the veneer of a person. Once you strip away color and speech and go past the stain of personal history, all any of us want is to belong in the world…and be loved for it."

Reverend Dorothy smiled. "You said 'us.'"

Abby thought about it. "When I got there I was more. Then I became less. By the time I left, I was the same. Everyone is vulnerable to sin…and everyone is worthy of salvation."

"How else but through a broken heart may Lord Christ enter in?" Reverend Dorothy replied.

This time Abby smiled. "Oscar Wilde."

Reverend Dorothy laughed then turned to Father Duncan who was chuckling. "I think she's going to fit in just fine here," she said then stood. "Let's introduce you around."

Chapter 38

A BIRD'S NEST

Everyone seemed nice and no one looked at Abby oddly, as if wondering why a twenty-five-year-old woman would want a job as a sexton.

After meeting the staff, Father Duncan made his farewells. He had a long drive back to Maysville, but he wanted to make sure Abby was settled. She assured him that she was and sent him off with effusive thanks. Then she and Reverend Dorothy set off on a short tour of the campus. The church administrative building housed not only offices, but also a meeting space, a commercial kitchen, and classrooms in the stucco addition with a small playground behind the building. It was much more spacious than the exterior suggested. The old stone church was much as Abby imagined it would be. It was a smaller version of St. Simon's, but boasted beautiful stained glass windows donated over the years. Off to the side, but invisible from the street, was a small, beautiful chapel with a small gold sign that read "The Mother's Chapel." Abby assumed it was a nod to Anglican Marian theology, which acknowledged Mary as a figure to be venerated, as well as a space dedicated to the saint the church was named for. She said as much to Reverend Dorothy who confirmed her assumption.

"You'll be living here," Reverend Dorothy continued as they approached the large house at the back of the campus. "It was the original rectory that was converted to meeting rooms and living spaces long before I got here. It is three stories with the meeting space on the first level, a visiting scholar's apartment on the second, and the sexton's apartment on the third. Both apartments have separate entrances on the outside as well as the inside. Are you OK with the stairs?" Abby realized Father Duncan must have told Reverend Dorothy about her injuries.

"I should be fine," Abby answered. Just then a short bark greeted them as they walked up to the front steps.

"And that's our resident guard dog," Reverend Dorothy said wryly. At the top of the steps stood a squat gray and brown dappled dachshund that was simultaneously growling and wagging his tail. "Meet Dashiell Hammett, but we call him Dash for short. He was a stray that adopted us a couple of years ago. He really answers to anything and will follow you anywhere, though he won't leave the campus. I hope you like dogs. Unfortunately he's part of the job."

Abby put her hand out to let Dashiell get a good smell. "I love dogs. We couldn't have one because my father was allergic to them. I'll be happy to take care of him."

"I'm glad," Reverend Dorothy replied. "I have cats that would not take kindly to having a canine addition to the family."

Abby and Dash made quick friends, and the little dog followed them in.

The meeting rooms were much as Abby suspected, but the kitchen had been recently updated and was beautiful. Reverend Dorothy skipped the visiting scholar's apartment and led Abby all the way up the outside stairs to the sexton's apartment.

It too had been renovated, and Abby commented on the high level of quality and the talent of the designer.

Reverend Dorothy nodded. "One of our parishioners owns a home construction firm and his wife is an art professor at the college. They renovated all of our buildings a few years ago. Luckily she decorated the apartment and not one of the previous sextons," she joked then continued. "Though this space could be considered the attic, it was originally built as a full living space for the original rector's house staff." Reverend Dorothy snorted. "Can you imagine a priest having house staff in this day and age?" She shook her head then continued. "Anyway, the ceilings are full height and luckily the space is large enough to have actual rooms. There are two bedrooms that share a bathroom. And as you can see the living area is open. You also have a full kitchen."

"It's beautiful. Thank you so much." Abby said sincerely.

"You are most welcome," Reverend Dorothy smiled. "Here's your key. I'll let you get settled in. You'll probably want to do some shopping. There's a grocer in the village, and all the big chains are back toward the highway. We'll meet tomorrow to go over your day-to-day duties. All right?"

"Yes, thank you."

"Welcome to St. Mary's, Abby." Reverend Dorothy gave Abby a reassuring smile then left.

Dash sat and watched as Abby surveyed her new home. The roof of the original house was shaped like a cross with four gables that all went in opposite directions from a large central space. The two bedrooms were at the front of the house with a small bathroom between them. The bathroom looked original to the house, but the plumbing fixtures had definitely been updated. Abby knew from all the home shows she'd watched in prison that people were paying top dollar to make their bathrooms look like hers. The living room comprised of two arms of the cross and was L-shaped with the entry door located in the corner. Abby noticed a steep set of stairs descending through the floor to the level below. At the bottom of the stairs was an ornately carved door with its own deadbolt. Abby assumed it was the interior entrance.

The kitchen occupied the last arm of the cross and was open to the living area. It was divided from the rest of the living space by a peninsula that, on further inspection, served as both a breakfast bar and home for the dishwasher. All the appliances were small, but they were stainless steel and looked brand new. The cabinets were an aged walnut with brushed nickel knobs, and the counters looked like a man-made stone. Further inspection revealed a small stacking washer and dryer in the closet next to the kitchen.

Luckily there were windows everywhere that let in lots of natural light. The bedroom windows faced the park in front of the rectory and the living area windows faced the cemetery. Abby had a bird's eye view of everything, and the best part about it, there wasn't a barbed wire fence in sight.

A quick look into all the closets revealed a full complement of linens. The iron beds in the bedrooms both had handmade looking quilts on them and towels already hung in the bathroom. The kitchen was stocked with dishes, pots, and pans. It only lacked food. Abby surveyed the living area, trying to determine what was missing. The furniture was an interesting mix of leather and dark woods; and something that looked like velvet but Abby hoped was microfiber. She stood there for another moment then realized the room did not have a television, which was fine with her. The only thing she would need to buy would be a computer. The police seized her computer after her arrest. By the time Jane got it back, it wasn't even worth salvaging.

Abby sank into an oversized oxblood velvet chair and looked out at the view of the cemetery. Dash walked over, sniffed her foot, and then, after determining she was worthy of his companionship, jumped up and settled in next to her.

Abby marveled at the abrupt change in her circumstances. She was sitting in dead silence in an apartment that looked like it was pulled from a catalog when just the day before she'd been in a noisy prison sleeping with six women and eating food from a hot plate.

She gave herself another minute to enjoy the quiet then got up to move and unpack her car.

It took several trips to carry everything up. She still had to move carefully. One trip up the steep steps of the dark interior entrance convinced her that the outside steps were the way to go.

By the time she carried the last box up, Abby was aching and starving. Since she needed to stock up on basics anyway, Abby grabbed her keys and went in search of a grocery store.

She had a good idea of the layout of Grayson from when she came in earlier, but figured she'd find more of what she would need at the larger chain stores near the highway. She stopped in at the electronics store first and bought a new laptop and smartphone. Then at the super-everything-store, Abby shopped for basic groceries and, as an afterthought, some food, a bed, and toys for Dash. At some point she would need to find a health food or vegan store for the things she typically ate.

It was late by the time Abby got back and the campus was deserted. Though it wasn't all the way dark, the electric streetlamps that ran along the drives were already glowing.

She carried up her purchases then took a brisk walk around the church grounds with Dash trotting along beside her. Even though it was cold, she'd walked most of the winding driveway. Then it began to rain, so Abby and her new roommate went inside.

After dinner, Abby spent the rest of the evening setting up her laptop and unpacking. Margaret Abbot had packed all of her clothes, most of which Abby didn't think she would ever need or even use so she sorted everything into keep and donate piles with the donate pile being considerably larger. She kept basics like jeans and twill pants, a few of her more professional pieces like skirts and blazers, and her nicer shirts and sweaters. Anything that was overly trendy or impractical for her current situation could go. Those got boxed up and placed near the door.

Finally, she was tired enough to go to bed. She spent a few minutes washing up then went into the smaller of the two bedrooms. It was cold in the attic apartment so she looked around and found another blanket in the chest at the foot of the bed and tossed it over the quilt. Abby crawled under the quilt to find warm flannel sheets. As she snuggled in, Dash appeared in the doorway.

Abby looked at him looking at her. "You can come in," she said.

As if he understood her and accepted her invitation, Dash trotted in and jumped onto the chest then onto the bed. He walked up to the head of the bed and burrowed under the blanket. He walked in circles to make his nest then settled down into a little curl of dog with his long nose resting near Abby's.

She smiled then lay there for a long while, eventually falling asleep as she listened to nothing.

Chapter 39

I THOUGHT I WAS
THE ONLY ONE

Abby spent the first few days of her new position learning the ropes. Since the church employed an outside service to clean and a parishioner donated the landscaping, her job was to oversee their work, manage the budget, and coordinate any repairs and improvements the church needed. Her only hands-on jobs were cleaning and maintaining the vessels used during worship, the various altar cloths, and securing the sacristy after every worship service. She also had the added responsibility of ensuring that the campus and cemetery were secure. The church had experienced some minor vandalism over the Halloween weekend and didn't want it to turn into an ongoing issue.

She was coming back from what she called her "graveyard walkabout" when Allison, the church's education director, intercepted her.

"Hey, Abby?" she called out as Abby approached the administration parking lot. She was a young woman, close to Abby's age, but her physical polar opposite. Where Abby was tall and thin, Allison was short and stocky. Her blond bob was a foil to Abby's long dark hair. During their brief meeting on Abby's first day, she appeared to be warm and very friendly.

"Hi, Allison," Abby replied.

"I thought I'd see if you'd like to go get some lunch with me? There's a really good café in town." Allison said, her face hopeful. "I'll drive."

Abby smiled. "Sure. Just let me change real quick. I've been pulling weeds in the graveyard."

"Oh, OK. I'll just pick you up at the rectory then."

Abby trotted over to the rectory and pulled off her jeans and sweatshirt. She found a mostly unwrinkled pair of twills and pulled on the sweater Sylvia knitted. Then she grabbed her jacket and met Allison outside.

The café was located on the ground floor of a converted bank. Abby and Allison didn't have to wait long for a table to open up since it was technically after lunch and most people were going back to work, or they were off to enjoy the remainder of their day. They were able to get a table in the window that afforded a view of the park that served as the town square.

Abby glanced over the menu and was surprised to see more adventurous fare than was typical in small rural towns.

A young waitress came over to take their order.

"I'll have the seared tuna and falafel on lavash with a glass of water," Abby ordered then looked at Allison.

"Um...I'll have the spinach salad, but can I have olive oil and sliced lemons instead of dressing? Oh, and iced tea?"

The waitress nodded then left to put in their orders.

Allison leaned over as she walked away. "I'm trying to lose weight," she said in a low voice. "My boyfriend likes me chubby but nothing fits anymore!"

Abby smiled politely.

"How do you keep so thin?" Allison asked as she blatantly eyed Abby up and down.

"I don't eat sugar," Abby replied. "And I run...well not lately. I had an accident and am still recovering."

"You mean the beating?" Allison's question was guileless.

Abby startled but didn't answer.

"I'm sorry. I really hope you don't mind, but we all know. One of the parish volunteers accidently intercepted a fax from your prison counselor to Reverend Dorothy." Allison looked stricken. "Oh my God, please know that nobody cares... I mean we care as Christians but not like in a judgmental way...oh, I am sooo sorry."

Abby shook her head but her smile was sad. "That's OK. I should probably get used to it. It's going to follow me for a long time."

Allison looked relieved. "When Reverend Dorothy found out about the fax mix-up, she gave us all an earful at the staff meeting. But she asked me to be extra supportive because the same thing happened to my brother."

"Your brother was beaten by a guard?"

"Oh, no." Allison shook her head and her blond curls bounced. "He went to prison for the same reason you did. But he went away for much longer."

Abby was surprised. "Really? How did it happen?"

"His roommate in college sold drugs to help pay his tuition. Some guy came up to Ben, my brother, and asked him how he could get some and, like an idiot, Ben took him up to their dorm room and introduced the guy. Then they got raided. My brother was sentenced to ten years but came home after eight."

"I'm sorry for your brother. That's a long time."

Allison nodded. "The worst part is he'd never used drugs before he went away, but he came home an addict. He had to go through rehab twice and now he's living in a residential facility. He's trying to finish his college degree but it's been hard."

"That's horrible!" Abby sat and imagined what would have happened if she'd been sent somewhere else, or even to another unit. Drugs weren't as much of an issue on B Unit. Hooch and sex seemed to be the main vices when she was there…last week.

Allison shrugged. "We were given free will. Sometimes we don't do such a good job with it."

The waitress arrived with their food and it was delicious. Abby ate as if she hadn't seen food in years, which in a way she hadn't.

"So," Allison began between bites. "My boyfriend and I are going to see a Journey tribute band play at a bar near Kenyon tomorrow night. They're really cheesy but super fun. Would you like to come with us?"

Abby felt terrible. Allison looked so hopeful. "I'm sorry, I can't. I haven't met with my parole officer yet, but I know I'm prohibited from drinking alcohol and visiting any bars or establishments that serve alcohol."

Allison slapped her head. "Of course not! What was I thinking? I'm so sorry."

Abby laughed. "You don't need to keep apologizing. It's OK."

"Ugh, I do it a lot." Allison smiled. "Stick my foot in my mouth, apologize, then do it again. It's kind of a pattern."

Abby laughed again.

Allison dropped Abby off at the rectory. Then before she could drive away, she stopped and got out.

"Since you can't sing like Steve Perry with us, would you consider going to see a horror movie with me? My boyfriend won't go and there are literally three other people in this town my age and they're all moms with little kids."

"You like horror movies?" Abby asked, surprised.

"Love them. Why? You too?" This time it was Allison who looked surprised.

"Love them. Sure, I'll go with you. Just let me know when." Abby waved as Allison drove off. She was suddenly happy. She felt blessed to have a new friend.

Chapter 40

JOINING THE FLOCK

The weekend had arrived, and with little to do, Abby attended both the Saturday evening and Sunday morning worship services. Father Tom performed Saturday evening's worship service. Abby wasn't sure about his style. Most priests she'd seen approached worship with a warmth and sincerity borne out of their love for God and a desire to lead His flock. Abby got the impression that Father Tom was quite proud of his role as priest. He looked as if he was putting on a show. The readers were very good though, and, aside from the sermon, Abby enjoyed the small, quiet evening service.

Sunday morning was definitely the Reverend Dorothy show. There were three services: 7:00 a.m., 9:00 a.m., and 11:00 a.m. There was an optional children's chapel during the 9:00 a.m. service. Abby was impressed by the number of parishioners attending the 9:00 a.m. service. When Reverend Dorothy began to speak, she understood why so many attended the service. Where Father Tom sounded like he was giving a lecture, Reverend Dorothy drew her congregation into a personal conversation. Sitting in the pew, Abby could feel a sense of love lift from the crowd and fill the entire space of the church. It was almost hypnotic how the Reverend's voice could move one to turn inward to reflect on the meaning of her sermon. As she spoke about God's call to do right by the world and His people, Reverend Dorothy wove a spell of words that fell on everyone like a benediction. By the end, everyone was at peace.

At the end of worship, Abby walked out and into Allison who was looking for a particular set of parents.

"What's wrong?" Abby asked.

"Ugh, I have this boy who I'm pretty sure is ADHD. He does fine at children's chapel then as soon as it's time to go to Sunday school he completely falls apart. I have too much to do to look after him *and* support the teachers. We've tried to be polite about it, but the parents won't do anything."

"I can help," Abby offered.

Allison looked surprised. "Are you sure?"

"Sure," Abby nodded then followed Allison to the administrative building. As soon as they stepped inside she could tell which kid was the problem. There were only a handful of classes serving different age groups. The boy in question looked to be about seven or eight and was practically bouncing off the walls. One of the teachers was trying to keep him from careening into the other children as the other teachers ushered the rest of the group into their classrooms.

"Which do you want, the kid or to pass out materials?" Allison asked, her face hopeful.

"I'll take the kid," Abby replied, affecting a serious expression and Allison thanked her effusively. "What's his name?"

"Damien," Allison called over her shoulder then hurried off.

Abby snorted. "Of course it is."

Abby walked over to where the boy was swinging on the railing of the stairs. She watched him watching her as she approached.

"Stop that," she ordered. Her voice was neither kind nor angry.

"What?" he asked, feigning deafness.

Abby towered over him and looked straight into his face.

"You're going to get off of that railing right now, and you are going to stand still and listen to me."

Damien crawled out from under the bar and stood there, almost still.

"You may call me 'Miss Abby' and when I ask you a question you will answer, 'Yes, Miss Abby' or 'No, Miss Abby.' Do you understand?"

Damien stared at the ground and nodded. His feet were doing a jitterbug.

"Let's try that again. When I ask you a question you will answer, 'Yes, Miss Abby' or 'No, Miss Abby.' Do you understand?"

"Yes, Miss Abby," he mumbled to the floor. Abby could see him practically vibrating with the effort to stand still.

"That's was very good, Damien," Abby said, which earned her a timid smile.

"Damien, did you eat breakfast today?"

"Yes, Miss Abby," he answered more confidently. "I had frosty flakes."

Abby figured as much. "Frosty flakes aren't good for you, Damien. You should be eating eggs and toast for breakfast, with fruit instead of cereal. Do you like eggs?"

"Yes, Miss Abby! I love eggs! I love fruit!"

Abby smiled. "Very good, Damien. Now, Miss Allison tells me that you can sit still in children's chapel but not in your classroom. Can you tell me why?"

Damien looked away, his face frowning but his body doing a little dance. "It's because God watches you when you're in church so you have to be still. But it's really hard sometimes."

Abby nodded. "Damien, do you take medicine to help you behave?"

Damien nodded, his frown deepening. "Yes, but it makes me itchy."

Abby thought for a minute. "Since you are having trouble sitting still, I think you should be a helper today. What do you think?"

Damien's face lit up. "Yes, Miss Abby. I can do that!"

"Come with me then." Abby walked away knowing that Damien would follow.

They found Allison in a large supply closet filling bins with items for the day's craft project.

"Miss Allison, Damien has volunteered to deliver the bins for you," Abby announced and Damien smiled proudly.

Allison was surprised. "Oh, that's great Damien. Do you know which classrooms they go to?"

Damien nodded then pointed to the bins. "It's written on the side."

"Very good. Then you can take this first one," she replied then handed him the bin for the preschoolers. Damien set off in a run.

Allison and Abby picked up the remaining bins and carried them to the hallway. When they were sure Damien knew where they were supposed to go, they let him run the hallways delivering the rest of them. When he was done, Allison sent him to collect all the attendance books.

"He can't do this every week," she said by way of protest. "He needs to be in his classroom."

"I agree, but there's no way that boy can sit still for that long. His brain and nervous system are working overtime right now. His parents really need to have his medication reevaluated."

Allison made a disgusted sound then immediately looked contrite. "I'm trying to be a good Christian about it, but they just aren't very receptive to their son's shortcomings."

"How about I take him out to the playground?" Abby offered.

Allison looked relieved. "That would be great."

When Damien returned from his latest task, Abby waved him over. "Come with me, Damien. You did such a good job that I'm going to take you out to the playground until your parents get here."

The little boy's face lit up and he happily followed Abby outside.

It was unseasonably warm, so Abby took off her jacket and laid it in her lap. Damien was one of those children who was perfectly happy entertaining himself, so Abby sat back and watched him for the twenty minutes remaining of Sunday school.

It wasn't long before his parents wandered over as if in the midst of a leisurely stroll. Abby stood and approached them before Damien realized they were there.

"Are you Damien's parents?" she asked knowing perfectly well they were. Damien was a carbon copy of his father.

"Oh, yes? Is he all right?" the mother answered vaguely. She squinted at the playground as if unable to see her perfectly visible ball of energy.

"He's unhurt, if that's what you're asking," Abby answered. She moved so that the mother had no choice but to look at her. "However, you need to know that he was unable to attend his Sunday school class today because he couldn't settle down without being disruptive."

"He takes medication for that," she said defensively and with more awareness than she appeared to have at first. Abby began to suspect the vacuity was an act. For his part, the father stood silent and practically invisible. Abby began to understand the dynamics in the family.

"You will need to take him back to his pediatrician and explain that his medication is over stimulating him." Abby advised her in a tone that was neither accusing nor conciliatory. "You also need to eliminate the sugar cereals from his diet. He should be eating protein, whole grains, and fresh fruit in the mornings. Unless his behavior improves, he cannot return to Sunday school."

Damien's father looked mildly concerned while his mother's eyes narrowed at Abby. "But this is the time we go to the Parents' Fellowship."

"And when you've parented Damien more effectively, you'll be able to return. It's for the good of your son. I'm sure you want that," Abby replied then turned her back on the useless couple. "Damien, you're parents are here to take you home."

"Yes, Miss Abby." Damien ran over and hugged Abby's leg enthusiastically. "Thank you, Miss Abby, for letting me be a helper." Damien's parents stared at him in surprise.

"You're welcome, Damien," Abby answered then planted her time bomb. "Don't forget to tell your parents that you need different medicine and that you want eggs and toast for breakfast instead of cereal."

"Yes, Miss Abby!" Damien yelled then ran off. His parents followed behind him reluctantly.

Abby found Allison inside standing with one of the volunteer teachers.

"Wow, Damien's mother is pissed," Allison said then apologized for her language. "What did you say to her?"

"I told her that she needed to take Damien back to his doctor to change his medication and to stop feeding him sugar in the morning. And I might have told her that he can't come back unless his behavior is under control."

Allison stared as the teacher snorted. "Good for you," the young woman said. "She's going to complain to the clergy so I'll go talk to Reverend Dorothy first. By the way, I'm Rebecca," she said putting out her hand.

"I'm Abby," she smiled as she shook the woman's hand.

"Nice to meet you. I'd better run and catch Reverend Dorothy before Damien's mother does."

Allison turned back to Abby. "How did you know to do that?"

Abby picked up the bins at Allison's feet and carried them to the supply closet for her. Allison followed.

"I wasn't a huge fan of the youth program at the church I grew up in. To be honest, I was really going through my obnoxious phase and they were happy to see me called elsewhere, so I helped my mother in her Sunday school class. By the time I was in high school I had my own class. I've had my share of problem children...and problem parents. The key is clear boundaries and positive reinforcement...for both."

Allison looked impressed. "Maybe you should be doing my job."

"No thanks. I've got my own job to do." Abby laughed then set off to tidy up the building.

Chapter 41

PAROLE AND PROBATION

On Monday, Abby drove to Medford early. She didn't know if there was such a thing as a Monday morning rush hour there, but she didn't want to risk being late for her very first visit with her parole officer.

She needn't have bothered though. There was very little traffic to worry about, and she arrived in time to go to the bank first. Jane had planned the visit well. The bank was located only steps from the Adult Parole Authority Office where her appointment was scheduled. It took a few minutes, but she had no problems getting set up as a signatory on the trust account. The bank manager was very attentive, but nervous, and Abby had to wonder if it was because she was a convict or because the trust held a pile of money.

She was done in plenty of time to walk to the probation office and still be early. It was a pretty day, colder than the day before, but sunny. The warm breeze that blew promised an early spring.

The Adult Parole Authority Office was located in an older building that was a bit of a maze inside. Abby followed the signs as best she could. She was happy to have gotten there early. Abby was starting to panic when she finally found the office and went in. She checked in at the front desk then took a seat. There were several other people waiting there. Most looked like they'd either just gotten out of jail or were about to go back in. A couple of them were clear meth or crack addicts. Abby doubted they'd be passing their drug test. A uniformed police officer stood in the corner watching them closely.

Abby was surprised to hear her name called so early. She looked over to see a larger twin of Captain Dennis waving her over.

"My name is Eugene Ash. I will be your parole officer. Follow me, Miss Blackwood."

Abby obeyed, and they wove their way through a labyrinth of doors and corridors until they reached a small office at the end.

"Please have a seat." Abby sat as he sank heavily into his chair. She was so intimidated by Eugene Ash that she couldn't come up with any other nickname than Mr. Ash.

"May I have your paperwork, please?" he asked, though it wasn't really a request.

Abby handed him the paperwork Jane had given her along with a copy of her employment contract that listed her address on the church's campus, and her college transcripts. She included her ID and car information for good measure.

Mr. Ash grunted his approval as he looked through her papers. He made checkmarks and notes on a file in front of him then handed back her ID, car registration, and insurance card.

There were no preliminary greetings or chitchat. Mr. Ash went straight to the point.

"The conditions of your probation state that you will be seeing me on regular basis until the remainder of your original sentence has been satisfied. Do you understand?"

"Yes, sir."

"As your conviction was based on a drug offense, you are prohibited from drinking or selling alcohol. You may not work in nor visit any establishment that is providing alcohol. You are prohibited from taking any kind of drugs that have not been prescribed by a physician to you personally, or purchased over-the-counter and taken in their original state. Do you understand?"

"Yes, sir."

"If you are given a prescription for medication of any kind, you will bring me a copy of that prescription before it is filled. Do you understand?"

"Yes, sir," Abby replied then sat in silence as he made notations in her file.

"You are not to carry a weapon of any kind. No guns, no pepper spray, and no knives. Kitchen knives are permitted as long as they stay in your kitchen. Understand?"

"Yes, sir."

"What was your highest level of education completed?"

"I finished my first year of graduate school."

"In what field?"

"Nursing."

"And have you reported for your first day of employment?"

"Yes, sir. Last week."

"Have you had any contact with any preincarceration associates since your release?"

"No, sir."

"Do you have a cell phone?"

"Yes, sir."

"Let me have it, please." Abby handed it over and watched as he put in numbers and poked at the various options on the screen. He seemed to know more about how it worked than she did. When he was done he handed it back.

"You will keep your phone on you at all times. I might call you, text you, show up at your job or home. These contacts are random and unannounced. If you do not respond or are not where you are supposed to be, I will hunt you down and put you back in prison. Do you understand?"

"Yes, sir."

"I've been going over your file and it looks to me like you are a way low risk, practically underground, so I want to see you every week for the first two months then we'll reevaluate your visit schedule." Mr. Ash leaned to the side and checked a calendar already filled with notes. "I don't want you to have a work conflict, but I'm pretty well booked. Are you able to see me? Ummm…Mondays at 2:00 p.m. will be opening up next week. Will that work?"

"Yes, sir. My work understands that I need to be here."

"Very good then," he replied and added Abby's name to his calendar. Then he turned back to her and put his pencil down. "Do you have any questions for me?"

"No, sir."

"You seem like a very smart girl. I know I don't need to tell you that I am your parole officer, not your friend. I'm not your therapist. But if you are having reentry problems, I need you to let me know. If you need an AA program, I'll find you one. If you need anger management help, I'll get it for you. You are not without resources, understand?"

Abby nodded.

"The most important thing we need for this to be successful is honesty. If you tell me the truth, I'll help you. You lie to me then I'm sending you back to jail. Understand?"

Abby nodded again.

Mr. Ash seemed satisfied. He glanced down at her file. "You were at Maysville?"

"Yes, sir."

"You got lucky," he remarked. "Maysville is better than most places."

"I spent eighteen months at county before I could go," Abby replied.

Mr. Ash's eyebrows went up. "Then you earned it. County can be rough."

"Yes, sir."

"What about hobbies. You have anything safe to occupy your time?"

"I like to read. And I run. I was training for a marathon before I was…hurt." Abby was embarrassed.

Mr. Ash looked sympathetic. "I know about the assault and I'm sorry. Like the priesthood can attract pedophiles, law enforcement can attract sadists."

"Yes, sir. Thank you, sir."

Mr. Ash closed her file. "I need you to submit for a drug test today. The cost for your test is fifteen dollars. You come up clean then you may go. You come up dirty then this meeting gets much longer and you'll be wearing handcuffs. Understand?" he asked then stood up.

"Yes, sir," Abby answered then stood as well.

"Follow me."

This time they walked in the opposite direction and stopped at a small exam room near the reception area. Inside was a young lab tech who looked up as they entered.

"Saliva and urine screen," Mr. Ash said to her then walked out.

The lab tech handed Abby a specimen cup and indicated a small bathroom to the side. There was no door, and as Abby stepped in, the lab tech followed. Abby realized the test had to be observed. It was difficult at first. Abby wasn't sure she would be able to go. The lab tech sensed her dilemma and leaned over to turn on the tap. As soon as the water started flowing, so did Abby. She finished, handed the tech the specimen, and then put herself back together. She washed her hands then sat at the end of the exam table. The lab tech placed the dip strip in her urine then changed her gloves to do Abby's saliva test.

Abby knew from her clinical rotations that the saliva test was redundant to the urine test and done only as a safeguard to false positives or negatives. If the two tests didn't match, they would have to do them again.

After she was swabbed, the lab tech sent Abby out to wait in the reception area. Abby knew she wouldn't be dismissed until the results of her tests were in.

The two addicts were still in reception, but now they were in handcuffs. Abby sat as far away from them as possible.

234

After only a few minutes, Mr. Ash called her back again.

Abby sat across from him wondering why she hadn't been dismissed. Mr. Ash regarded her silently for a moment then dropped a bombshell.

"Your urine test indicates that you are pregnant."

Abby's mouth fell open. "What? Are you sure?"

Mr. Ash nodded then turned the paper in front of him and pushed it toward her. Her litmus strip was taped to the front. She'd read enough of them to know that the indicator was dark enough to not be a false positive. She was pregnant.

"You were released a week ago. These strips don't pick up hormone levels well, so you may be at least eight weeks along. Were you eligible for conjugal visits at Maysville?"

Abby shook her head, which was still reeling. "No, sir." Her voice was shaking.

"So I'm going to assume that your situation is due to contact with a guard then."

Abby said nothing.

"Abby, if you were assaulted by a guard then this is rape. If you engaged in consensual relations with a guard, it is a relationship based on implied intimidation and still a felony for him."

Abby remained silent.

Mr. Ash's expression was stern. "Are you going to tell me who got you pregnant?"

Abby answered his question with her own question. "Does my being pregnant affect my parole or negatively impact the terms of my probation?"

Mr. Ash regarded her silently for a moment then answered.

"No."

"Then no, I have nothing further to say."

Mr. Ash sighed then pulled a piece of paper over and scribbled something on it before handing it to Abby.

"That's the name of an obstetrician here in Medford. She's very good. If you are still going to be pregnant at your next visit, you need to start seeing her as soon as possible. Your drug test was clean. I will see you on Monday. You may go."

"Thank you, sir." Abby took the note then stood up and walked out.

She was in a daze as she made her way to the exit. It wasn't until she was sitting in her car staring out at nothing that she realized she had no recollection of leaving the office.

I'm pregnant…I'm going to have a baby….I'm going to have Quinn's baby…

The thoughts kept running through her head as she drove back to Grayson.

Still on autopilot, Abby pulled into the parking lot of the administration building rather than the rectory. She sat staring at the stones on the wall, contemplating her options. She realized she only had one real option in front of her, so Abby got out and went inside.

Instead of an elderly volunteer, Blaine sat at the reception desk. He looked up as she walked in.

"Hey, Abby," he greeted her with a warm smile. "What's up?"

Abby had liked Blaine immediately. He was about her age, thin, and extremely pretty for a man. Abby assumed from his mannerisms that he was gay.

"Is Reverend Dorothy in?"

"Sure. She's just having a late lunch. Come on." Blaine jumped up and Abby followed him down the hall.

Blaine opened the Reverend's door and stuck his head in. "Do you have time to see Abby?" Abby couldn't hear the response but assumed it was positive when Blaine stepped back and waved her in.

Abby stopped short as the door closed discreetly behind her. Reverend Dorothy sat behind her desk wiping her mouth with a napkin, a half-eaten salad in front of her. Abby had indeed interrupted her lunch.

"I can come back another time," Abby began, but Reverend Dorothy stopped her.

"Nonsense," the Reverend said as she stepped from the desk and waved Abby over to the couch. "You saved me from overindulging. How was your visit?" Abby had adopted a policy of full disclosure with her new boss, so Reverend Dorothy knew about Abby's visit with her parole officer.

"It went well," Abby began then stopped. She had no idea how to continue.

Reverend Dorothy seemed to sense her conflict. "What's wrong? Did something happen?"

Abby sighed. The enormity of her situation hit her suddenly and hard. "I'm required to submit to a drug test during my visit as a condition of my parole."

"And that didn't go well?" Reverend Dorothy asked, surprised.

"It showed that…I'm…pregnant."

Reverend Dorothy sat back in shock. Abby appreciated the look of worry on her face.

The Reverend recovered then sat up again. "Can you tell me how that came to be?" This time her expression was all business.

Abby was quiet for a moment. She felt like she could trust Reverend Dorothy so she told her everything.

When she was done she was relieved to see Reverend Dorothy looking at her sympathetically.

"I hear your words and I understand your feelings of betrayal, but I get the impression that you still love this young man," she said quietly.

Abby shook her head, but didn't answer.

"The fact that you didn't name him to your parole officer is very telling, Abby. If you didn't love him you wouldn't hesitate to hold him accountable for his role in your predicament."

"I'm not in a place emotionally where I can look at things objectively," Abby said carefully.

"Trust me," Reverend Dorothy laughed. "No one is capable of looking at love objectively, but let's revisit that later. Have you made a decision about what to do about your 'situation?'"

Abby was confused. "I don't understand," she said.

"You are facing a potentially difficult situation. I will make no judgments should you decide to terminate your 'condition' early."

Abby shook her head. "That's not an option for me. My difficulty lies in where to go now?"

Reverend Dorothy frowned. "Now it's my turn to not understand."

"You can't want me to stay here." Abby didn't dare assume that she would be welcome. She was already a parolee, now she was a pregnant parolee.

"My dear, if we haven't cast out a convict, we certainly won't cast out a mother," Reverend Dorothy said, chuckling.

"Are you sure?" Abby suddenly felt a glimmer of hope. "The parishioners might feel differently."

Reverend Dorothy laughed, setting Abby's mind at ease. "Well, then they're not very good Christians then, are they? You needn't worry about that. We are blessed with a mostly loving group of families. The few who might take issue with your situation are welcome to come see me."

"I can't tell you how much I appreciate this," Abby began but Reverend Dorothy interrupted her.

"We are called to serve *all* of God's children, not just the easy ones."

Abby thanked Reverend Dorothy again then left.

Abby knew the news of her pregnancy wouldn't be a secret for long, so she went in search of Allison to break the news to her first.

Abby found her in the Sunday school's supply closet doing inventory for the next class project. Allison looked up when Abby poked her head in.

"Hey! How was your first meeting?" Abby had told Allison where she was going figuring it was better to be truthful than to be considered unnecessarily prevaricating.

"It went OK. Do you have a minute?" Abby asked.

Allison put down her list. "Sure. You want to go outside? It looks nice."

Abby nodded and the two women went out to sit at one of the benches in the Sunday school's playground. It had gotten warmer and Abby appreciated the additional privacy.

"I had to submit to a urine test and I wanted to let you know first...well second actually, I told Reverend Dorothy first...but...I'm pregnant."

"Oh my God!" Allison jumped up and hugged Abby fiercely. "That's amazing! I'm so happy for you...wait..." Allison sat down suddenly. "Is this happy news or 'uh oh' news?"

Abby smiled sadly. "A little of both, I suppose."

"Oh," Allison's face fell. "Is there a decision you have to make?" she asked carefully.

"Other than which obstetrician to use?" Abby shook her head. "No, there's no decision to make."

Allison smiled. "I'm happy for you then. Actually, I'm kind of excited. I've never had a friend going through a pregnancy. It'll be like a trial run for me, you know?"

"Uh, OK," Abby said with a laugh, "if you say so. I'd better let you get back to work."

The women stood and Allison impulsively leaned over and gave Abby a hug, surprising her.

"Congratulations, Abby. You're going to be a great mom," Allison said warmly.

Abby wasn't sure about that, but she returned her hug. "Thanks."

Abby bypassed the administration building and took the long way back to her apartment. She was tired and wanted to sit and think about her situation. Dash was waiting for her on the front porch. He followed her as she climbed the outside stairs. She realized that the fatigue and lethargy she'd attributed to her injuries were more likely due to her pregnancy. Abby was ready to lie down the moment she opened the front door. Dash trotted in before her and jumped into the oxblood chair as if in understanding that she needed to rest awhile.

Abby delayed resting to send Jane an email detailing her predicament. She wasn't surprised to hear back almost immediately. Jane was understandably alarmed and ready to fight the prison on Abby's behalf. In soothing language, Abby wrote that it wouldn't be necessary. She was happy with her pregnancy and just wanted to move on. Jane's reply took longer than Abby anticipated, but when it arrived it simply stated that whatever Abby wanted was fine with Jane. She'd asked nothing about the father and for that Abby was grateful. Abby sent a thank you in reply then shut her computer down. Exhausted, she sat down with Dash, happy to be able to close her eyes for a few minutes.

An hour later, hunger drove her up, and a quick peek in her refrigerator revealed a distinct lack of food. She went to her computer to pull up a list of recommended meals. She found it very similar to her current diet with the exception of dairy and salmon, which weren't currently part of her regimen. Abby wrote out her list and set off.

She returned to the cluster of big name stores to visit the bookstore first where she picked up a pregnancy book, and then for good measure one on caring for babies, both from the Mayo Clinic. Then, with the diet recommendations list in hand, she wandered over to the grocery store to stock up more dairy foods and some canned salmon.

She was exhausted by the time she returned to her apartment but rallied enough to feed Dash then make her own dinner. Afterward, with Dart's warm little body curled up against her, Abby went to sleep.

Chapter 42

SEEMINGLY IRREVOCABLE CONDITION

Abby made an appointment for the following Monday with the obstetrician Mr. Ash had recommended. Dr. Graham was a young, soft-spoken woman with her own practice in Medford. Abby liked her immediately. She checked Abby thoroughly, declared her perfectly healthy, and sent her off with a prescription for prenatal vitamins and a full schedule of monitoring visits. Abby paid her bill and was grateful that the fee wasn't unmanageable. Abby didn't have health insurance yet, but she felt the urgency to resolve that issue now that she was pregnant.

She met with Mr. Ash afterward, and other than officially informing him of her plans to have the baby and showing him her vitamin prescription, the meeting went on without incident.

Back in Grayson, Abby settled in to live a quiet life. As her days passed, she enjoyed the solitude of her work at the church and her few friendships. It was such a departure from her time in both the jail and the prison. She missed the women in her unit at Maysville, yet she loved the quiet of her little apartment among the trees.

She wasn't surprised that she did not miss her friends from her life before her arrest. No one had contacted her after her arrest or during her time at either County or Maysville. And despite the fact that many of their parents were also parishioners at St. Simon's, none had shown up for her father's funeral. Their abandonment cut deep, so Abby emptied her heart of the hurt she'd felt, forgave them, and then set them aside in her mind. She had someone far more important to occupy her time with now.

Dr. Graham had warned her against the extreme levels of training she had indulged in while in prison, citing the miracle that she'd gotten pregnant in the first place. She encouraged Abby to take up prenatal yoga and slow down to a walk. The doctor also advised Abby to gain a little bit of weight by increasing her caloric intake to 2000 calories. Abby augmented her diet with more healthy fats like avocados, eggs, and olive oil on her daily fresh spinach salad, and she invested in a blender to make nutritious protein shakes.

Dr. Graham had also warned that she would feel tired more often, which Abby found to be absolutely true. She started going to bed just after her evening walk with Dash, and she took short naps in the afternoon before going into the church to attend to the cleaning and maintenance of the sacristy.

Abby had also fallen into the habit of visiting the Mother's Chapel at the end of her daily visit to the church. It was always empty and its small, enclosed space was comforting. At first glance it was just a small version of the larger chapel, but on further inspection it was subtly more ornate. It had the same exposed beam ceiling but intricate moldings followed the arches like strings of pearls. A large statue of Mary sat in an alcove filigreed with gold, as were the ends of the six small pews that faced her. The gilt fleurs were painted in regular patterns on the wall. Colorful natural light spilled across the pews from two small stained glass windows. One depicted Mary at her son's birth and the other at his crucifixion. Abby would sit and gaze at the windows, her hand on her tiny belly.

Despite the comfort and peace she felt in the chapel, Abby found it difficult to pray. She didn't know if it was a silent crisis of faith or a sense of failure to fulfill God's purpose for her. She came to the chapel as a penitent, but she could not bring herself to ask for forgiveness. She'd been taught long ago that whenever it was too hard to pray, just talking to God became its own form of prayer. But Abby found she had a harder time talking to God than she did to Mary, so she spoke to the mother in intercessory prayer, hoping that her thoughts would be accepted by God.

Often she found her thoughts going to Quinn. She was usually successful in suppressing that part of her heart, but every once in a while his face flashed before her unbidden. She didn't want to think about him. She didn't want to acknowledge the guilt that was growing in her at having kept her pregnancy a secret from him. She wanted her time in the Mother's Chapel to be about God, and not Quinn.

During those times that she wasn't in chapel, Abby wandered the campus and cemetery with Dash following close behind. She took it upon herself to weed around the graves and throw away the dead and deteriorating offerings families left behind. She noticed that, despite regular mowing, the graves that had markers set into the ground rather than headstones were disappearing in the overgrowth of the grass. So every week she knelt before each grave and carefully trimmed the grass away from the marker. Dash would sit next to her, watching her. From a distance it looked like the two were paying their respects.

When she wasn't working, Abby ate and rested. She felt her baby growing inside her. Despite being so thin, she was almost eighteen weeks along and she still wasn't really showing. Abby was hopeful that she could keep her pregnancy private. So far only Mr. Ash, Reverend Dorothy, and Allison were keeping tabs on her progress. Mr. Ash routinely called her and texted her, though he'd only made a couple of unannounced visits to the church. She continued to see him weekly and understood that his attention was borne as much out of his desire to ensure her well-being as his duties as her parole officer.

The only real unwanted attention came from Father Tom. Other than their initial introduction, Abby rarely saw him. She couldn't say why, but she found him somewhat off-putting. Her efforts to avoid him had been mostly successful until she found herself crossing paths with him more often than before. It was as if the larger she got the more he went out of his way to "accidently" run into her. Their encounters weren't particularly enjoyable. His comments and backhanded compliments routinely rubbed Abby the wrong way. He would say things like:

"You're doing surprisingly well at such a masculine job."

"You're so physically fit, if it weren't for your hair, one might mistake you for a man."

"You certainly look like you're eating better now that you're out of prison."

"It's so refreshing to meet someone who doesn't care how they look!"

"It's unfortunate your education went to waste. It's probably a blessing that your parents aren't here to witness such a disappointment."

And so on.

Dash seemed to dislike Father Tom as much as Abby did. He would bark wildly whenever Father Tom was nearby. She'd come to rely on Dash as an early warning system, and went out of her way to venture in the opposite direction as soon as Dash started to growl.

Abby was in the cemetery cleaning up litter when she had the misfortune of another Father Tom encounter. The previous day had been windy and someone's trash had broken loose of its bag and blown across the gravestones. Abby walked the rows with a garbage bag and a long metal trash picker she'd found in the church's storage shed.

243

Dash began barking hysterically sending a frission of dread through Abby's body. She looked up to see Father Tom approaching, his face a moue of distaste aimed at the yapping dog.

"Dash, hush," Abby ordered. The little dog stopped barking and walked away from Father Tom to sit next to her. She said nothing as she watched him approach. He was the most ordinary looking person she'd ever seen. Slightly pudgy, he had a pale round face with blue eyes that pulled up slightly in the corners. His hair was a nondescript brown that was cut very short, emphasizing his weirdly low hairline. He looked like one of those people whose neighbors would state that they never would have guessed he was a serial killer ("He seemed like such a nice guy.").

He was sweating slightly as he walked up.

"You're looking very casual today," he said by way of a greeting. Abby looked down at her smock top and cargo pants. She was more than six months pregnant and had finally broken down and purchased maternity clothes.

"I *am* picking up trash. Should I be wearing a dress?"

Father Tom chuckled. "Of course not. A dress would be a complete waste of an outfit."

"On you," Abby finished in her head.

"Is there something you needed?" she asked, impatient to finish her task.

"Oh, I was just out for some fresh air when I saw you nearby."

Uh huh, Abby thought to herself.

"I thought I'd check-in to see how our lady maintenance man was doing," he said benignly.

"I'm doing well," Abby replied. "Thank you for asking."

"You're most welcome," his smile was more a smirk. Abby wondered if he realized how patronizing he looked.

"Are you settling in well?" he asked. It was an odd question since she'd been with the church for a few months already.

"I am," she said with a tinge of strain in her voice. She was getting tired and she really wanted to finish. "If you don't need anything, I should be getting back to … this….before it all blows away."

"Oh, of course," he said backing away. "I just wanted to offer you any support you might need during your transition."

"Thanks, but I'm OK," she replied then turned her back, dismissing him. She knew she was being rude, but there was no other way to get him to leave.

Then he lobbed his last grenade.

"Well, don't work too hard," he warned as he moved away. "A woman in your condition needs to rest. Your baby only has one parent after all."

Abby stared at his back as he made his way back to the church.

"Asshole," she mumbled then apologized to the tenant at her feet.

Chapter 43

UNFORTUNATELY DESIRABLE

Abby saw more and more of Father Tom over the next few months after he dropped his bombshell. As much as she tried to avoid him, she found him around every corner and behind every door. Her efforts were more difficult as her pregnancy progressed. Abby's ungainly body got in the way of her desire to flee quickly. And the slower she moved, the faster he did.

She mentioned it to Allison at the movies one night and was concerned to see Allison looking guilty.

"I should have told you, but it's my fault he found out," she said in a rush. "Blaine and I were talking about how beautiful you look, and I said I hoped I look half as awesome as you do when I have a baby. I didn't know it, but Father Tom was standing right behind me. I'm sorry."

"Don't worry about it," Abby sighed. "It's not your fault he's such a creeper."

"He is isn't he?" Allison exclaimed. "And have you ever noticed how insulting his compliments are? He told me once I was lucky my boyfriend liked large girls."

"That's just rude," Abby was suddenly incensed. "He has no business commenting on anyone's weight. Have you seen his belly? He's more pregnant than I am."

"I know, right?" Allison agreed. "And he keeps finding reasons to bring you up at all the staff meetings."

"What do you mean?"

"He'll say things like, shouldn't we all be concerned about you being at the church at night by yourself, or talk about how much time you spend in the Mother's Chapel. He also said, since you're due soon, that we should be looking for a replacement for you. And once he brought up your talking to Damien's parents even though it was months ago, and Reverend Dorothy cut him off. She was professional about it, but she basically warned him that he shouldn't be speaking with the parishioners about you and that any issues should come directly to her."

"What an asshole!" Abby was furious.

"Please don't be mad," Allison entreated. "We all have your back. Even Ella got mad at him and called him a…" Allison lowered her voice, "dickhead."

Abby snorted at the image of the lovely and genteel Ella calling Father Tom a dickhead. Abby didn't think she used that kind of language.

"I'm not mad. I just wish he'd leave me alone. I don't understand why he's always around. It's like being back in prison."

Allison looked at her sympathetically then the two women went into their movie.

Abby didn't have long to wait for Father Tom to declare his intentions. She had just finished meeting with the buildings and grounds volunteers when he waylaid her on her way back to her apartment. They were having an Indian summer and the weather was unmercifully warm. Abby's obstetrician had advised her to take it easy in the heat. Although Abby wasn't huge, her feet and ankles had swollen badly. She was hobbling along the path when she felt a damp palm take her elbow, startling her.

"Here," Father Tom said in her ear. "Let me help you."

Abby firmly but politely pulled her arm out of his grasp. "I'm fine. I don't need any help." She could see Reverend Dorothy coming out of the church and hoped she was on her way back to the offices. They would cross paths shortly and hopefully end this uncomfortable situation.

"I'm happy to help," he insisted. "In fact, I was wanting to speak with you about your plans going forward. You'll be having your baby soon and you'll need someone to serve as father to your child."

Abby stared at him. "What are you talking about?"

"Well, it's not the most orthodox of arrangements, and I'm willing to deal with the 'raised eyebrows,' but you're going to need a husband to raise your child for you."

"I can raise my child myself," Abby said carefully. She glanced over her shoulder, but Reverend Dorothy was still too far away.

Father Tom chuckled. "I'm sure you can understand that you might not be the most suitable person to parent a child. I'm willing to overlook your shortcomings. Since I am currently unattached, I think it would be most advantageous for you to have me as your mentor…and your husband."

She heard a voice behind her. "What do you think you're doing?" Reverend Dorothy sounded angry and incredulous at the same time.

Abby didn't realize that Reverend Dorothy had come up behind her. She was about to answer when she felt a snap like a giant rubber band break deep inside her. Water began to pour out between her legs as a massive cramp doubled her over.

Father Tom looked at her in horror. "That's disgusting! Stop doing that!"

Reverend Dorothy quickly put her arms around Abby as she slowly crumpled to the ground.

"Abby's water broke, you idiot. Go tell Blaine to come here immediately," the Reverend snapped.

Father Tom turned and hurried away.

"What the hell was he thinking?" Reverend Dorothy said, more to herself, as she pulled Abby's cell phone from her pocket. "What's the name of your doctor?"

"Graham," Abby panted as another wave moved through her.

Reverend Dorothy found Dr. Graham's number and called her as Blaine came running across the campus with Allison close behind in her car. Father Tom was mercifully nowhere in sight.

"Yay, a baby's coming!" Blaine cheered. Allison stopped the car next to them. Blaine and Reverend Dorothy carefully lifted Abby and helped her into the backseat.

"I'll go get your bag and bring it shortly," Blaine offered.

Abby nodded weakly then waved as Allison drove off.

Chapter 44

GOD, THE CAREFUL MECHANIC

Allison made it to the hospital in record time. Dr. Graham determined that Abby was fully dilated and rushed her into the delivery room. Less than three hours later, Abby was a mom.

Exhausted, she lay with her son in her arms as Allison snapped a picture. He was tiny and swollen and perfect. She could not stop looking at him. Her most precious baby had arrived, and Abby loved him with every cell in her body.

"I'm worried that he's so small," she said to Reverend Dorothy.

"He might be a little early," the Reverend admitted. "My daughter was six weeks early and was healthy for the most part. A few tummy problems, but otherwise she was fine. He'll be fine too. We were created to withstand quite a bit."

Abby stared at her son, memorizing every feature of his face. It was too early to tell whom he looked like. Right now he looked like a baby.

With no family, there was only Blaine, Allison, and Reverend Dorothy at the hospital to help Abby celebrate. Abby wished her friends from B Unit could have been there to see the baby. She smiled as she imagined them making a fuss over him. Even though it wasn't allowed, Abby knew she could send Mad T's daughter a picture to forward to her mother.

As it grew later, the nurses ushered everyone out so Abby could get some rest. Her baby was taken to the nursery to be checked over by the pediatrician, so Abby closed her eyes.

When she awoke, Jane was sitting in the chair next to her bed. The baby lay sleeping in his bassinet next to her.

Jane looked up and smiled. "Hey there," she said quietly.

Abby smiled back. "You came."

Jane nodded. "I wouldn't miss it. Especially since your Reverend Dorothy offered us the use of...I think she called it a 'visiting scholar's apartment?'" she whispered.

"Us?" Abby asked.

"I made Matt come with me," Jane laughed quietly. "He knows I hate driving long distance. Plus we're going to be here for a little bit."

"Why?" Abby was confused. "For me?"

Jane glanced at the baby to make sure she wasn't disturbing him then leaned closer. "I don't want to get too much into it right now. I know you're tired, but Eugene Ash and I have been working together to have the court release you from your probation early. We had to wait until after the baby so the judge could rule without prejudice. Once that's done, I can file to have your record sealed or even expunged."

"That's wonderful. Thank you so much," Abby whispered.

Jane smirked. "Don't thank me yet. I need to get you into court next Wednesday. Your doctor said she'll release you and the baby tomorrow, so that gives you almost a week to recover. Do you think you'll be OK by then?"

Abby nodded.

"Great," Jane leaned over and gave Abby a hug. "Congratulations, Abby. You're getting your life back."

Abby smiled. A tear rolled down her cheek as Jane left the room.

The next few days were a whirlwind. In order to be discharged, Abby's son needed to be seen by his own pediatrician. Luckily, the only pediatrician in Grayson was a parishioner at St. Mary's and came immediately when called. He declared both mom and son to be perfect and they were sent home.

While she was still in the hospital, Blaine and Allison had been busy getting a bassinette set up next to Abby's bed in her apartment. She was still sore from the delivery, so they happily volunteered to be her gophers until she felt up to conquering the stairs on a regular basis. For his part, Dash merely sniffed at the baby then sat quietly as if declaring him acceptable.

Mercifully, Father Tom stayed away after receiving a thorough dressing down by Reverend Dorothy. Blaine reported with great satisfaction that Reverend Dorothy warned Father Tom to stay away from Abby or suffer termination. Abby knew the reprieve would be short-lived, but she appreciated the effort. He still hung about but avoided any mention of marriage.

A week later her court date arrived. Allison offered to babysit as Jane and Abby drove the distance to Medford. They met Mr. Ash there, and together they all went in to meet with the judge. What she thought would take hours only took minutes. When she walked out, Abby was free. She gave Mr. Ash a massive hug and thanked him.

"No offense, sir, but I hope I never see you again," Abby joked.

Eugene Ash laughed out loud. "Same here, hon. Same here."

Abby and Jane returned to Grayson with the good news, and then Abby said goodbye to Jane and Matt.

"I can't thank you enough," Abby said.

Jane hugged her back. "We're not done yet. You let me know what you're going to do going forward. I'll let you know if we can get another hearing date set up to have your record sealed."

Abby nodded then waved as they drove away.

Reverend Dorothy, Blaine, and Allison were all smiles when Abby walked into the offices to pick up her son.

"Yay, you're free!" Blaine cheered, waking up the baby.

"Blaine!" Allison scolded him as Abby went over to pick up her son.

"I'm going to guess that it went well," Reverend Dorothy smiled.

Abby nodded. "They discharged the remainder of my probation."

"Congratulations. But I hope you're not planning on going anywhere soon," Reverend Dorothy cautioned. "You can't leave us without a sexton." Blaine and Allison stood behind her shaking their heads. Blaine tried to look serious but failed miserably.

"Are you sure?" Abby ventured. It was too much to hope that she could stay.

"Of course," the Reverend exclaimed. "You're welcome to stay as long as you need to. We were hoping to keep you forever."

"What about Father Tom?" Abby didn't want to be the cause of any more discord in the parish.

Reverend Dorothy snorted. "As long as he stops trying to marry you, he can stay too."

Abby smiled. "Then we'd love to stay."

Chapter 45

AS THEY SHOULD BE

The old church was cold; but even with the blizzard blowing outside it was silent, except for the cooing of Abby's son.

The baby sat in his stroller near the altar rail staring at the toys hanging from the handle as Abby carefully removed the handmade altar cloth. She smiled as he sang behind her, his babbles and squeals resounding throughout the old church. He had pulled his hands free of the heather blue blanket Sylvia had sent as a baby gift. Abby was glad she'd put a pair of soft scratch mittens on his hands before bringing him to work with her.

Abby's mind wandered while she set about polishing the front of the large walnut altar. As much as Reverend Dorothy wanted her to stay at St. Mary's, Abby knew she needed to stop stalling and make a decision about what to do now that the remainder of her parole had been discharged. She was a mother now and needed to think about what kind of life she wanted for her son and herself. Her job as sexton wasn't a good long-term solution; but with a felony on her record, Abby knew it would be difficult to get a job elsewhere. She knew she couldn't go back to Springfield, and she certainly couldn't go back to prison. She didn't really fit in anywhere. She'd deliberately avoided touching the bulk of the trust in hopes that it would last her and her son a long time. Worse, she knew her situation was still of great interest to Father Tom and desperately hoped he wasn't gearing up for another proposal attempt.

Behind her she heard the door to the church open. She felt the icy wind blow over the pews. Abby figured it was Father Tom coming to pester her again, so she ignored him and finished her polishing.

Abby turned when the baby's singing stopped. Fear wrapped its icy fingers around her heart. Quinn stood next to the stroller holding her son, staring into a face that was a mirror image of his own. He smiled as the baby stared back at him with his father's stoicism.

Abby held her breath, her emotions were somewhere between hope and terror. She was desperately afraid of what Quinn would say. She had never told him about the baby.

Quinn's smile dropped as he put their son back down. Abby's heart was pounding in her chest as Quinn stepped closer, his expression alternating between anger and hurt.

"He's mine, isn't he?" Quinn asked quietly. Unable to speak, Abby simply nodded.

"Why didn't you tell me?" he asked, his voice cracking from the hurt of betrayal. Abby didn't have an answer.

"You can't keep him from me, Abby," he stated. "I want my..."

"He's all I have," Abby interrupted. "You can't take him away..." Angry tears spilled from her eyes making shining cuts down her cheeks. Her worst nightmare was happening. Quinn's words were a stab to her already fragile heart. Her vision blurred as she began to shake her head. Hope and terror had given way to anger. She was both furious and heartbroken.

Quinn moved over toward her and pulled her close. His lips rested against her ear. Abby could feel the pounding of his heart matching hers perfectly. His arms held her tight. His body was warm in the cold church. She felt the icy shell surrounding her heart melt.

"Shhh, not like that... I came here for both of you," Quinn whispered. "I couldn't stand not knowing what was happening to you. I came to ask you come back with me. But I didn't know about the baby, Abby...not until I told Redfern I was coming here. She and Hamilton hid your test results when you were discharged. They knew you were pregnant. When she told me...I didn't want to know whose baby it was. I thought when I found you...I didn't know what the baby...if he was mine or not. You didn't say anything...I thought it was because it was Tobin's. Then I saw the picture. Sheronda had it taped over her bunk."

Abby shook her head against Quinn's shoulder. "I didn't know until I got here. She didn't say anything to me. I'm so sorry, Quinn. I should have written you...told you."

Quinn pulled back. His hands were on her face, thumbs wiping away the tears.

"I'm the one who's sorry. I knew the minute I saw you that I loved you. And it was wrong of me to want to be with you…to take advantage of you like that. Then Victoria…the things she said. And like an idiot I believed her. Sheronda told me I was stupid and she was right. I betrayed you in the worst possible way and I pray that you can forgive me. I love you, Abby. I love you so much I can't leave here unless you come with me." Quinn pulled her close. Abby wrapped her arms around him and held him tight.

Behind them the baby started singing again. Quinn smiled into Abby's eyes as their son's voice echoed in the rafters.

Abby stepped over to fetch their son from his stroller. He gurgled then pressed his face into the hollow of her neck. She hugged him close then moved back to Quinn. "What's his name?" Quinn asked.

"Ian. I named him Ian," she answered.

Quinn started. "That's my name."

Abby smiled as she handed Quinn his son. "I know."

Abby watched him nuzzle their son. Then he reached over to pull her into his embrace. She knew at that moment where she finally belonged.

ABOUT THE AUTHOR:

K. Wiley Sider lives in Ellicott City, Maryland with her husband, two beautiful daughters, and two deeply spoiled dogs.

Other books by K. Wiley Sider:
The Things That Fall Away
Solitary
Servant
Boy Toy, Book One of the Dead Husbands Series

Learn more about the author at:
www.kwileysider.com
www.facebook.com/kwileysider

And on Twitter at:
@kwileysider